INSPECTING THE ISLAND

BY THE SAME AUTHOR

Reaching Peckham – a narrative sequence of poems

INSPECTING the ISLAND

Hylda Sims

Seven-Ply Yarns

Published by:

Seven-Ply Yarns
PO Box 217, Ipswich, IP4 2NZ

In association with:

Libertarian Education
Phoenix House, 157 Wells Road, Bristol, BS4 2BU

ISBN 0-9538797-0-4

Cover design by Matt Wooding
Cover photograph by Liz Simcock

Printed and bound by:

Short Run Press, Bittern Road, Sowton Industrial Estate,
Exeter EX2 7LW

for Viv, Rom, Lily and Wilfe

Acknowledgements

Coralford School is loosely based on Summerhill School, where I was educated, but is not a photocopy. The character of Muir is mostly derived from A. S. Neill, its founder and first head. Those who know of Homer Lane will recognise his ghost in Plato Tewson's brief appearance. Other characters are entirely fictional as are all the events and situations described.

I would like to thank Peter Hore, Brian Docherty, Tony Butten, Jill Bates and Lynette and David Gribble for their generous and close attention to the text and Wilfe Gorlin for many dives into a cold pool on a rainy day.

Hylda Sims

"This is an island. At least I think it's an island. "

(Piggy, in *Lord of the Flies* by William Golding)

Prologue

*Twenty years ago, first time I went up the big tree. Fourteen,
I was. Grows their side of the wall, hangs over it. Easy. You
grab the low branches and swing yourself up. You can just walk
in there down the drive, but I prefer to climb up the wall
straight into the tree, sit there secret, watching them.
Remember it, hot in my head still. Changed out of my uniform,
sweaty and itchy where I'd been sat all day, and into my cadet
gear, my camouflage stuff. Got my dad's binoculars from his
drawer. He hadn't got home yet to give me one for not making
my bed properly or something. Hadn't got the stick at school
either, not that day. One of my better days.*

*Some of them were sitting around on tree trunks in front of
the school. Boys and girls. Some had their arms round each
other. This old man comes up. They don't stand up or stop
touching the girls. "I'm the school inspector," the old man says
with a serious face. A boy says, "Fuck off, Muir. We all know
you're only the gardener." They all laugh. The old man sits
down with them and they offer him something, chocolate or
something.*

*You see the swimming pool from the tree, round by the side of
the house. Kids floating about in old car tyres. Couple of girls
lying on towels. Nothing on. You can see their tits! Could hardly believe what I was looking at. Made my head thud. I
focussed the binoculars and took a good long look.*

*This little kid comes towards the tree riding his bike over the
humps. He jumps off the bike and lets it fall onto the grass.
The wheels carry on spinning. There's a rope hangs down from
the tree with a loop in it. He climbs up to the fork. I flatten
myself against the trunk of the tree on the road side. He never
sees me. He puts his foot in the loop, hangs on to the rope and
goes swinging out over the grass. The rope swings back, he
pushes against the tree with his free foot and goes swinging out
again.*

1

I look down through the leaves. The bark's scratching my face, I see the top of his head, long hair flying out. I can feel the wind through his hair, the way the rope takes him. I feel dizzy, sick. Eight times I count him do it. Then he takes his foot out of the loop and holding on just with his hands he swings out again, lets go in mid-air, lands on his feet on the grass, grabs his bike and rides off. I know I'll never get rid of him, this kid, this scruffy, jammy little bastard of a kid, hair shining in the sun like a lit bulb, flying through the air, flying up and down the humps on his old bike.

I shin down the tree, brush my fatigues down and get the bus home. Get there before my dad gets in, put the binoculars back. I'm careful to wipe them clean so he won't suspect I've touched them. He's rough when he catches you touching his stuff. I'm up in my room, doing my homework and the fatigues and the school uniform all hanging clean and straight in my wardrobe by the time I hear him come in, slamming the door and shouting out for me in his loud, angry voice.

PART ONE

CHAPTER ONE

Maz shot out of the undergrowth between the inspector's legs as the inspector stood gazing at the hillocks of uneven grass known, he understood, as the hockey field. The inspector brushed a piece of grass from his knee.

"Where should you be, lad?"

Maz shook the leaves out of his hair. He looked puzzled. He took in the well-polished leather shoes, the tie, the refusal to move, the practised unsmiling stare. He shrugged. "Sorry, didn't mean to mess up your clothes. You the inspector?"

"I don't think that's any of your business, do you?"

Maz's frown deepened to hurt. He wriggled backwards, away from the inspector, jumped to his feet and ran off.

"Hey you, come back!"

The inspector was feeling in his pockets, as if worried for the safety of his money – or was he fumbling for a sweet ?

Maz disappeared behind the main house.

The inspector knew he hadn't played it right, but he didn't know how else to play it. These children unnerved him with their level gaze and their straightforward serious questions. A lot of the time they didn't seem to notice him at all. His presence didn't change their behaviour in the slightest. They joked, swore, offered him biscuits from their food parcels as if he was one of them. When he couldn't respond in kind, finding himself saying something patronising with a false matey smile like "I won't let on you said that," they looked at him pityingly and drifted off – to the tree swing, to their rooms, to their lessons, to the art room, to God knows where.

He looked along the front of the house. Victorian, he supposed. A modest Victorian manor, originally the country seat of some successful industrialist. Once it would have been staffed by a dozen retainers – gardeners, cooks, skivvies. Now it was shabby. The crumbly red bricks had initials and dates scored into them going back to the thirties. A few cars were parked in front of the windows on the hard baked earth, which must turn into mud when it rained; in front of that a stretch of grass which had been recently mown, with some handsome ash and beech trees; around the house unkempt grass, paths, more trees, a number of one-storeyed outbuildings, and the weathered wattle fence of the swimming-pool. Visible behind the house in the distance was a steep green hill with the black towers of Eliston Castle silhouetted against the summer sky.

No-one else in sight. He didn't know what to do or where to go next. He had the feeling that kids must be watching him out of the row of sash windows that blinked through the ivy and virginia creeper hanging from the eaves or perhaps they were simply looking through him. Then he noticed two girls leaning out of an upstairs end window. They were watching housemartins flying into a nest under the gutter carrying food for their young and winging away again towards the trees.

You were lucky to find more than half a dozen kids together at any one time, except at the meeting.

Ah yes, the meeting! A bedraggled looking youngster of indeterminate age and sex emerged now from the front door and ran round the grounds clanging an old brass bell. Kids straggled into the house in response, taking their time. The boy Maz shot round the side of the house on a bike too small for him, scuffed to a stop, propped the bike against the bricks and ran inside. The inspector followed him into the lounge, a large room with several exits which seemed like a kind of junction for the rest of the building.

The kids were settling onto the floor, propped against the scarred oak-panelled walls. Some sat in tiers up what must have once been a rather grand staircase curving out of the room. Some were cuddling each other – even boys and girls, even boys. A few staff and older children had younger ones attached to them like limpets, ensconced between their knees, lolling on their shoulders. There were – the inspector gave a surreptitious head count – about sixty of them, a scruffy looking bunch of all ages, as well as about ten equally scruffy looking adults. It wasn't too easy to tell the one from the other.

Could you compare it to assembly? To those tidy rows of chairs with the uniformed children, the line monitors, the adults seated facing them but just that bit higher on the rostrum? Other teachers stationed strategically down the sides of the hall, the head ready, waiting for the murmur of voices to die down respectfully so he could give his simplified message about quiet bravery and loyalty and God, make his announcements about the after-school clubs and have his usual moan about the graffiti on the stairs? You could assess that sort of thing. Did the head speak pleasantly but authoritatively? Were the staff in control at all times? Did the ingress to the hall and the egress to the classrooms proceed smoothly with a minimum of opportunity for pushing and shoving? Were the pupils in their lessons and on task within the five minutes allotted for changeover? You could assess that sort of thing. It fitted in with the notion of targets, training, right and wrong.

But here?

Muir himself, about to become one hundred years old, was helped to a wooden armchair in one corner, where he took out his baccy and slowly filled his pipe. The chairman, a girl of fourteen or so with long, straight blonde hair and kneeless blue jeans, and the secretary, a boy of the same age who looked Japanese, were conferring over an exercise book.

"OK," the girl said, straightening up, "meeting come to order. Kevin, shut up, I said come to order."

Kevin (he was the maths teacher, the inspector recalled) grinned at her warily, "OK, OK," and propped himself on the wall opposite the secretary.

The room gradually went quiet. A few people were knitting. Apparently that was the current craze. Even Maz, he saw, had acquired knitting from somewhere; a large white object – a sweater, he supposed – was draped over his crossed legs like a pet sheep. A thick wooden needle was tucked under one arm, the other needle clicked in and out.

"OK," the chairman said. "Any visitors?"

A little girl with a dirty, round, freckled face nudged the inspector helpfully. "You're a visitor, aren't you?"

7

The inspector raised his hand uncertainly.

"Could the visitors wait outside," the chairman said, "through that door, in the lobby?"

The inspector and a couple of other visitors did as they were told. Through the glass door the inspector could see the voting on whether to allow the visitors to attend the meeting. It appeared to be a rubber-stamping process, for within a minute a girl opened the door and called, "You can come in now."

No chairs were left, so the inspector sat awkwardly on a ricketty bench next to a little boy extrovertly chewing bubble-gum.

Another visitor, a small woman about his own age with greying hair, stepped carefully over the children on the lower treads and sat on the stairs. She looked at home with the place and its customs, though the inspector had not seen her before in the three days he had been there. Now for the first time he looked at her properly, across the scratched bannister rail. He thought afterwards that it hadn't been the face itself but the small, sideways twist to her smile, which made her unmistakable, even after all these years. He coloured up. His heart floated, then sank. He wanted to run out and hide or rush up the stairs and grab her. Her indulgent lopsided grin was pitched towards the chairman.

"OK," said the chairman, tossing back her hair. "First business: Brendan versus the Carriage Kids for keeping the Shack awake after lights out. Brendan."

A thin boy with wiry red hair spoke in an intense voice. "Last night the Carriage Kids were playing their stereos after Shack beddies. I told them to shut up and Simon told me to fuck off. These kids think just because they're in the Carriages now they can break the fucking law."

The inspector, beaming insincerely, suppressed an automatic wince. A few hands went up.

"Simon," said the chairman.

A tall older boy with rimless glasses moved a smaller child sitting on his lap on to the floor and stood up to speak. "Those guys weren't trying to sleep. They were making a hell of a noise themselves. Try asking *them* to shut up. I kicked

8

Brendan out of my room because he was messing with my stuff and then he just wanted to get his own back." He sat down again and the small child snuggled back on to his lap.

"Katie."

A plump girl wearing a long red dress spoke up from the stairs. "That's beside the point, Simon. What's the point of having a silence rule if you guys don't keep it? You big kids are supposed to set an example." She giggled. "Anyway we could hear you right over at the house".

"Hear, hear." A murmur of voices went round.

The inspector took out a small book labelled "Coralford School, July 1999" and wrote the words, "conciliation techniques via student exchange. Teacher input?" He disliked the words he had written, they seemed stilted and irrelevant.

"What are you doing?" the little boy next to him asked, and pouted out a livid pink balloon.

"I'm . . . er . . . trying to write down what they're doing."

The boy popped his gum. "The secretary does that." He indicated the Japanese boy who was sitting on the floor next to the chairman, writing in the exercise book. "What's your name ?"

"Er . . . Mr Bignold," the inspector said.

"No, I mean, your first name. What are you called?"

"I don't think that's any of . . . " The inspector checked himself. ". . . Er, Jasper . . . Bit of a silly name," he finished lamely. "What's –"

"Quiet !" The chairman looked over at the bench sternly, "Next person to make a noise, one p fine. I'm taking proposals now."

The inspector coloured again and glanced over at the other visitor on the stairs who appeared to be following the business intently.

"Aaron."

The boy next to Jasper took the bubble-gum out of his mouth and stretched it between his fingers. "I propose the Carriage is fined late beddies next Saturday."

"I second that," Maz said, parting his short hair with a knitting needle.

"I propose we get a strong warning and if we do it again we're fined beddies," Simon said. The meeting laughed.

"Any more proposals? OK, all in favour of Aaron's proposal?" The chairman repeated it carefully. Half a dozen hands went up and she counted them. "All in favour of Simon's proposal?"

Almost everyone put a hand up, including, the inspector saw with surprise, the boy Brendan, who had brought the complaint. He wrote, "Defused confrontation via student-centred decision-making process. Teacher input?" Muir sat puffing pensively on his pipe, having voted for the first proposal.

"OK, carried." The chairman looked deliberately in Simon's direction, "Simon and other carriage kids: strong warning not to make a noise after beddies. Do it again and you'll get fined. Next business?" She glanced down at the secretary.

"John staff versus Class Three for not putting the woodwork tools away." The secretary's l's sounded very faintly like r's.

The businesses proceeded, first the discussion, then the proposals, then the vote. The worst that seemed to happen to anyone was a ten pence fine. Aaron was "gated" for two days for leaving the school grounds without a big kid or staff to look after him. He stuffed his chewing gum back in his mouth, looked sulky and said nothing.

"Any other business?"

Jasper saw the woman visitor's hand wiggling above the bannisters.

"Charlotte."

"I'm here for a couple of weeks to do some interviews with Muir for his hundredth birthday. Is it OK if I tape the meeting next week – is that all right?"

"I expect so," the chairman said. "All in favour that Charlotte can tape the meeting next week?" Most hands went up. "All against?"

Muir raised a shaky arm and spoke. "You guys are too generous. A tape can fall into anybody's hands. With you lot swearing and talking about your love life, once *The Sun* got hold of it, the school could get closed."

"Muir, the meeting's been taped loads of times," the chairman said kindly. "We know Charlotte, she's an ex-pupil for God's sake. Anyway, it was overwhelmingly carried. Business closed."

"Ombudsmen," said someone.

"Oh yeah. Who wants to be ombudsmen next week?"

Simon and Katie put up their hands as well as Kevin, the maths teacher. The secretary wrote their names down.

"OK, meeting closed."

Maz stuffed his knitting under his arm, scrambled one-handedly up a ladder in a corner of the room and turned a switch. There was an electronic buzz. A fusillade of bass guitar and drums ricocheted startlingly round the lounge. Some kids wandered out of the French windows into the warm evening air. Katie and Simon walked towards each other and started moving to the music.

Muir tamped out his pipe and put it in the pocket of his baggy corduroy jacket. Half-supported by two of the bigger girls, he made his way over to rescue Jasper. "Come over to the cottage for a whisky," he shouted in a hoarse whisper, cupping a paper-thin hand over his mouth and leaning perilously towards him.

*   *   *

If you don't live, you die, and if you don't die, you live. The choice seemed stark to Muir. Living he had his stiff joints to contend with; what he called his century itch – a kind of scratchy, tingling sensation over his skin as if it were allergic to the pressure of air; the mornings, when he would wake monotonously early and drift into a snoring, uneasy doze while he waited for someone to come and haul him out of bed and shuffle him to the bathroom for his pee, which never seemed to be the full satisfying gush it had been. It was as if his bladder had dried out like an ancient stream across a rock, the source mysteriously retreated in against itself. As for his penis having any other function, he had difficulty some days recalling the concept of sex, the spike of adrenalin, the stiffening of

11

flesh. Perhaps, he thought, that itch of his was the diaspora of his sexual urge, spread and trickled over his whole crinkled body, causing his skin to prickle and irritate pointlessly rather than concentrating itself into one erect wholesome desire. Perhaps it scattered off you like dandruff when you died, made the ground itch, grew into trees . . .

His head jerked up – he'd been dozing in the old grey armchair again.

Then there was death – a consummation devoutly to be wished, Hamlet had opined. He couldn't think of it like that. A nothingness. After all this time he was afraid of nothingness, leaving everything, never knowing how things turned out. What things? How could anything "turn out"? He would have liked a third option, a sort of flying eye, a watching brief without any direct involvement. Something that didn't include the weariness of struggling far too often to have a tiny pee, to get to a chair, the utter boredom of the hundred thousandth time of washing his hands, maybe the millionth time of a word, any word, say the word "I", dribbling weakly through the divide of his lips, without anyone actually understanding who "I" was, what "I" meant. A third state would be the thing, an option you could take to hang around without this hideous shape that had settled on him like an unironed, scratchy blanket. If one could have believed . . . but that would entail so much bullshit, make a nonsense of his entire life, let in all sorts of ridiculous notions – received truth, original sin . . .

"Muir. Muir?" An anxious voice. He felt a hand on his knee. It had no quality. "Muir, are you all right? Can I get you something? A little more Scotch?"

He started and opened his eyes. "Why not –" he couldn't remember the name " – laddie? Just a wee dram." He found he often lapsed into this music-hall Scots which had been normal when he was himself a laddie.

"It's Jasper Bignold." The voice identified itself. "You were telling me about future plans, for when . . ."

"Aye, I dropped off."

"I think it's time I went. I'll come over again tomorrow if I

12

may."

Muir blinked up at him. He was struggling hard to remember who he was, to place the slightly uneasy feeling he had about the man's presence here.

"You're the . . . the inspector chappie ?"

"Yes, but just an informal visit, just interest really."

Muir noticed the swift reassurance and felt more uneasy. "Och weel. Comfortable are you, over there in the terrace?"

"Yes, fine." Jasper backed towards the door. "I'll find you tomorrow then."

"I hope so laddie."

Jasper made his way in the dark across the front lawn towards the pair of terraced cottages on the edge of the school grounds where visitors were accommodated. He guessed Charlotte would stay for the dancing. He also guessed she would be sleeping in the next house. He couldn't face her tonight.

CHAPTER TWO

Saturday night is late beddies. Sunday starts lazily. Two little kids are sitting in the sandpit and another sitting on one of the swings by the swimming pool fence. Everyone else is having a lie-in. If they bother at all, they will skitter down to breakfast in their pyjamas at the last minute for some cornflakes and a mug of tepid tea.

Maz is always up early. Somewhere he has the feeling that if he doesn't get up and blink the day into existence it will never appear. It is his task in life to open the cupboard where the forthcoming day's events are contained and let them out into the light.

He sat now in the dens, a part of the grounds concealed behind a hedge at the far end of the hockey field. The dens had been there for several generations, an extensive earthwork, a warren, shored in place with pieces of wood and large stones. You went down some roughly planked earth steps into a central hollow leading off which were smaller cavities dug out of the ground. Legend had it that the first dens had evolved from an old shelter left there at the end of the war. Some of the smaller cavities had boards across their entrances with people's names and notices such as "Keep out. Private" scrawled in biro or felt tip. The soil which had been removed formed a low wall round the outside of the area. When it rained heavily things would cave in and run together into a muddy trench and the dens would be abandoned for a while. Come summer and drier weather and somebody would start up the dens craze again; there would be hours of digging, dredging, scraping, propping and tidying. There was a school rule that you couldn't sleep overnight in the dens: Muir worried about safety, kids getting buried or drowned in their sleep, and his wife Helga fussed over health matters – rheumatism, colds and the dirt and mud that got caked on people's clothes.

Maz had been carting stuff to his den for some time now –

flat stones from the surrounding fields and pebbles and shells from seaside trips. He was building a kind of mosaic floor. He liked working alone on it in the early mornings, the sun shafting almost horizontally across the hockey field, a light breeze goose-pimpling his arms until the exertion of shifting and setting the stones made his skin tingle with warmth.

You couldn't stand up in your den if you'd roofed it over, but you could sit there in a private cosy box. Some kids joined up to make bigger dens so that you could sit in them together and play cards or fivestones, but Maz had a one-kid space. He was vaguely aware that soon he would be losing interest in the den, becoming a big kid, chairing meetings, listening more to music, spending more time rehearsing with the school band. Already he intended to give the sweater he was making to Katie. She was exactly two years older than him and he liked her a lot – he liked the way her hands kind of fluttered as she spoke and the tiny giggle with which she concluded almost everything she said. He had an urge to finish his den, make it as nice as he could and then trade it on to one of the younger kids – maybe Aaron, who was just coming up to a dennish kind of age. The current rule was that if you didn't use your den and keep it in good repair somebody could ask in the meeting to take it over, but most people preferred to trade on. At present values a good den like Maz's was worth two weeks poc, six puddings or three weeks' bike loan. The floor would be unique when finished though, so Maz was thinking he might do a rather better deal.

"Hello, you're up early."

Maz looked up. Preoccupied with moving the stones he hadn't heard Jasper's quiet step. The forced friendliness of Jasper's tone immediately irritated him. Maz nodded at him and continued working.

"What are you making here?" Jasper jumped lithely down from the grassy edge. He was wearing a dark tracksuit and discreet black trainers.

Maz picked up the biggest stone left on his pile and clunked it into place between a large shell and a piece of old brick.

"Finishing my den."

"Need a hand?"

"It's all right thanks." Maz carried on working, his back to the inspector.

"Look," Jasper said, "I'm sorry if I spoke to you a bit sharply yesterday . . . it's not easy for a grown-up, a teacher from an ordinary school, being here . . . It's very . . . different."

Maz said nothing. He wished the inspector would go away.

"I hope you won't hold it against me," Jasper said.

"It's all right," Maz said. "I've got to go to breakfast now."

He backed out of his den on his knees, stretched and ran off up the steps. Behind the hedge he stopped and looked back at the inspector who poked around looking at the dens for a while, then walked up the steps, sat on a log and wrote something in a notebook which he took from a large pocket in the front of his tracksuit top.

Maz began to construct an intriguing fantasy about the inspector. Maybe he was not an inspector at all, but had his own reasons for being here. Maybe there was Venusian treasure hidden somewhere in the grounds. It was the inspector's brief to smuggle it out and trade it to the Martian Mafia for a fortune. Maz knew this fantasy would amuse him for a while. He, Maz, he decided, would be Mazola von Strumm, the famous half-Venusian boy sleuth. MvS's mother was a Venusian time-traveller who intended, on Muir's death, to reveal the treasure's whereabouts and donate it to the school. Maz realised he would have to track the inspector, if necessary befriending him for the time being.

He ran over to the house and emerged with a piece of bread and jam in each hand in time to see the inspector walking towards the back drive. Munching from each hand alternately he loped along after him, keeping his distance. The inspector took the road for Eliston, Maz hopped across the stile and took the way through the fields. When the last mouthful was gone he wiped his sticky hands down his jeans and began to run. The sun was now quite high in the sky, the breeze ruffling his hair as he pelted down the field. Drops of dew still shone on the coarse grass. The idea of Venusian quicksilver flashed through Maz's head. Once or twice he tried a kind of rolling somersault through the quicksilver as he ran. At the bottom of the field it had gathered into the fast burble of a stream. Maz took up two handfuls and pressed the liquid into his mouth. He sprang on, invigorated by the magic fluid, and wriggled easily through the loose hedging in the corner of the field. Mazola von Strumm tipped his head cautiously over the town stile. The inspector was striding up the hill towards the castle just ahead of him.

*   *   *

Jasper went into the Coffee Pot, a double-fronted cafe in Eliston market square. He was, he knew, avoiding Charlotte. For the previous three days he'd gone across to the school for breakfast, queuing at the hatch with the children for a bowl of cornflakes and a slice of toast. Sometimes a member of staff would make a point of sitting beside him in the dining-room making desultory conversation, but mostly people ignored him, intent on their own morning thoughts and plans.

The Coffee Pot had six round well-polished tables. Jasper sat at the corner one facing into the room.

"Will you be wanting the full Sunday breakfast?" The waitress's words wove up at the end of the sentence and stopped suddenly.

"No thanks, just coffee and toast."

"It's a nice day for the time."

"Yes."

Jasper felt isolated, marooned.

Jasper Bignold, BA 2.1, MA, Manchester, secondary school teacher, deputy headmaster, author of *Geography in the Classroom* (now updated and tied in with National Curriculum levels, still standard issue in many schools), headmaster, ex-local authority inspector, Ofsted inspector, married, two grown-up children, shortly to be divorced.

Jack, his younger child, had completed his university course in business administration and modern languages and almost immediately found a job with a firm in Holland. At around the same time the authority had disbanded their inspectorate and Jasper had been given his redundancy notice. Under the new system he and some colleagues were setting up a freelance team of inspectors that tendered for school inspections.

How do you tender for an inspection, Jasper had wondered. The two words seemed like opposites. Tender, he thought, that's how I feel, bruised, tender, brittle. He wondered if, pre-occupied by a mixture of anxiety and exhilaration, busy with the detail of closing the old service and setting up the new, he had simply failed to notice what his wife, Kay, was doing, thinking, planning . . .

"Jas . . .," she had said to him using that voice that meant he had to sit down next to her and give her his full attention. He closed a glossy Ofsted booklet entitled *Inspecting Schools, a Guide to Good Practice*, and glanced across at her. She had on her serious and determined look.

"Do you think we've ever . . . er . . . really loved each other, you know, really passionately?"

Jasper went pale in the pit of his stomach. It came to him that he'd been waiting for this question for thirty years. He'd gradually come to expect that it would never be asked. He'd gradually forgotten what the question was.

"What do you mean?" He didn't raise his head, ashamed of his classically evasive enquiry.

"That's what I mean. You don't know what I mean, do you? You don't know what it means to really love someone, to real-ly . . . live in them – live through them. I mean we're buddies, friends, but we're not . . . lovers. We've never really been lovers." She moved towards him and put her arms awkwardly round his hunched torso. "I've been trying to tell you for so long. I mean, you're a nice man, such a nice man."

But he did know what she meant. He'd always known only too well what she meant.

Then she told him how she had been Don's lover for years. She refused to specify how many. Don was Jasper's squash

18

partner and best friend. Now that the children were "off their hands," as she put it, she proposed to go and live with him. "I felt sure you must have realised, I always felt you wouldn't really mind, but I kind of couldn't quite tell you. I mean it was pretty obvious."

But he hadn't noticed. Why hadn't he noticed? Had he not cared enough to notice? Had he always taken it for granted that she loved him utterly, while he . . . did the best he could, kept his bargain with himself, more or less? He started to cry. He started to get angry. "Why the fuck didn't you tell me? Let me off the hook before? What am I supposed to do now? You're a cow! A cold, selfish, middle-class, fucking cow!"

She backed away. "You can have the house, I don't want anything from you, Don has enough. I'll just get out of your hair." She walked into the bedroom, her head up at an unusual angle – self-conscious, defiant it seemed to him. He heard the wooden scrape of drawers opening, the click of suitcase lids, the soft thwack of clothes landing on their bed.

Scruff's whine drilled into Jasper's forehead. He was pressing his nose against the French windows, pawing at the wood and whining atrociously. He found the dog's lead and walked him to the park. Jasper felt, or rather not-felt, mechanical, like the sputtering engine of a car about to be towed to the junk yard. The dog fussed around him in the park, offering sympathy. Jasper stroked his stiff fur, let him off the lead and sat on a bench for a while. The park seemed to be full of couples, old, young, holding hands, arguing comfortably about inconsequential things. Everybody had somebody with them. He called Scruff and walked back home with him.

Kay's VW was parked in the pebbled drive and she was carrying two taut, shiny, plastic bags out to it. He picked up Scruff, shoved him in the back seat of the car. The dog's front feet slithered into the well, then it recovered its balance, sat on the seat and stared at him, shivering. He threw the lead at Kay.

"Take the fucking dog as well. What do you think I am!"

"Oh dear," Kay said sadly, as if commenting on the utterly

unreasonable nature of his behaviour.

He went out of the gate and strode off down the road as if he had a purpose. "Hello Jasper," one or two neighbours said to him as he went past their hedges. "Oh hello." He forced his smile on and turned his head towards them. "All right? Bit of a hurry." He forged on till he came to The Mason's Arms, a gloomy cavern where he knew nobody, and bought himself a beer. The pub was almost empty. It was six o'clock. A few men in business suits were chatting at the bar. He found the darkest, remotest corner table and rapidly downed his beer, went to the bar and bought another. The businessmen left and the pub began to fill with a younger, hipper clientele. He fetched another beer, and another. The juke box started up. He bought another beer, vacantly deflecting the barman's efforts at conversation. The double doors at one end of the pub got propped open and people started bringing in amplifiers and mikes and instruments. He bought another beer and a whisky chaser and took it back to his refuge in the corner. Snatches of raucous noise, sudden high-pitched squeals of feedback invaded the bar as the musicians and their sidekicks padded round the stage in a spaghetti of cables. The musicians took up their places and a great fireball of sound rolled over him, scorching his mind of content. At ten o'clock he eased himself through the crowd of pulsing bodies and out into the cool, disconcertingly quiet, night street. His ears rang. He slid home. His road was empty and still. Nobody was out in their front gardens.

He fumbled with his key. Scruff was whining and scrabbling on the other side of the door. For a moment he had wondered if it was all some peculiar dream.

There was a note: "I'll be in touch. I do care about you. Anyway, we have to explain to the kids. Kay. P.S. I've had to leave the dog for the moment – sorry."

Jasper tore up the note, and put the bits tidily into the fireplace. He stood on the heavy embossed rug from John Lewis's and stared round the room aggressively. He could see nothing he liked. Nothing in the room had anything to do with him. He had been driven deep into enemy territory. No, he was in a no-man's-land of his own construction, he had dug the trenches himself. The room was preparing to attack. Enemy snipers everywhere: the pink shaded lamp Kay's aunt had given them for Christmas, which Kay insisted on keeping, the Clarice Cliff ginger jar her mother had left her, the half wall of dull-coloured hardback books on education, knitting and art with no science fiction or poetry or novels or music. And as her father's grandfather clock tocked on menacingly beside the French windows, in the women's trenches he knew they were waiting the hour to spill over the top, with their barbed, cof-feed tongues lacquered with innuendo and false sympathy.

"He never had the least suspicion, poor lamb."

"Must have been blind then."

"Blind, yes, blind to everything, old Jasper."

"She got so bored. No passion in him apparently – you know, the bed thing – no good, she said . . ."

Jasper snatched up a green enamelled clock from the mantlepiece and hurled it at what he took to be some kind of machine gun emplacement on the piano – his piano – a pre-dictable tortoiseshell-framed picture of himself and Kay posed in front of an ugly, red-brick, Victorian Church, Jasper smiling his embarrassed grin in a black dress suit, Kay tacked onto it like a long lace curtain. The clock thwacked to the floor short of target. Scruff rushed over to it wagging his tail, sniffed it and sat down looking hopefully to his master for more. Jasper crossed the room in two swift strides, grabbed the photograph and hurled it at Clarice who, caught on the side, toppled over, rolled to the end of the bookcase, arced gracefully towards the parquet and smashed to pieces. Scruff scampered to his feet, slithering on the polished floor, whimpering in expectation. Jasper lifted a foot onto the soft flesh of the armchair and pushed it over on to its back on top of the remains of Clarice.

He sped to the kitchen for weapons, returning with a Sabatier knife and a pair of scissors. Scruff scampered behind him misguidedly hoping for food. Jasper made his sorties among the dead and wounded, slashing, lunging, cutting down, finishing off, here a cushion, there a lampshade, here a

pouffe, there a plant. Finally, making his last lunge, he strad-
dled the nest of occasional tables by the fireplace, raised the
Sabatier high above his head in both hands and brought it
down with full force piercing at one mighty stroke the appliqué
cloth Kay had made soon after they married and all three
tables. He'd always said they were rubbish.

The knife juddered violently and was still. Silence collected
itself like dust falling over no-woman's-land. Scruff snuffled
round the conqueror's feet submissively and rolled over on to
his back for a stroke. Jasper stepped over him, carefully avoiding some spilled black loam from a punctiliously watered
peace lily lying on its side and staggered over to re-occupy his
piano, his beautiful upright mahogany piano with inlays of
paler wood curving all over it in the shape of leaves. He swept
some glass shrapnel and a vase of pink roses off its surface
with a single swing from the shoulder, grabbed a pile of *House
and Gardens* that were holding down the lid, flung them over
his shoulder and opened the piano. Whimpering, Scruff crept
out on his belly from under the splayed, shiny pages and sat
patiently beside him. Jasper sat down at the piano stool and
launched into *Mood Indigo*. A hideous travesty of its haunting
chord sequence filled the room. Jasper lowered his face sideways onto the keys and moaned. Scruff licked his ankle hopefully. After a while Jasper carefully unfolded himself and lay
down in the foam oozing from the Heal's sofa. Scruff sprang up
next to him, laid his head lovingly across Jasper's heaving
chest and stared trustingly, enquiringly into his eyes. Jasper
closed their lids protectively.

Who the hell am I? Jasper the inspector curled up with his
dog like a homeless person sleeping rough in a doorway. What
the fuck am I doing here? The question rolled itself towards
the ornamental ceiling and hung there.

"Did you want the bill sir?"

Her voice tailed up at the end again in that north-eastern
way.

Maz caught up with him halfway up the hill, walked beside him in silence for a while, and then said, "Are you staying around for a bit?"

"Couple of weeks, I think."

"You have a car, don't you?"

"Yes."

"Any chance of you taking a few kids to Newcastle to get stuff for Muir's party?"

"I'd like to." Jasper felt a little tug of satisfaction at Maz's request. "As a matter of fact I have to go into Newcastle tomorrow in any case."

"Great. See you later." Maz speeded to a run and disappeared down the drive.

Back at the school Jasper scanned the grounds for signs of Charlotte. He felt disappointed and relieved when there were none.

"I'll show you the guineas if you like." It was the girl in the meeting who'd let him know he should put up his hand. "I'm Tamara."

"Yes, please." He smiled his encouraging teacher's smile. "I'm Jasper, by the way."

Tamara led him to a hutch beside the school workshop. He could hear the sound of hammering and banging.

"They're making Muir's present," Tamara said. "It's a secret. Could you help me feed them? One got lost, so we're not allowed to take them out by ourselves."

Jasper bent down, undid the mesh door and fished around in the straw. He got out a brown guinea pig. It sat, warm, peaceable, on his hand and sniffed his fingers gently; he could feel the tickle of its delicate thin paws on his palm as he stroked its shiny, slightly curly fur with his other hand. Tamara had picked some grass and held it out to the guinea pig. Another voice said, "That's Cocky, the other one is Lucky. He's black and white." Aaron crouched down and got out Lucky. "Let's put them on the lawn."

The three of them sat down on the grass and watched the two guinea pigs snuffling and munching. Tamara knelt, knees

23

together, lower legs splayed behind her in a posture only comfortable to young children. Aaron sat close to Jasper. "I'll show you my Space Bandit after this if you like. It's in my room."

Jasper nodded and smiled at Aaron, his body untensing itself. He stretched it sideways across the grass and watched Lucky scrabbling carefully along the sole of his left shoe. "I'd like that very much," Jasper said. A sense of laziness and wellbeing, a feeling he'd almost forgotten, was seeping along his legs. "In a little while."

*   *   *

"Tell me about how you got started, Muir."

Charlotte switched on the neat little battery tape recorder on her lap. The story wasn't new to her, but she needed the detail.

Muir dived with relief into the warm sea of the distant past, remarkably easy to do these days. Deep below he felt the damp, calloused hand of Fergus Mackie, a ploughman's son, aged nine, inside his own. His other hand was already in the clutch of Mary Brown, daughter of a servant from the manse. (Reverend McVeigh, in his Christian charity, had found Margaret Brown a cleaning job after she "fell".)

"Sir, can we not be off doon the auld green and play, sir?"

Muir sometimes thought he could never again love any children as much as he had loved these poor, innocent, ignorant first pupils of his.

"They were misguided enough to make me temporary Head of Kirkstone Village School back in the thirties after the previous chap had had a nervous breakdown. I couldna bring myself to do to them what I'd had done to me. Really I always intended to become a writer not a schoolmaster, so I thought, och, I wouldna really care if they gave me the sack, gave me a bad testimonial." Muir contemplated his pullover for a while. "On the second week I took the tawse, the strap they had there

24

up in Scotland. I went from one class to the other holding it in my hand. The bairns cowered, they thought it was a threat – do as you're tellt or else.

"I made an announcement : 'We won't be wanting this any more. We're going to bury this in the corner of the school playground tomorrow at playtime. Donald, you can dig the grave, Kirstie, you can say the service.' Kirstie and Donald were the worst kids in the school, always in trouble. I wanted to show I was on their side.

"I saw them all in little groups after school chattering together, looking over at me. They didna ken what to make of it.

"At playtime next day I handed Donald a spade. There was a wee plot of garden, the only place that wasn't tarmacked over. He looked up at me. He was a bright wee lad, cheeky.

"'Are you sure sir?'

"'I am Donald.'

"I'd taken in my old military bugle and I gave them a wee fanfare.

"He dug up a few spadefuls. I handed him the tawse. He ran it across the palm of his hand a few times contemplatively, gave me a wink and threw it in the hole. He spaded back the earth and stamped it down with his boots which were about three sizes too big for him, hand-me-downs from his brother Tam.

"'Kirstie.'

"Kirstie stepped forward in her ragged dress and planted crossed sticks bound together with rushes on top of the grave and said in a sepulchral voice,

"'Tawse, tawse, rest in peace.
 You never gave us nane.
 Even if Reverend McVeigh tells us
 We'll nae dig you up again.'

"The bairns had all gathered. They cheered and threw their bonnets in the air. I thought it was a fine effort, that funeral."

"And you wrote a book about it, that school ?" Charlotte had heard the story of the tawse many times before.

"Aye after the year was up we were like a big family. We never stayed in the classroom unless it rained. We'd be off in the woods, or sitting in a cornfield picnicking and sketching and telling stories."

Charlotte remembered that he had written in the book, "I've turned a hard-working school into a playground and I rejoice."

"After the year was up," Muir said, "I decided that as soon as I could I'd set up on my own but it took me a while before I could get the cash together, so that was later. I started off with about five so-called problem children in a little house down in Somerset. I'd decided I wasna going to teach them, I was going to let them teach me."

"And Coralford grew out of that?"

"Aye. The first years were the hardest of course. Shortage of money, and we had some tough guys. They'd been repressed and beaten and all they wanted to do at first was let off steam. We got a lot of destruction, broken windows, abuse, while they were getting their own back on adults."

A somewhat more recent face swam into Muir's head. It was a girl's face, contorted with rage. "You're a bastard, Muir !" She had Muir's favourite dinner plate in her hands and she smacked it against the wall of his living-room, where he used to give the more difficult kids therapy, known then as PL's or Psychology Lessons. The plate broke in two with a satisfying clap and fell to the floor. Muir rummaged around on the dresser and handed her another plate sneakily picking one that already had a crack in it.

"Try this one my dear."

The girl put the plate down on the table and burst into tears.

He told Charlotte this story. Charlotte was laughing.

"Muir, that was me – don't you remember, after the newspaper?"

Charlotte's friend Winnie had a PL every week and Charlotte had felt jealous. Winnie said anyone could get one, you only had to ask. When Charlotte went for her first PL Muir was sitting in the same big chair as now and he motioned her to another. He said nothing. Charlotte waited. Muir waited. Nothing happened. After a while Muir lit his pipe, put the matches on the arm of his chair, picked up a newspaper from a nearby table, opened it out and disappeared behind it. Charlotte sat watching and waiting. Muir carried on reading.

"Aren't you going to ask me some questions?" Charlotte had said at last.

"Nope."

Muir turned a page. Charlotte could hear the sucking noise of his pipe. A thin cloud of smoke floated up from behind The Times. Charlotte grabbed the matches, lit one and set fire to the corner of the back page. Without haste, Muir lowered the Times to the floor and placed his large square-toed shoe over the flame, reducing the corner of the page to blackened ash. "Good," he said. "I didn't think you had the guts to do that. Might have picked the front page though, I hadna quite finished the crossword."

After that came the scene with the plate.

"So you were the wee besom who broke my favourite plate. Och weel, you've turned out not so bad considering the school you went to."

Muir leaned back and closed his eyes. The room went still and Charlotte wondered if Muir had fallen asleep. She had a slight fear of his closed eyes, thinking he might just drop off to death one day soon. She couldn't imagine how people of a hundred died. But Muir opened his eyes and spoke.

"I had a pretty awful upbringing myself: the tawse, the prayers. If they thought you might have even been thinking about masturbating (I never knew how they could tell) you got the strap. I wanted to do away with all that. I've lived here, trying to set children free for nearly seventy years, but I'm not free myself. I have the scars of childhood across my whole personality. I'm not a Coralforder like you lot. What's it like to be free, free from all that?"

"I don't feel especially free," Charlotte said, realising suddenly that she was the one being interviewed, being required to explain herself. She was thinking hard. She wanted to be absolutely truthful, to get at the crux. "It's too abstract, the idea of freedom. I suppose if you're in prison and someone lets you out, maybe you feel free. But if not, maybe you just feel — well, normal. It takes a long time to realise your normal might not be the same as other people's. You have a different set of questions and answers I suppose. That can make conversation difficult."

"With me too?"

"In a way. In a way you are a conventional man reacting against a conventional world. Writing a history of twentieth century thinkers we can put you in a category – Russell, Wells, Shaw – iconoclasts, rebels, enfants terribles. And of course they were your friends, you had a set, a coterie. But me, I'm one of about five hundred people that might have been here at one time or another, but most of them are doing something else. They're housewives, librarians, office workers, university lecturers. They're assimilated, on the face of it, just like the rest of the population. Yours is not a philosophy that produces disciples – well not among ex-pupils anyway." Charlotte smiled at him. "You should be glad, disciples always get things wrong."

Muir gave a faint groan. "Aye, I don't want disciples . . . but I wouldn't mind them doing something a bit . . . different."

"What?" Charlotte had considered this problem many times. "What could they do that was more different than what you'd already done? What for? What would they want to do anything different for? Like old Isaiah Berlin said, freedom's a negative power – freedom not to do things is what matters. Surely you are the supreme exponent of that notion, even if you've never heard of it." (Muir was always claiming to be ill-read, Charlotte remembered.) "You've given us the freedom not to do anything in particular. We haven't felt . . . driven . . . most of us . . . driven to change things, driven to action, driven to may-hem, driven to revolt. We haven't got that enormous electrify-ing charge that comes from feeling inadequate or angry, or regretful, or deprived or neurotic.

"So, I've produced a bunch of friendly cabbages ?"

"A friendly cabbage isn't such a bad achievement as a matter of fact. Most cabbages are not friendly. Isn't that the over-riding message of the twentieth century? Give the average cabbage a football match, a couple of pints, confront it with a foreigner, someone who worships strange Gods, and he or she – yes, or she – will leap out of the patch with a machete, encouraging the rest of the cabbages to do the same."

Muir's attention was wandering. A small blue butterfly had come in through the open window and landed on his knee, perching, wings folding and unfolding, on the brown corduroy, making the lines of the fabric suddenly seem like a ploughed field. Charlotte wasn't sure Muir had seen it.

"It's a butterfly. Shall I put it out ?"

She leaned across, cupped the butterfly in her hands and put it out of the open window. It fluttered away, and was lost in the blue of the sky.

"Will it be like that I wonder, dying?" Muir said.

Charlotte was surprised he'd followed the flight. But the old were long-sighted. "Merging, sort of, you mean, with a blue sky?"

"Aye."

Charlotte tried to imagine the sky as an Escher-like anti-world of pressed butterflies, each with its wingspan of soul. "I don't see why not. One could hope."

Muir changed the subject suddenly, "Will they let it survive me?"

"They?"

"Whatever they call themselves these days – I lose track – the Education Department, the HMIs."

"Ofsted now, I think they call them. I don't know, Muir. Maybe Coralford isn't a threat anymore."

"Because I don't write books and letters now ?"

"Maybe."

"Charlotte . . . do something for me, dear."

"Of course."

"Find out what that inspector chappie is up to. He says it's a private visit, but I'm not so sure."

"Jasper Bignold?"

"Aye."

"I know him from university, by coincidence. I'll have a chat with him."

Charlotte didn't feel entirely comfortable with Muir's request but couldn't avoid it. She switched off the tape.

"Shall I bring you some coffee, Muir ?"

CHAPTER THREE

Mazola von Strumm sat cross-legged in his underground safehouse below the hockey field, planning his next move. Outside the door there was a loud chirping coming from the trees, which MvS knew would be the sparrows. They were relaying information to Earth from the Venusian Embassy on the small planet Strumm after which his mother had been named.

He understood that when these noises became audible to his Earthling ear, it meant his instincts were correct. Much of his success as a sleuth depended on the virtually trance-like state he fell into when working, which allowed the rhythms of the Universe to flow into his mind. He had partaken of the quick-silver fluid again on the way back to school, before he caught up with Jasper. This had enabled him to note Jasper's relief at being offered the hand of friendship, and his pride at being given an assignment. MvS did not intend to join the Muir's Birthday Committee and Jasper on their trip to Newcastle. It was his intention, in Jasper's absence, to make a careful search of his things. At the same time, he felt pleased to know that MBC would be enjoying a comfortable ride in Jasper's BMW. He suspected that Jasper, like most visitors anxious to ingratiate himself, would probably stand them to a generous tea somewhere in town. Though he regretted missing this, for he was perpetually hungry, MvS found the prospect of the search more exciting.

The noise of an amplified guitar and a set of drums being thwacked merged with the planetary chirruping. Maz inched forward, still in lotus, using his hands, and rose to his feet in one swift movement by pressing onto the outsides of his feet, uncrossing his legs with a sort of leaping pirouette and made for the sound which was issuing from the lounge.

*　　　*　　　*

The piano wasn't that good. Someone had taken the front off and its iron framed grid of strings was covered in dust. Jasper was sticking to a basic twelve-bar, all he felt capable of after such a long absence from the keys. A kid he hadn't noticed before, probably because he was so small, was struggling to get his arms and fingers round what looked and sounded like a home-made electric guitar. A girl was thrashing a kit which consisted of snare, high-hat, bass drum and tom-tom. Jasper felt she was speeding and tried to hold back the beat. A crowd of onlookers was gathering, tapping their feet encouragingly. Aaron stood quite close to the piano, staring intently at Jasper, chewing again and looking rather sulky. Jasper became aware of a bass struggling to find the right key, finding it, and setting up a rhythmic stair-climbing riff under the piano chords, holding down the tempo. He looked up and saw Maz, a bass guitar slung round his neck like a postman's bag, an ear close to the keyboard, and his fingers, still less than full-sized, walking steadily up and down the frets.

Jasper couldn't quite remember how he got into this situation. Aaron, he thought. After they'd put the guinea pigs away, and he'd been to Aaron's room in the house to see the Space Bandit, Aaron had taken him over to the lounge where the kids were practising, and Aaron had asked did he play anything and someone else had said did he know such and such a tune.

Maz's arrival had lifted the musical quality of this scratch band considerably. Jasper suggested *Perdido,* a slightly more complex number, and then some Latin American stuff. Maz, he noticed, kept glancing at him with an odd, slightly critical expression. But Jasper knew he wasn't critical of the music, it was something else, some underlying suspicion, prejudice even, that Maz had towards him. But he could see that the kid had exceptional talent. They recognised it in each other, this musicality. Finally the other kids stopped playing and Maz and Jasper moved into a complex piano and bass duet that was interrupted by a kid running through the lounge ringing the bell for second lunch. The onlookers gave Maz and Jasper a big cheer. Maz put down his guitar and strolled off towards the dining room to be near the front of the queue.

And now Jasper was to be a featured member of the Coralford band when they played their spot at Muir's party and was committed to God knows how many rehearsals before the event took place. Kids came up to him saying, "That was great." Suddenly everyone seemed to know his name, his nickname even – "You playing for the party, Jasp?"

Aaron tucked his arm through Jasper's and saw him to the dining room, where he left him. "See you later, Jathpy", he lisped and ran off.

Jasper was a man of his time, a conventional man of his time. He'd left his grammar school and gone to university, northern, unglamorous, hung around on the edges of the sit-in in '68, been on a couple of student committees that had trickled down from these events, had his first real affair with a woman a few years older than him, a woman of experience – Charlotte. She had been one of the founders of the Libertarian Socialist Group, a woman of independent mind. She had charisma stemming from her background: her father had been in the Free French Navy during the war, her mother had a mysterious job in British intelligence. Most fascinating of all she had been a pupil at the world's most famous, most free school – Coralford. Jasper had never met anyone quite like her before and felt his heart and head were opening out into the sunlight of freedom, of over-arching love. Then he'd moved back into the mainstream middle class life where his family had been for a number of generations: small tradespeople in the late Victorian period and by the 1960's comfortably off, running an engineering works, pillars of their local community. There was a powerful network of them and they hauled Jasper back aboard the boat that they saw as essential for his successful navigation of the river of life. His was the first university-educated generation in the family and they weren't going to let him fritter it all away being some sort of drop-out, some sort of hippy, messing about with some woman who was

33

certainly no better than she should be, and not the kind you married.

And Jasper had stayed in the boat. Having dunked a toe into the swirling psychedelic waters he had stayed aboard the boat. Well, what else was he to do for God's sake? What was to be gained by slogging round India wrapped in a bedsheet filling yourself up with some mystical claptrap or other? Jasper was too bright, too practical, too fond of comfort for that.

But he felt bad, guilty, regretful about it all nonetheless – still. Essentially he felt bad about two things, the piano and Charlotte. He used to play the piano every day – no, every night, through the night, in smoky pubs and student parties and then stagger back to bed and sleep, lectures missed, essays not finished. When he did wake up his head would be full of chords and tunes and riffs, his hands itching to feel the cool, creamy, soothing keys beneath them. He used to hate the bitch when she never quite sounded like the miraculous music in his head. But he worked at her, tamed her, almost made hands and head meet. He had a jazz trio for a while, MJQish. He was good and he knew it. To Jasper it made him and Charlotte equal somehow: her experience, her style, her free-ranging mind and his knowledge and talent. He could have taken a different boat, the music boat, and he knew it. He let his parents pull him aboard this comfortable, monotonous steamer chugging along some smooth, featureless waterway for no particular reason. But why did he let them? What did he want there that was worth having?

He gave up Charlotte and the piano like last season's unfashionable clothes.

The piano he had kept with him, like a coffin containing his long-dead self right there, in the front room of his well-appointed home. And he kept her tuned, meticulous over her maintenance, angry if the kids thumped on her. At first he'd opened her lid, tried to continue his conversations with her, tried to understand her wide, toothy grin better. But he played more and more rarely, never having solitude to practise, never having gigs to practise for.

34

And Charlotte – Charlotte was dust on the wind, a speck on the sun, a splinter in his heart.

He caught sight of Charlotte now, walking slowly with Muir towards the dining room. He hastily finished his tinned fruit and custard and went over to his flat. "See you Jasp," the kids sang out. Ms Piano had given him the in.

But he was not there only to play the piano, Jasper reminded himself uneasily as he dodged into the back drive just in time to avoid Charlotte.

He made himself a cup of tea in his kitchen, took it upstairs with him and sat in front of his laptop, meaning to type up his impressions of the place so far. He typed a heading –First Impressions and then a sub-heading – The Meeting.

After that he could think of nothing except Charlotte's twisted smile hovering above the battered staircase. He drank his tea and stared at the screen for a while. He felt dozy in the little back room with the sun scorching through the window onto his back. He gave up and switched off the computer.

An hour later Jasper stood on the chipped concrete slabs by the side of the swimming pool. A plump, naked, elderly woman was doing the breaststroke up and down the pool – Muir's wife, Helga. Muir himself, wearing a pair of ancient elasticated trunks, floated on his back in the deep end near the rail. His body looked like the bleached trunk and primary branches of an ancient, indestructible tree. A few kids were splashing about, some naked, a few boys in cut-off jeans or loose shorts, some older girls clothed in thin T-shirts which clung wetly round their breasts.

Maz surfaced from a dive, swam to the car tyre floating in the middle of the pool and hauled himself into it, trailing his arms and legs over into the water.

Jasper was relieved to see not everyone was naked. He stripped his outer garments down to his trunks and hung them carefully over the wattle fence with his towel, walked to the deep end, jumped into the pool and came up close to Muir, treading water.

"Afternoon laddie." Muir raised a stick of arm and let it fall back into the pool.

"I wondered when it would be convenient to have another chat."

Muir lowered his legs carefully and hung on to the side. His white hair, darkened by the water, clung to the folds of his neck in thin strands. "You could drop in for a while after supper."

"That would be fine."

"OK, laddie."

Muir let go of the rail, paddled cautiously across the pool and floated again, next to the other rail.

Jasper did a strenuous crawl up and down the pool for a while and stood up at one side of the shallow end.

Charlotte came through the gate in a white towelling robe. Her eyes seemed to swoop over Jasper's head like a swallow. She threw off the robe and stood naked on the edge of the pool. Charlotte's body was a little looser, more dimpled than he remembered it, the breasts angled down. She jumped into the pool, her sleek head emerged after a second or two and she swam over to Muir.

A fierce and uncontrollable pang shot through Jasper's belly, an intolerable wrench as though an old wound had ripped open. He fell forward and swam across the pool several times with his face in the water, hardly daring even to raise his head for breath, climbed up the steps in the shallow end and began rubbing at his hair with his towel.

He didn't want to look round. And he could sense somebody standing there, waiting for him to end his ostrich preoccupation with his hair. He pulled the towel off his face and opened his eyes.

"Hi Jasp."

She stood next to him in her white robe. She looked him straight in the eye. He could sense the others in the pool, looking across at them.

"Charlotte . . . I thought it was you . . ."

Her hair looked much darker again when it was wet. She

looked more like the image that had been hanging in his head most of his life.

"You knew it was me. No point in not saying hello."

"Of course not . . . We just . . . kept missing each other."

They looked at each other in despair, as if nothing they could say could disguise what needed to be said. At the same time, a sense of excitement, of suspense, came to Jasper, a sense of shadowy curtains at last about to rise. It was too much for him. He put his head on one side and flicked some water out of his ear. He bent over, balancing on one leg while he dried first one foot, then the other.

Charlotte stood still, waiting. At last she blurted, "Don't I get a kiss then?" She turned her face up.

He straightened himself and their wet cheeks met.

"You here on business?"

"Not exactly . . . Sort of . . . er . . . resting." He busied himself with drying his shoulders.

"Maybe we could meet for a drink," Charlotte said with that decisive air of taking command that he remembered with both admiration and irritation.

"Yeah, that would be nice."

"The Dirty Bottles in Eliston then. Tomorrow night. You know The Dirty Bottles?"

"Yes, I know the Dirty Bottles." He eased his tracksuit back on over his wet trunks. "I've got to go and rehearse now, they've roped me into this birthday celebration. I'm in the band." He gave an embarrassed laugh. "About eight thirty then, in the DB."

"Yup."

Maz was waiting by the gate, a towel wrapped round his waist. "Jasp – tell them I'll be there in five minutes."

Jasper made his way over to the band rehearsal, which was in the old theatre building by the back drive.

*   *   *

"What did you do after Kirkstone?" Charlotte said, switching

37

the tape on.

Muir had put on his old grey and black lumberjacket. Charlotte felt sure she could remember it from childhood, the feel of the rough wool against her forehead as he danced with her in that absurd pre-war, pre-wars pump-handle style, her short arm stretched to its full length, his accommodatingly bent, his big square feet turned in.

"Och, they gave me the push of course. I stayed in Kirkstone for a wee while, got a job as a hand on one of the farms. It made the locals pretty uncomfortable – in those days the village dominie was a cut below the manse, but gentry none the less. You weren't expected to get your hands round a cow's udder. Then I heard about Plato Tewson's place, Commonfold, in Devon. He ran a kind of community for adolescent delinquents along democratic lines. The kids had a meeting, a bit like here. But he ran into trouble and the place was closed."

"What for?"

"Two of the lassies there accused him of sleeping with them. The court had never believed these two before, not when they were accused of shoplifting and soliciting, but now they believed every word."

"Was it true?"

"Plato denied it".

"What did you think?"

"Oh I believed Plato. He loved the lassies mind, but he wouldn't have lied about it. They were over eighteen in any case, so they couldn't charge him with a crime."

"So what did you do next?"

"Plato had discovered Freud by then. He became a psychoanalyst and I became his pupil." Muir felt round for his baccy and began to tell Charlotte a story she'd heard many times about how he had fallen in love with psychology and believed it would cure everything, until he discovered that freedom was more effective than psychology.

"That came later, with the experience of Coralford?"

"Aye, the problem kids got better, whether I gave them PLs or not."

"But you carried on giving them."

Muir looked down at his pipe and smiled his leathery smile, "It was a way of keeping in touch, finding out what the kids were up to, who was courting whom, who'd stolen what."

"And you got the meeting idea from Commonfold?"

"Yes and no. I was impressed of course, but really the kids more or less developed it themselves. When we first started there were only a few kids – about seven if I remember right, so you didn't need a chairman and voting and rules. That all came later, when we got more kids."

"I remember when you declared a dictatorship and tried to disband the meeting," Charlotte said. "Nobody took you very seriously, just one of your occasional tests to see how serious we were about our rights. I even remember thinking that at the time."

"Och no, I just fancied total control for a while, shoot kids for not turning off the lights, not returning my screwdrivers, that sort of thing. But you wouldna have it. After two days you called an emergency meeting, if I remember, confined me to the cottage for three days."

"Why didn't you just ignore us and carry on?"

"Well you know, a dictator can't function without an army, and I couldn't conscript anyone to my side. Tried bribing them with late beddies, chocolate, extra poc. Didn't work. Basically I couldn't inspire fear in anybody." Muir sighed with satisfaction.

In the distance Charlotte heard the clanging of the bell for second lunch. "Are you going over?" she asked Muir.

"Aye." He put his arm out for Charlotte to help him up.

After lunch Charlotte went over to her visitors' house, finished reading Johnson's biography of Tewson, and made a few notes:

Plato Moses Tewson (my God, what names those Americans gave their poor kids!), born 1888, Pittsburgh, Pennsylvania, USA, son of a railroad employee. (Do I have to go into all this? But it fascinates me.) Plato was a bit of a rough diamond, bit of a maverick, fond of the women but an absolute

39

charmer and a genius with delinquent kids. He was taken on in Britain to run a newly established venture, Commonfold, master-minded by the ninth Earl of Tenbury on land donated by the eighth Earl of Tenbury. (What would we do without the liberal, landed aristocracy?) It was intended to salvage young delinquents from our, shall we say, rigorous prison system and encourage them towards normality. Tewson built it into a kind of democratic community plus Freudian analysis. (Not that he had any psychiatric qualifications, just a natural talent, a woodwork certificate and plenty of balls.) It was his self-government meetings which gave Muir the idea, or so people claim. Muir seems to think it was mainly the kids themselves who thought of it.

Plato had been running things for a few years when a couple of the girls that were there on licence from the Magistrates' Courts accused him of sexual abuse (or whatever the term was then) and though it was never proved and Tewson was never found guilty, the Home Office stepped in smartish, withdrew its support and the place had to close down. (Baby out with the bathwater again.) Some people felt the Home Office wanted to do this anyway because the place was too free and too successful, and poor old Plato was just a scapegoat. He was a great survivor and a great improvisor so he became a psychoanalyst on the London scene and Muir became one of his analysands. So did lots of lords and ladies and a few clergymen too. Lots of ladies. Plato could charm the bloomers off women and he almost certainly charmed them off some of his "students", so there he was in court again and the papers were full of it. Finally, broken and under threat of deportation he took a walk on the Wilde side – fled to Paris and died in 1934 before he even made fifty.

Muir was under Tewson's spell for a long time even though he'd worked out quite a lot of things for himself about loving kids and letting them play, in Kirkstone, before he even met him. Only some time after Plato's death did Muir feel sufficiently free of him to start up his own school.

(Funny, all this time I never knew the term PL came from Tewson – apparently, because he had no qualifications, he couldn't officially "analyse" people, so he called them pupils and gave them "psychology lessons", or PLs. It doesn't seem totally clear as to whether he was the latest, suitably persecuted

Christ, or a randy old . . . er . . . faker. Maybe it doesn't matter. Muir loved him and seems to think he was a genius with kids even if he was a randy old faker. More research needed. This article seems to be developing into a treatise as usual. Amazing how the fight for freedom goes around and around, always coming back to the same place, always dependent on some individual's reputation, always vulnerable to scandal. Muir of course is very careful about his own reputation, hence his longevity. Saintly and self-effacing revolutionaries – is that what we need? Boring. Not very nice for them. So many strands of thought, forgotten men and women, half-realised buried ideas that fed into this little island of Coralford, once influential and famous and now about as close to our education system as Tahiti is to Alcatraz.)

CHAPTER FOUR

Jasper met the members of Muir's Birthday Committee who were going to Newcastle with him in front of the house after breakfast: Katie, Leah, Brendan, Tamara and Aaron. He felt more relaxed about Charlotte. Behaving like no more than a friendly next-door neighbour she'd offered to check his back window for him, which, with a growing absent-mindedness, he felt sure he'd left open.

"You all look pretty smart," Jasper said.

Leah curtsied. "Thanks Jasp. I like your suit, by the way."

Jasper wore a dark suit and a tie because he had inspectorate business in Newcastle.

Aaron was wearing clean jeans and check shirt and his hair, just washed, was slicked back. A well-brushed and combed eleven-year-old with no chewing gum.

Katie looked at him sadly. "Aaron, it's no good, you're gated."

"So? I'm on the committee."

"Tough. You can't go out if you're gated. School rule."

Aaron looked appealingly at Jasper. "You want me to come Jathpy, don't you?"

"Of course Aaron, but – well, a rule's a rule." He felt bad. He felt for Aaron: his loneliness, his sulkiness. He tousled Aaron's damp hair. "Never seen you looking so clean too . . . It's a pity, but . . ."

Aaron ducked his head away from Jasper's comforting hand. "Fuck off, jutht fuck off !" Tears began to spout from his eyes, and he ran off in the direction of the hockey field.

"Oh dear ! Should I go after him?" Jasper asked.

"No," Katie said, "he's always having hairies. It's because he's new, still breaking out. It's usually like that for the first few terms."

"Hairies ?"

"Hairy fits."

"Oh." Jasper smiled to himself at the combination of psychological sophistication and childish slang.

A little crowd had gathered to wave them off as though they were going on safari to a distant land. Jasper's BMW slid smoothly over the rough gravel of the front drive. The three younger kids sank into the back seats, Katie sat next to him.

The day felt muggy with a grey and deeper grey bank of clouds around the edge of the sky. Jasper had not driven anywhere during his five days at Coralford. He'd not been anywhere further than his walk into Eliston to the Coffee Pot and an occasional drink in the Dirty Bottles after his evening meal at the school, when he sat in the front bar letting the upending brogue of the locals rise soothingly around him. About nine o'clock he'd edge out, waving and smiling, and walk back, past the gloomy shape of the castle against the star-glutted sky, down the steep hill where you heard the burble of water over stones in the quiet carless night, and back up to the little terrace. He'd look out of the back window across to the school, where just a light or two was showing on the upper floors, make himself a cup of tea and a sandwich in the kitchenette at the back of the downstairs room and be in bed, foetal and relieved by sleep, before Eliston church clock finished tolling ten.

He swung the BMW off the access road onto the A1 and headed south behind a tall maroon truck with LONG VEHICLE and MORPETH ELECTRONICS written in yellow lettering on its rear. After a while they got onto the dual carriageway and he began the game of mirror glancing, waiting for a chance to swing into the fast lane. The kids encouraged him – "Go for it Jasp." He pulled out, put the BMW into fifth and was soon speeding along in his commodious capsule through the space allowed by the solid, slow-moving trucks on his left, and a phalanx of assorted vehicles passing back towards Scotland. Jasper shoved a CD into its slot on the dash and the car's excellent sound system surrounded them with Coleman Hawkins' deep-blue tenor sax. Jasper reflected that his own offspring, even now, would have complained at this old-fashioned self-centred choice of music, but these kids seemed contented enough. They sped through thickly wooded valleys and hills, sheep-dotted meadows, past the tidy roofs of isolated houses which all seemed to be part of some other dimension, a constant green rhythm flowing around and under them, a sombre bowed cello under the relaxed beat of Hawkins' *Body and Soul*, disconnected from the A1, its white glare, its speeding and slowing, its hazards.

Chimneys and pylons signalled the outskirts of the city and soon the grey haze approaching them revealed its interior structure: a Novotel, a school with peeling, blue-painted railings, St James's Park football ground and the Newcastle Brown Brewery; ramps, traffic lights, signs, bus stops, the spire of an old church like an ancient nagging finger against the high-rise flats.

A large roundabout sieved them into the crowded casserole of the city centre, its imposing civic buildings and massively wrought stone bridges silent and brooding above the litter of dry, scarred pavements, garish shop signs, and intricate loops of graffiti. Everywhere people, activated by who knew what unseen machinery, hurried about the streets and others leaned and lolled as if nobody had got round to changing their batteries. A group of teenage lads in Disneyish T-shirts and baggy jeans tumbled out of a hired van and swaggered about the pavement, swearing and pushing.

Weariness and unease took hold of Jasper. It reminded him of long past Mondays, when he was on his way into school after a weekend in the garden. It was like flying Concorde from Fatu Hiva to Heathrow, emerging into the metallic dayglo airport still half succoured in the restful green of exotic forests, the mind still lush with holiday dreams.

Well, you could sell up and become a musical version of Gauguin, he mused, plant your piano in the jungle, like some exotic cultivar; run a school for half-clothed native children . . . How many native children left on Fatu-Hiva, he wondered. He took his place in a queue of cars and drove slowly over the High Level Bridge towards Gateshead.

"The bridges, look at the bridges! I love the bridges," Katie shouted.

Jasper took a quick glance to his left and saw a series of huge arcs over the sluggish Tyne far below and then they were suddenly in the complex of freeways and roundabouts taking them towards the Metro Centre, its mirror-glass cubes eerily offset by an enormous and rusting scrap-metal yard on the opposite side of the freeway. He swung the car into the car park and arranged to meet the kids in the McDonald's at half past four, reminding them fussily to be careful of their money, to watch the traffic, to keep together.

"Yeah, yeah, Jasp – it's OK, we've done this before, you don't need to worry."

They seemed invigorated by the city.

"Let's check out the arcades."

"Not me, I want to go round Toys R Us."

"Don't be feeble ! Let's go and get a coke first. How about . . ."

He watched them in the driver's mirror till they disappeared among the crowds of shoppers and sat on in the car looking through his notebook, trying to bring his mind into educational focus. After a while he drove back into the centre of Newcastle, parked on a meter and walked towards the river down a steeply sloping street oddly named Side, to meet Denise Roxborough, HMI, Ofsted, for lunch at Dinette's. She was already there, sitting on a sofa next to the entrance. She wore a well cut navy suit over her well-kept figure; a pair of pearl earrings, which seemed chosen for propriety rather than decoration, were buttoned on the small pink ears which nestled into her thick, short-cut grey hair.

"Jasper, hi." She rose, shook his hand and bussed him on one cheek. She smelt profoundly clean. They sat down at the table she had booked. She looked over at him with a sympathetic smile.

"I was so sorry to hear about, you know, things at home. How are you coping?"

"Fine," Jasper said. "It's more or less over. I haven't seen Kay face to face for about three months. Just a few legalities now."

"I understand that Coralford is some sort of recuperative

45

trip. Doing something you've always wanted to do."

"Sort of . . ."

"Is it . . . helping? It must be a fascinating experience. Marvellous in its way. Pity not to see it in Muir's heyday of course. Something like that must depend so much on the quality of leadership, don't you think?"

Jasper's eyes flicked over the watercolours on the wall which depicted vineyards in Southern France. Their table had a single yellow rose (real) in a narrow-throated glass jug. The tablecloth over the small square table was impeccably white and starched. Jasper had noted some informal little bistros and pasta houses as he'd walked down Side but this wasn't one of them. He felt that Denise and the restaurant were allies, effortlessly maintaining standards of spotlessness and middlebrow taste to which he could no longer aspire, no longer wanted to aspire.

"I'm enjoying it. A bit disconcerting at first, but now I'm getting to know a few people, especially the kids. It works very well in its way."

"Such a pity Muir never adapted to currently perceived needs, never let his project be monitored, properly researched with control group comparison and so on. There must be so much potential value there."

"Not really Muir's job to do all that." Jasper felt rattled. "I mean the idea hasn't been patented by him, nothing to stop others doing it in their own way. Anyway, nobody monitored anything in those days."

"True." Denise ignored the menu which the waitress handed her. "I'll have a Caesar Salad and some mineral water. Jasper?"

"I'll have the same," Jasper said, taking his cue from her.

"Of course, we've taken a lot of his ideas on board over the years, but it's hardly appropriate today, not when children need to know so much more . . . don't you think?" Denise looked across at him, head cocked for a reply.

"Quite so," Jasper murmured, filling his mouth with bread roll and chewing it slowly to avoid a longer response.

46

The salads arrived, an artistically arranged mixture of lettuce, bacon and croutons on large oval plates.

Denise checked her perfectly manicured, unvarnished nails on their way to her knife and fork. "Look, I know your visit is informal, but as I mentioned in my letter, it would be helpful if, while you are there in that . . . er . . . unstressing capacity, you could find a way to report on a few pastoral aspects of the school – whatever could be potentially concerning, damaging even, to the department and the good practice we're committed to encouraging."

"With respect, how could Coralford be damaging to the department?" Jasper said, aware of a risky touch of cynicism in his tone. "I could imagine the department being potentially damaging to Coralford, but the reverse . . . You know the place is becoming more and more obscure, irrelevant. Muir doesn't publish any more, there are no LEAs who send kids there. An eccentric anachronism in the middle of nowhere."

Denise speared a small piece of crispy bacon from her salad and combined it with a pale-green crinkle of lettuce. Jasper thought for some reason of a park-keeper with his pronged stick clearing left-over detritus from the night before. She ate delicately, slowly, while she composed an impeccably diplomatic response.

"We can't avoid the fact that, like all regulatory bodies, we're involved in a rather complex public perception exercise. Well, you know that. In general of course we are about seeing that government guidelines with respect to standards in the mainstream are in place and implemented, but we do have to look to our own performance indicators, and this will include our role of guardianship with respect to the independent sector."

Jasper had never fully got his head round the concept of performance indicators. He therefore nodded understandingly and murmured, "Absolutely right."

"There could be developments in the independent sector which cause the public, and by extension ourselves, justifiable concern."

"Coralford is hardly a development," Jasper said. "It would

47

appear to have scarcely changed in sixty-five years. It's an evolutionary cul-de-sac; it's like the flora and fauna of Madagascar: fascinating, worthy of study, beautiful even, but unable to reproduce itself on the mainland even in a zoo."

"I think perhaps you misunderstand my thinking on this." Denise, amazingly, seemed to have almost finished her salad whilst Jasper had been speaking. His own plate was still half full. He drank his mineral water and bent his head respectfully.

"Coralford of course had things to teach us in the past," Denise continued, lining up her knife and fork on her cleaned plate, "but what was of value has already been largely subsumed and what remains is inappropriate in the contemporary, multi-cultural, techno-sophisticated world. Schools today must be, in the last analysis, vocationally targeted . . . wouldn't you agree?"

Jasper took a deep breath on her behalf whilst she took a contemplative sip of mineral water watching him over the rim of her glass. She was not looking for an answer to her question. She continued, "I'm suggesting that we could be reaching an appropriate moment to encourage the closure of an institution which contains, to say the least, some distinct worry-clusters."

He let her breathe for herself while he worked in a last trailing forkful of lettuce. She eyed a passing waitress to their table and ordered coffee.

"One of them is Coralford as a focus for disaffection in the after-phase of government restructuring. And another is the under-monitoring of youngsters, advocated, it would seem to me, as a matter of principle at Coralford."

Jasper nodded in what he hoped was a non-committal way.

"That could leave Ofsted in difficulties if an accident waiting to happen finally . . . er . . . happens. You see what I'm saying?" Denise looked across at him, pushing her lips lightly together, turning up the corners of her mouth, and screwing up her napkin with rhythmic precision, as the waitress gathered up the plates and brought a pot of coffee and some tiny white cups and saucers.

"Your informal visit to the school could, we hope, provide us with a scenario for proceeding." She blinked lightly, apparently pleased with her prose. "Of course, important for your team, in view of your intention to tender for the Coralford inspection, would be that you would be well-placed to obtain the contract. One would want to avoid being pushed down the road of offering it elsewhere."

Denise sipped her coffee, sipped it again, put down her empty cup, and waited.

The pause lengthened. Jasper, although he hadn't smoked for twenty years, longed for a cigarette. Worse, he longed for a big sharp slug of whisky, any whisky, to go with his cigarette. In fact he longed to be sitting at a piano in a smoke-filled room playing *Moonlight in Vermont* with a whole bottle of the stuff standing on the piano and a fag drooping out of his mouth as his fingers languorously felt its velvety chords – doo di doo di dah . . . Charlotte's young face floated transparently across his mind and sank away.

"Was there a particular . . . er . . . worry cluster you'd like me to, as it were, declust?"

Denise leaned her navy elbow on the table and her chin on her discreetly ringed hand. She permitted herself a small grimacing smile over "declust". "Well, the question of prematurely active sexuality of whatever orientation, whether student to student or something more . . . sinister must always concern us, as well as insufficient supervision in areas where mental or physical safety could be compromised. Much of this would, in the long term, be investigated by Social Services, but I suspect that certain pastoral problems will emerge in the course of Ofsted's inspection." She smiled at him openly for the first time, showing a set of gleaming white teeth and the extreme tip of her surprisingly red tongue. "I'd be very surprised if you didn't bring to light difficulties in the area of supervision. I don't need to stress to you that concern for safety must always be top of our agenda – together with an adequate curriculum, of course." She looked firmly in the direction of the waitress who hurried over instantly. "Could you put this on my card, dear?" She laid her credit card on the table. "Jasper, I'm afraid I have to run. I have a meeting in Leicester this evening, trainee inspectors' thing. Why not give me a ring in, let's say two weeks . . ." She pulled a slim Psion organiser out of her bag. "Let's say Monday the twenty-first? Morning would be best."

Jasper suddenly felt angry.

"Just a moment, Denise. You know it's Muir's hundredth birthday in a couple of weeks. Do you not feel Ofsted should, might . . . I dunno . . . a congratulatory telegram at least, some sort of recognition? After all he is a world-famous figure, tremendously important . . . perhaps the most . . .'

Denise's blink developed a hint of seductive flap and marginally increased speed. Her lips turned up again.

"I hear what you say, Jasper. Of course, Ofsted should, in an ideal world be doing just that sort of thing . . . However, being seen to be impartial rather precludes gestures of that sort –" she smiled apologetically "– and I'm afraid the department does keep a rather tight rein on budget, I'm not sure which account would be . . . But yes, it would be a good thing to do. I'll mention it, of course, in the office. Yes, thank you for that.' Her lips recomposed to a pleasant horizontal, suitable for departures. She picked up the card and receipt, reclasped her bag and rose. "In two weeks, then. Thank you so much for taking time to come over."

Jasper remained at the table, called over the waitress and said with a sarcastic tone he scarcely knew he possessed, "Now that Auntie's gone, perhaps you could bring me a packet of Marlborough and a double whisky."

If someone had asked Jasper if he was interested in education he would, if being honest, have said, "Good God, no." The word conjured uninteresting, unattractive sights, sounds, smells stretching back into the mists of his childhood: the chalked, stiff looking fingers of his elderly maths mistress as they squeaked out trigonometry problems on the blackboard to be copied; the hideous day when six of them had been caned for smoking after waiting thirty minutes outside the head's study with every passing fifth year hissing, "You're for it, Big Nose!" Then those unspeakable years at Yarborough Comprehensive, going through the geography books on Sunday nights. "No, Freddy, Mexico is not in Antarctica. Consult your atlas!" And as his pen ticked and crossed and underlined and exhorted, that sick feeling of knowing that the following morning he had 4 G, which meant his weekly run-in with James Postman and Co., who sat at the back and took a mile if he gave an inch. Everything to be pointlessly checked out yet again: where were their books? Left at home, so that would mean a detention then. No, they couldn't go to the toilet, it would soon be break. Yes, he did insist Postman moved up to the front where he couldn't hold a conversation about birds all the way through his lesson.

Then being in his own office at the front of the school with a constant timid staccato of knocks on the door – "Please sir, Mr Jones says could he . . ."

And then trailing round artificially cleaned-up classrooms after obsequious heads and deputy heads, sitting through lessons frantically overprepared by nervous teachers, asking predictable questions of nonplussed children.

Sitting in meetings, endless meetings, listening to the platitudes, the lame theories, the excuses, the unrigorous assumptions about what children could and should do. No, he wasn't, had never been, interested in education. He couldn't imagine why he had spent more than twenty-five years of his life pretending to be interested in education, in order to keep his unexciting, unexcited family in their unremarkable semi with its built-in garage and utility room, and his piano trapped behind the pink lampshade.

And now he was expected to be an informer, a pedagrass. He was to bite the hands that freed him. He was to smack his host, a kind, wise centenarian, in the dentures. He ordered another double whisky and lit another cigarette. At three-thirty he remembered he had to meet the kids. He ordered black coffee and wondered whether the only safe way to get them home would be by taxi.

*   *   *

Mazola von Strumm, wearing his dark glasses and baseball hat, looked speculatively over the red brick wall confronting him. He didn't think it would present him with any difficulties. His piercing half-Venusian eyes could see clearly that the window on the first floor was two fingers open. He noted the potential footholds where the brick had crumbled and the pointing was missing, and the series of heavy-looking iron hooks which had once, he seemed to recall, supported the creeper which used to go up the wall. It had been better with the creeper, he thought; his half-planetary parentage had made him peculiarly averse to the heavy, ground-hugging quality of earthling structures.

Giving a quick glance around and seeing nobody about, he went immediately into lunar climb mode, moving his elastic legs lightly from crevice to nail, nail to crevice. In seconds he was levering open the window with his fingers, easing in head first on his stomach, and entering the room space with a perfect forward roll which left him sitting in his lotus in the centre of a furry red and black rug. His eyes pierced all four corners of the room simultaneously looking for tell-tale signs of – anything.

The scene around him was suspiciously tidy and ordinary. A single bunk took up most of one wall, with a sheet and duvet folded at the head of each bed. A small table had a director's chair pulled up to it. A neat little laptop in its case lay on the table under an anglepoise lamp. A miniscule chest of drawers completed the furnishings. Two metal coathangers hung from a hook on the door.

MvS checked the drawers and found them empty but for a newspaper lining. He looked under the rug, but found nothing except a solitary woodlouse. His sensors told him that it was immobile with terror, so he carefully replaced the rug and avoided stepping on the spot as he moved stealthily out of the

52

door. He found himself in a small dark space with a steep set of stairs going down, an opened bathroom door ahead of him and another door at his side. A typical earthling warren, MvS thought with a certain sense of superiority as he gently turned the handle of the closed door. A double bed, slept in but made, filling most of the space, another chest of drawers – underpants and socks, reasonably plain – M and S, MvS guessed, another table with an old-fashioned clock on it, still ticking, and some male clothes – tracksuit, jeans – hanging behind the door. On the small bedside table a shiny booklet, large, saying *Ofsted Guide to Inspections*. MvS picked it up and noted some underlined passages. The code system was far from obvious, he thought. Ofsted? Old Farts System of Terrestrial Detectives? But he'd heard the word before somewhere, a sinister bunch of mobsters from the wild planet Steddo he rather thought. "Crimbollocks," he muttered, suppressing a smile as he wiped the booklet clear of prints with the bottom of his T-shirt.

Downstairs, a single, good-sized room filled the entire floor, with a kitchen at one end and the front door at the other. A mug and plate were washed and draining on the sink. On the otherwise empty kitchen table lay an opened envelope. MvS picked it up delicately. 'Jasper Bignold, MA, 24 Huxtable Road, Bromley, Kent KV3 6NX.' He peered intently at the postmark but could read nothing. His fingers slid inside, felt the fold of paper and pulled it out.

"Crimbollocks !" he hissed again. His veins pulsed. He sat in lotus on the table and began to unfold the sheet of faintly scented paper.

A door opened at his back. MvS pirouetted round in an instant, allowing the letter to fall to the floor. He stood on the table, index fingers pointed at the intruder.

"Maz ! What in hell are you doing?" Charlotte said, standing in the doorway, with a slightly alarmed expression on her face.

MvS had vanished into his twin-jet quicksilver transporter, and Maz felt a bit embarrassed. He jumped lightly off the table. "Just popped in to see if Jasp was around."

Charlotte wasn't impressed. "You know he's gone to Newcastle." She was holding the keys in her hand. "Come on Maz, what are you doing here?"

"I was . . . er . . . just taking a look around. I don't quite trust him, Jasper, he's always snooping around and writing things in his notebook."

"Jasper's OK. As a matter of fact I was at university with him, I know him quite well. He's OK."

Maz picked the letter up and put it back on the table. "Well, in that case . . . He plays the piano good. It was . . . just a bit of a game I suppose. I quite like the guy, actually."

He backed towards the door. "See you Charlotte."

Charlotte waited till he'd gone and opened out the letter. It was a long time since she'd opened a letter of Jasper's. It was on DfEE notepaper:

Dear Jasper

Thank you for your letter of last week. I was interested that you are proposing to visit Coralford School. You will be no doubt interested in tendering for the inspection in due course. We feel that in view of Mr Muir's age it is important to have a project on line without delay, and your visit might give us some notion as to how to structure the inspection. What seems clear is that our normal guidelines as to performance, staff input and so on might be difficult to apply. However it is important that our standards are not lowered on behalf of what may have become an institution out of touch with contemporary trends.

A propos the above, it would be helpful to have a person to person chat with you shortly. I'll be in the Newcastle area over the coming month. Perhaps you could telephone at the office to arrange a lunch.

With all good wishes,
Denise
Denise Roxborough, HMI

Charlotte folded the letter carefully, took it over to the school staffroom and photocopied it. There was nobody much about. The kids would mostly be in their lessons, she thought, though she caught sight of Aaron hanging about on his own by the back drive. She replaced the original carefully in its envelope, put it back on Jasper's kitchen table, locked the door behind her, went to her room, put the photocopy in a drawer and sat down on the bed and thought about Jasper.

The last time she had seen him was as his train had pulled out of Manchester's Snow Hill station, taking him back to his parents for the Easter vacation. Charlotte had had to turn and rush out of the station forecourt into the drizzling northern daylight and gasp in mouthfuls of smoke-scented air to stop herself from screaming or fainting. Jasper was going back home for a week or two. There was nothing unusual about that. It had been, she thought now, as if there was a sensor buried somewhere in her head that felt into the future, understood that the letter, not this letter, that letter (well in a way this letter too) was already posting itself into Jasper's head.

She had not thought about Jasper much for many years, in the way that, after a time, grown up, you don't think about your height, or the colour of your hair. The pain of Jasper was like your hair going grey, or your waistline thickening. You made a point of not thinking about it, but there they were, grey hair and disappearing waistline and lack of Jasper imperceptibly changing you into someone else. Lack of Jasper was an undercurrent, an underlying state of being, no longer an acute illness but a chronic sense of dislocation. And you no longer remembered who you had been, how you had looked, what you had thought, how you had felt. You became sensible and conciliatory, or reckless and carefree, but you had changed colour in the way chameleons might change when moving from a well-watered, flowery garden into a desert.

CHAPTER FIVE

The Dirty Bottles was divided into a number of small rooms leading off a central corridor. It got its name from a pile of dusty green glass bottles in the front window, reputed to have lain there undisturbed since 1876. The locals were friendly and talkative, used to opening conversations with strangers. When Jasper had gone in there, tentative, on his first evening at the school, they had quizzed him gently.

"You'll be staying up at the school then?"

"That's right."

"You'll be from the TV mebbe?"

"No, just visiting."

And they would tell Jasper they'd been up there once or twice; their sister once worked in the school kitchens; the kids seemed a nice enough bunch once you got used to their rough appearance.

"But they're all the same these days, kids. We used to have to polish our boots every day before we went to school."

And they'd ease a few details out of him – where he lived, how long he was staying, what he did, although he was canny about revealing his occupation too clearly.

So tonight the barman greeted him familiarly. "Hello now, will it be the usual ?"

"I think so."

Jasper glanced around, saw that Charlotte wasn't there, took his pint of MacEwan's and found a table, glancing over into the other rooms on his way. The Dirty Bottles was carpeted and cosy. It reminded him of a little place round the corner from Charlotte's flat in Manchester. The gist of it was, he supposed, that he had been pared back to that time, that picture of the two of them, sitting opposite each other in a pub, just come from bed and just going back to it, full of complicit togetherness, naked for each other. All the rings that had grown round his trunk since had been viciously hacked off almost at a stroke – no wife, kids flown the coop, no secure job, nothing to buffer the imminent confrontation, to give validity to the way he had lived his life to date, to give him a credible point of view. He felt at a disadvantage, a potential recipient of I-could-have-told-you-sos, you-made-your-beds, I'm-glad-I'm-not-in-your-shoes and other gloats of that kind.

And he was in Charlotte country here at Coralford. He need-ed to avoid letting out the secret of his quasi-alliance with the other side. Not that he had decided to co-operate, not so far. Yet he couldn't imagine Charlotte gloating. On the other hand he couldn't imagine her sympathising. In fact only one vision of Charlotte filled his mind, and it was not of this Charlotte but of that Charlotte: lying locked with him on a striped Indian bedspread on the floor of her flat. Was it that he had been frightened, overwhelmed by the intensity, the inevitabil-ity of their knowledge of each other? "Little Death" he thought, the Elizabethan term for sex, for orgasm. He could have lain there forever, locked in little death with Charlotte, never left the room, never eaten a crumb, never spoken to another soul – forever. Once every thousand years they would have risen together, walked together around their walled par-adise, and walked again to their bedspread and declaimed to the sun, Donne-like,

"Shine here to us and thou art everywhere;
This bed thy centre is, these walls, thy spheare."

As his father pointed out (not knowing the half of it), you can't go on like that. You've got to do something, be someone. It's all right for this Charlotte, she's a woman. Some women are like that. We've spent a lot of money on you, Jay old boy, given you a lot. Don't want to lean on you old son. We all had our fun, I had my fun, at your age, before the war. Oh yes, lad, I wasn't born yesterday. But you can't live your whole life hav-ing fun. Got to be someone, knuckle down.

Jasper was back there with Charlotte, watching himself and her on the bedspread, when he saw a woman walking from the bar towards the table holding a glass of beer, her face a little serious, determined, a woman who looked exactly like

Charlotte would look one day, one day in the distant future. He felt suddenly ashamed as if he had somehow caused this woman to grow old overnight. The woman sat down silently at his table. He felt his face smile. His voice blurted a strange, unpremeditated question at her, in an eager, climbing tone, which seemed to parody the buzz of conversation around them.

"You got the letter then?"

The woman's face froze in shock. The lines around her eyes deepened and lines appeared at the sides of her lips and separated her chin from the rest of her face . She looked at him for some time before she spoke. Jasper began to drum his left hand on the table uneasily, realising vaguely that it was the first four bars of *Eleanor Rigby*.

*   *   *

Charlotte considered Jasper's present appearance in some detail, aware that she was making him feel uncomfortable and able to enjoy the knowledge without guilt. He was still good-looking, she had to admit, but he'd lost that sexy, straight-boy-on-the-loose charm. Hardly surprising, she thought, trying to be objective. The open, enchanting smile with which he greeted her was almost vintage, but the tender, indulgent look in the eyes which had always accompanied it was blurred over, replaced by a wary cleverness. He looked kind, careful, diplomatic, but firm, not to be vanquished.

And there was pain there. No, she thought, not exactly pain, but a not quite concealed irritation, as if there was something he couldn't quite catch constantly blipping for attention in the back of his mind; an away-ness, a sad kind of not-there-ness, a let's-get-this-over-and-move-on-to-the-next-point-on-the-agenda-ness. A meetings man. A partings man.

She checked for familiar and unfamiliar habits, and found one of each – the way he ran the fingers of his right hand into the hair at the back of his head (now completely grey, in plentiful, cropped curls), whilst drumming some tune with his left. But now it was accompanied by a slight tensing of the muscles around his mouth, as if making a barrier to hold back incautious words. And he looked dazed, as if shocked into silence at the fact that these particular words had squeezed through his own lips into the smoky air of the Dirty Bottles.

"You damned idiot," Charlotte thought. She too felt shocked. "What letter?" she said, a hint of subterfuge intervening because of this morning's sly photocopying.

"I'm sorry, I was just . . . it doesn't matter."

"Yes, I got the letter."

"I always hoped for a reply . . . Pretty stupid under the circumstances, I suppose." His mouth tensed again.

"I'd say so."

Charlotte had received the letter approximately thirty years previously. It had come in a long white envelope and had consisted of a single sheet of white Basildon Bond embossed with his parents' address:

> I'm not coming back to Manchester next term. I can't see you again. Don't ask me to explain – family stuff. I just don't have the courage, just don't have the guts to walk away from them. They've put everything into me and I can't let them down. I love you and I always will. J.

A young man's letter, Charlotte thought. Today he would have been more diplomatic, "Let's have a cooling-off period, a trial separation . . . think it over . . ." And she'd had a young woman's reaction, hadn't had the courage to get on the train, go down there, take him by the hand, lead him back to her. Hadn't fully understood that there were no more Jasper fish in the sea . . . and she'd tasted a few fish since then, quite a few. She sipped the half of lager she had brought with her to the table and changed the subject.

"Why are you here J? Just looking?"

Jasper felt wrongfooted. He closed his eyes momentarily, then fixed them on his pint of MacEwan's on the polished mahogany table.

"Kind of. I've always wanted to see the place, ever since – well, ever since you."

"No hidden agenda then, from the Department?" she looked hard at him, pulling his eyes level with hers. "Come on Jasp, you're not a busman's holiday man. Why aren't you in The Gambia or San Francisco enjoying a well-deserved break with the wife, away from it all?"

To Jasper the possibilities for their conversation seemed to fork, both directions leading to embarrassing revelations. He decided to avoid the family route for the moment. "Muir's birthday is an important occasion, even to the Inspectorate, believe it or not. He is, after all, a seminal figure in the history of British education."

"Come off it Jasp. Don't tell me they're looking him over for next year's honours list."

"Not exactly. They're wondering about the status of the school, its potential to continue after Muir dies. It – well, it might be a time when the school . . ."

"Could easily be closed."

"Not necessarily."

"But possibly."

"It's on the cards I suppose."

"So you're here to suss it out."

"Not really."

Charlotte spoke bluntly. "Jasper, are you here on holiday, or at work?"

Jasper's eyes had dropped to his glass again. He picked it up and emptied it, noting meanwhile that he could and should divert back to the other fork. "Well, both and neither really. Actually I'm on sick – no, sort of compassionate leave." He found it odd talking to this woman who spoke just like Charlotte always used to speak. Strange how the body changes but the voice remains the same, as if signalling some indestructible essence. Was his voice still the same, he wondered. He felt his voice was overlaid with caution, cant.

"You're ill? Somebody died?"

"Not quite. I've just been under some personal . . . stress lately."

"Oh, sorry. Want to talk about it or not?"

"Let me get us another drink."

Jasper felt he had done well to divert from the work road. He didn't feel able to grasp that nettle with himself or Charlotte. What's more he suddenly felt a strong desire to open up to Charlotte about the other business, make his situation clear to her. He put their new drinks on the table and sat down again.

"It's – well, Kay, my wife and I have recently split up. It's . . . after nearly thirty years. It's . . . quite a thing, I suppose. Not all that terrible, but . . . quite a thing."

"You're on your own?"

"Yes I am." He shrugged. "I'm afraid . . . for . . . for the moment." He was aware of his brief, self-conscious laugh. More like a sigh.

Then silence.

"How weird," Charlotte said at last. They looked at each other, each one noting how the other's face had acquired a tight-lipped stare.

"And you?"

"Sort of," Charlotte said, playing her cards close. She felt they were like twins, separated soon after being born, the one sent out to work, the other sent out to play. Jasper staying in the same job, carefully working his way up, enduring the frustration, the boredom but lulled by the security, the comfort, the safe sex with one woman only, while she wandered from place to place, man to man, struggling to bring up her boy, lost in petty adventures, meaningless activities, till their original similarities were all but lost, encrusted with habits and assumptions, pandering to other people's notions of who they were.

"You've got kids?" she asked.

"A boy and a girl. Grown-up now of course. You?"

"I've got a boy, twenty-seven next month."

She imagined Jasper's and Kay's offspring, carefully coaxed and shepherded, making their way, being a credit to their parents.

"But you're not still with the father."

"No. Finished a long time ago. We're still friends – well that's all we ever were really, looking back . . . A guy I lived with for about five years. . . . after you . . . it –" she hesitated "– just wasn't quite enough for either of us. All I can say."

Charlotte's tone didn't invite further questions and Jasper felt relieved not to have to pursue the subject. He just wanted her to put out her hand and give his a sympathetic squeeze, to forgive him. He felt her touch would either merge this woman back into Charlotte, or prove to him that she was someone he had only just met.

"Was that *Eleanor Rigby?*" Charlotte said. She drummed the first bar lightly with her fist.

"What?" Jasper giggled self-consciously. "Oh, . . . I suppose it was." He looked at his fingers.

"Shall we . . . get a little drunk together, just a little, cut the crap?" Charlotte said.

Jasper shrugged his assent.

"I'll get them."

Charlotte got up and went back to the bar. Maybe that's why I left, Jasper thought, because of the way she always took the lead, made all the decisions.

She carried the two pints carefully across from the bar.

"Tell me how it's been for you, darling," she said with forced brightness.

*   *   *

Aaron had managed to hang on to his mump all day. He hadn't allowed a smile across his face when people spoke to him and the most he'd said to anyone was "Shut up!"

He'd taken Space Bandit into the woods along with his piece of blanket and sat under a tree most of the day talking to it. The woods were on the far side of the dens and he'd watched the kids coming and going. Nobody had come to find him or ask him what was the matter. Well, I don't want to see any of them anyway, he'd said to himself. He'd meant not to go into first lunch either, but he'd got pretty hungry and run out of gum, so he joined the end of the queue and said, "Shut up !" to people when they said, "All right Aaron,?" and gave him a friendly punch on the arm.

Jane had come up and put an arm round him but he'd shrugged away from her. She shrugged too and said, "Be like that, then." She was used to Aaron and his sulks, no point pushing it.

At bedtime, which seemed to take ages to come, nobody said anything much, except for Jack and Albert who sang, "Aaron's got the gru-umps, Aaron's got the gru-umps," dancing round him in their pyjamas while he was getting undressed. Aaron said, "Shut up!" and got into bed, turning his face to the wall. Jane came in to give them their goodnight story and kiss and he kept his face to the wall hugging his piece of blanket. Jane planted a kiss on his cheek anyway. He put out a hand and fended her off, hiding his pleasure, stifling the wish to reach out to her and have a good cry.

"I knew you were awake all the time," she grinned down at him. "See you in the morning." She put out the lights in their room and went off down the corridor humming.

"It's all right for her," Aaron thought, guarding his mump. He'd been planning to keep it until Jasper got back, hoping Jasper would come up and make a fuss of him, maybe bringing something back from Newcastle for him to make up for leaving him behind. But Jasper hadn't come back till second supper. They'd been all excited and pleased with themselves, carrying lots of bags and parcels, but none of them were for Aaron. Jasper hadn't spoken to Aaron, he was too busy joking with Katie. Katie hadn't noticed him either. They'd all been hanging on to Jasper's arms, full of what they'd been doing in Newcastle. Aaron had gone back to the woods with his mump and Bandit. Then through second supper he'd waited outside to see Jasp but Jasp had just said, "Hiya Aaron," the way people do when they're thinking about something else and don't want to bother with you. "I'll see you tomorrow, OK? I'm busy now."

Aaron drifted off to sleep and when he woke up it was very dark in the room. It was up to him, he thought, if he went downtown. He'd go downtown now if he liked, it was up to him. The idea of going downtown right now excited and scared him, almost de-mumped him. But then he thought everything would be shut and he'd have to go past the hedges in the dark. So what? Only chickens are scared of hedges, and anyway, he'd take Space Bandit and Blanket. Take them where? Everything would be shut. Then he remembered the garage on the other side of the town. He remembered Jane telling Kevin, the maths teacher, it was open all night when Kevin said he'd run out of cigarettes.

Aaron got his clothes on really quietly, pushed his feet into his trainers and velcroed them across. He got Bandit and Blanket. Then he remembered he'd need money for his gum. That meant fiddling in his jeans pocket for his key, feeling under his bunk for the edge of his box, sliding it out without making any noise and feeling along the front of the wood to find the keyhole. He fished about among his letters from home and the remains of his last parcel being very careful until his fingers felt the little box in the corner where he kept his poc. He felt the corners of two 50p pieces piled one on top of the other. He left one there, quietly locked the tuckbox, slid it back under his bunk and pushed the 50p down into his jeans pocket. Then he stuffed the pillows down his bed, pulled the duvet right up over them, crept out of the door, down the back stairs and out of the house.

Everything was pretty dark and the air felt chilly, but the sky was full of stars and there was a slice of yellow moon up there too. Like melon, Aaron thought, I love melon, and he felt his mump draining away as excitement and hunger and nerves took over.

The hedges were bad, but he stayed out towards the middle of the road keeping Bandit between him and the hedge in case anything was dumb enough to try and jump him.

The castle was the worst, completely black and old, blocking out the melon moon. Aaron ran going past it, slowing down as he came into Eliston itself. The town was empty. Perhaps it had been raining a bit because the streets were damp and shiny under the streetlights. The toy shop was all closed up and so was the Sweet Box, except you could see boxes of chocolates in the window when you put your head right up against the glass. Aaron heard a rumble coming from the Dirty Bottles as someone drew back the bolts on the door. He hid himself in the doorway of the Sweet Box, crouching down behind an empty newspaper stand. He saw Jasper and Charlotte and a few other people coming out of the Dirty Bottles. Jasper and Charlotte were laughing and saying goodnight to people. They walked off towards the school.

Aaron walked on through the town towards a bright focus of lights in the distance and a big illuminated Shell sign. He speeded to a run, checking the 50p in his pocket, slowed across the forecourt, shoved open the big door and went into the shop.

The man looked up from behind the grill as he pushed his change through the plastic hole.

"Out late aren't you? It's nearly midnight."

"It's all right," Aaron muttered, pushing his change and gum into his pocket and making quickly for the door.

"Wait a minute laddie. What's your hurry?" the man called out after him.

"It's all right, he's with me."

Another man had intercepted Aaron by the door, giving him a wink. He caught hold of Aaron's elbow and propelled him towards a crummy-looking van next to the pumps. "You're from the school, that school, aren't you?" The man had a beard and thick glasses through which his eyes looked little.

"How do you know ?" Aaron asked.

The man winked again. "Seen you up there. I'll run you back, get in." He urged him towards the van.

"No, it's OK, thanks."

Aaron edged away and suddenly began to run, darting across the forecourt out of the circle of lights and into the darkness beyond. Glancing back he could see the man getting into the van and the shop man coming out to speak to him.

Aaron ran and ran till he could hear his own breath coming in hard short gasps, almost drowning the noise of the van roaring closer behind him. He dodged into the alley behind the Sweet Box where cars can't go. He heard the door slam. He pelted down the alley, turned into the little lane at the end and back onto the road. He ran on, clutching Bandit and Blanket to his pounding chest. His footsteps seemed to slap and echo on the wet road. He heard the door slam again and a motor throttling and revving, then the burr of the approaching van. He was past the castle now, down at the bottom of the hill. From behind him a sudden flare as the headlights came over the brow. Aaron caught the sound of the weir as the vehicle swooped down the hill towards him. He lunged for the stile,and scrambled over the rough wooden step into the field.

The van slowed and stopped. Then the horrible sound of the door shutting, quietly this time, as if the driver didn't want to disturb his prey. Aaron began to run across the black slippery field. Somewhere about the middle of the field he dropped Blanket, but he ran on, staggering, panting, clutching Bandit.

CHAPTER SIX

Jasper woke up to the sound of a bell. For a moment he couldn't remember where he was. There was a band of pain across his forehead. He groped for his watch, held it away from him and squinted at it long-sightedly. It was seven o'clock, too early for the breakfast bell. He went downstairs pulling on his bathrobe and put the kettle on. The sound of the bell got nearer to the terrace and a child's shrill voice could be heard shouting, "Special meeting, special meeting." There was a bang on the door and the voice shouted again. Jasper heard the footsteps receding along with the sound of the bell.

By the time he got to the lounge most of the school seemed to have assembled, the kids still in their nightclothes, the staff in dressing-gowns. Maz, like Jasper himself, was wearing his tracksuit, muddy from his continuing labours in the dens. Katie and Hiroshi came in with their arms round each other. Charlotte came in behind Jasper with a brief "Hi, J." Jasper leant up against a door unsure whether he was allowed to be there or not, but nobody questioned his presence. He looked around at them, shivering with sleep, wrapped in what they could grab – sheets, duvets, towels; snuggling up together on the stairs, on the floor, they looked more like refugees than schoolchildren. His mind slewed back to Denise, in her immaculate suit, sitting at the white tablecloth. He couldn't imagine how her disciplined mind and body would react to this rag-tag gathering, what professional phrase she would coin to describe them. Two or three bodies had hopped in through the French windows in their sleeping-bags – they had been camping out in the hockey field.

"Who called this meeting?" the same chairman as before, wrapped in a bedsheet, demanded sleepily. "Better be something important."

There was a small giggle.

"I did," said Muir's wife, Helga. She had a bustling authority about her. A kind but stern Mum, an elderly, no-nonsense, plump, domestic presence you might find in any boarding-school. She stood next to Jane, the younger children's house-mother, a tall, thin, young woman with spectacles. "I've just been told that Aaron didn't sleep in his bed last night and nobody seems to know where he is. Can anybody throw any light on this?"

Katie put up her hand. "He was pretty miffed because he couldn't come to Newcastle. He rushed off in a mump. That's the last time I saw him."

"Didn't anybody notice he was missing at beddies?" Simon asked.

Jane spoke, in a high, nervous voice. "He wasn't missing. I put him to bed as usual, and the beddies officers said he was there at lights out. He must have crept out in the night."

Maz's hand went up. "Quite a few kids get up to play early, in the woods, in the dens. Probably no big deal."

"We've already looked. The big deal, as you call it," Helga said briskly, "is that he stuffed his bed with pillows. Everybody would think Aaron was still in bed if Jack hadn't jumped on him and found he was jumping on a pile of feathers."

A half-nervous giggle went round the meeting.

"It's not funny," Helga said. "Either we find this kid in the next thirty minutes, or I have to call the police. It's not exact-ly what I want to do most, call the police and let everyone in Eliston think that Coralford kids aren't safe in their beds."

"OK," the chairman said, hefting up her sheet. "Anybody else, before I take proposals?"

Jasper felt responsible, guilty towards Aaron. Denise's words were feeding his headache, "An accident happens, that's wait-ing to happen. A lack of supervision," and he felt angry. Why had no one seen how unhappy Aaron was, how homesick, how vulnerable? He felt angry with himself. Why hadn't he imposed his adult authority and experience and taken Jasper to Newcastle with him? Because that was what he needed; to be special, to be given a treat, not to be bored, lonely, hanging round this place with nothing provided for him, no boundaries.

Then another wave of anger shook him. Why weren't these teachers doing something right now? Why didn't they simply take charge and get out there beating the bushes, searching round Eliston, telephoning the parents, checking the fields around the school instead of going through this pseudo-democratic farce, deliberating and theorising as if they had all day? He noticed his hand was waggling urgently in the air.

"Jasper."

"The best thing is for each grown-up to pick a few kids, the ones nearest to them. Give everyone five minutes to get their clothing on and then start fanning out in groups to the edge of the grounds and beyond. One party goes into Eliston to ask and look around. Everybody meets back here in half an hour. After that the police and parents must be told. You should do it straight away without any more argument. Just do as a member of staff tells you." He heard his old headmaster's voice ringing out. Impatience tingled down his arms and legs. He knew that underneath he felt guilty, guilty about Aaron and about the way he had so rapidly relaxed into the easy self-indulgent life of this island. To his surprise, nobody seemed to take exception to the sharp bossy tone of his voice.

"Does everybody agree with Jasp's proposal?" said the chairman.

All the hands went up.

"OK, carried. Right, stay where you are while a staff picks you."

Soon ten groups of children were standing in front of the house, fully clothed, carrying an assortment of sticks and broomhandles and hopping about excitedly. Under directions from Helga, they began slowly walking out from the school, poking around with their sticks as they went. Jasper, Katie and three younger kids poked and scanned their way out of the back drive, checking the bushes at the rear of the terrace on their way, left the school, climbed over the stile and fanned out across the field towards the stream and the weir. Jasper pulled a stick from a tree and began to prod along the hedgerows. One of the kids shouted from the middle of the field and held up a tattered piece of cloth.

"It's Aaron's blanket!"

"Oh God!" Katie put a plump hand over her mouth. She ran along by the stream. About halfway across the field, the stream gathered itself to a small river, spangled down the precise stone steps of the weir and lost itself in overhanging trees.

Jasper heard her calling and ran over, his trainers slipping and squeaking in the wet morning grass.

"What is it ?"

His heart was thudding.

"I can see something down the river, through the trees."

Jasper put his foot into the soft mud at the edge of the water and felt it squelch up over his socks. He peered along into the gloom of overhanging branches. He could see a red thing held in a bundle of reeds and twigs in the middle of the river. He looked at Katie and saw unwiped tears on her white face.

"He had red pyjamas."

"OK, wait there, I'll go."

"It might be quite deep, there's a school rule you can't –"

"It's OK." Jasper was already forcing his way along the bank, holding on to the underbranches of the trees, his body almost doubled, his legs sinking deeper into the yielding mud, the vegetation scraping his face, his arms, clawing at his tracksuit. Something detached itself from the bank. The water moved. A water rat, Jasper thought. He'd lost sight of the red thing now, it must be beyond a large trunk, low to the water, which stretched almost the full width of the river. Heaving himself above the trunk, he caught a glimpse of red through the secondary branches which grew along it. He forced himself over the trunk, through the foliage which whipped his face, snatched at his hair, snagged his sweatshirt.

He splashed down on the other side. He could see the red thing now. It was a garment of some kind, sodden, bulging, held fast in a clump of vegetation in the middle of the river. Jasper looked about for some kind of stick, but everything within his grasp, awkwardly bent down under the trees as he was, seemed brittle, bendy or rotten, snapping and breaking at

his touch. His head swam with pain. He had a sense of claus-
trophobia and doom, bent double out of the sun in this absurd
grotto. He felt he would be here forever in this dark slimy cave
of rotten wood and sudden, sleek rodents. "Hell, this is hell,"
he muttered. Then he remembered his stick, stupidly left up
on the bank.

"Katie!" he bawled.

"Yes, Jasp? Have you . . ." Her voice tailed off into sobs.

"No. Find me that stick I had, float it down to me, throw it
lengthways into the middle."

Clenching onto the bank, peering back, he watched the stick
ride the water. Taking the current from the weir, its progress
was rapid and straight, until it caught against the down
branches on the other side of the tree trunk. "Oh fuck!" Jasper
edged back to the tree and fought his way back over. "Fuck, oh
fuck!" he sang as the branches scratched and tugged at him.
Then back over for the third time with the stick.

He glanced back towards the weir and saw Katie's face and
the scared, excited faces of the other kids, heard the sound of
the weir burbling past them. The sun emerged from a cloud
and framed the shape of their heads. He felt as if he were
glimpsing angels out of a prison window.

He stretched the stick out towards the bundle. It was too
short.

"Jesus Christ!" Jasper pushed the stick down into the water
a couple of feet in front of him. The stick touched something
solid – about six inches of it was left poking out. For Christ's
sake, the river was shallow, quite shallow. He could probably
have waded down the middle of it without danger. He waded
now towards the reeds, carefully testing the riverbed in front
of him, and parted them. An old red blanket. He touched it and
the threads gave way. It was rotten, completely rotten, only
held together by the stagnant water, the enclosing reeds.
Underneath he saw a few coke tins, a plastic bag or two, a
lemonade bottle. The jetsam of an ancient picnic had somehow
recomposed itself upside down in the middle of the river.

"It's not him!" he shouted, and heard an answering chorus of joy, "Yay!!" He walked back up the centre of the river, waist high in water, probing ahead with the stick, and let Katie and the others hand him to shore. They were laughing.

"Jasp, you look like the Creature from the Black Lagoon." All five of them collapsed on the bank, laughing, and the kids hugged him despite his wet, smelly clothes.

"I'm going to the terrace to change. You might as well go straight back to the meeting. I'll join you there".

His tracksuit clung to his legs, his face was bleeding and he exuded a dank, mossy odour. He peeled himself out of his clothes, left them on the kitchen floor, went upstairs, took a shower, put his robe on and went into the bedroom. He was thinking about how Aaron had attached himself to him from that first moment in the meeting, about the guinea pigs, the Space Bandit, the comfort blanket, the way he stood by the piano. And the way he, Jasper, had only half-liked him, this sulky kid with his grubby face and whiny voice. He'd been flattered by the attention, and he'd understood that he was a lonely, homesick, scared little boy, for Jasper was a professional adult. He'd categorised Aaron, without consciously thinking about it: one of those kids other kids bullied, at least in normal schools, because they hung around teachers, sucked up to them, grassed on their mates. But Aaron had seen something in Jasper – a protector, a friend . . . Well, he hadn't been enough of a friend. He shoved his jeans and a shirt on and looked around for his notebook and a pen. It was important to write all this stuff down, to have a record, whether he used it or not. He couldn't find his notebook. He wondered if he'd left it on the table by his computer. Jasper's headache had loped down the back of his neck and was straddling his shoulders. Probably on the kitchen table his mind muttered thickly, but I'll check.

On the bottom bunk in the spare room a boy was curled up asleep wearing muddy day-clothes. A Space Bandit lay on the floor beside the bunk. Its helmet had rolled off and its guns were pointing to the ceiling.

PART TWO

CHAPTER SEVEN

Jasper was not an intellectual. He was a how man, not a why man. There was a job to be done, he did it, didn't ask whether it needed doing or where it would lead, he got on with it in his efficient way. Odd, he thought, here he was in this school which was apparently utterly unintellectual and unacademic and it was forcing him to ask why. Why was he asking why? He was standing on the edge of the hockey field with a head full of why's, watching the kids put up their tents, the latest craze. Ostensibly, he told himself, he was there to keep an eye on things as Denise had asked him to do – "just in case", as he excused it to himself.

It was late afternoon, the sun hanging over the far end of the field like an orange balloon. Jasper had a sense of weakness, of giving-in-ness, as if all his life he had maintained control of himself because it was the correct thing to do, and now that self-control was slipping. It showed, he thought, running a hand though his hair. It needed cutting. His tracksuit had bulging knees, the bum he knew was grass-stained where he had been sitting on the front lawn with the kids, playing with the guinea pigs again. He knew he would put the same clothes on tomorrow without really caring. He had not made his bed that morning. He had a sense that he was gradually sliding down a steep smooth hill, and though, like a child, not really having any notion what was at the bottom, being prepared to slide down just for the fun of it. There was a sense in which self-control could only be maintained if one didn't question why. To question self-control was to lose self-control.

The kids were laughing and joshing, stumbling about over guy ropes; plastic igloos were inflating like blue and khaki moles emerging from the ground.

Would they have been better off in their classrooms looking at, say, the open-field system in medieval England? Jasper hadn't witnessed any lessons at this school whereas at other schools that was the central thing you were expected to do, your main function – looking at the lessons. He'd noticed that here most of the lessons seemed to take place in shabby huts around the perimeter of the grounds as if peripheral to the life of the community. He didn't know what they did in their lessons. Maybe they too studied the open-field system – when they felt like it, when they weren't rolling about on their own open field. It didn't seem to matter. Jasper couldn't bring himself to intrude on their lessons. He'd had enough of lessons. Lessons bored him. All over Britain kids were sitting in their classrooms attending to their National Curriculum and these kids were putting up tents and messing about on the grass. Why not? Jasper asked himself this simple question, a question which had never occurred to him before in all his years associated with schools. Were they missing something or were they experiencing something important that the others were missing? If so, what? Fun? Life? Fresh air? Independence? What? Just the experience of being themselves, unfettered, unhindered, doing what they felt like doing at that moment? Or were they merely falling under the spell of another set of instructions, the spell of whoever had decided to have a camping-out craze? Or were they under the spell of Muir? Doing what you felt like doing at that moment – it seemed to Jasper that his experience of this had been very brief and was now impossibly distant.

His mind filled with a picture of himself as a little grey schoolboy, with his cap and long shorts waiting to go into school. Over in the corner of the playground, pushing its branches over from the house next door was a large tree. He saw a squirrel launching itself, as if flying, from one upper branch of the tree to another, and then appearing again, running down the trunk. Jasper wanted to run over, throw off his cap and scratchy school blazer and climb the tree, see where the animal had gone, see if it had a nest. He had gazed over at the tree, screwing up his face to look for the squirrel.

"Bignold, turn your head round, look to the front," a stern voice said next to his ear. "This is no time for daydreaming.

Playtime's over."

Christ! he thought, watching the tents mushroom, was that why he had been so irritated with Maz when he crawled out of the bushes that day as if he had nothing better to do with himself? Jealousy, sheer jealousy? But the last thing he wanted to do was scrabble around in a bush – but he had, he had. That's what he had wanted to do, scrabble around in bushes. But they'd made him sit in his grey suit at a shabby little wooden desk (even the tree had been humiliated – made into a horrid desk) and told him to keep his mouth shut, put up his hand when he wanted to speak, wait to be chosen.

Jasper, trying to build up a cross-section of case-histories of the children, determined to at least take Denise's concerns seriously, to consider the evidence from all sides, had chatted to Helga about Maz when he had seen her in the pool earlier in the day. They'd coincided at the shallow end, Jasper slightly out of breath from his twenty brisk lengths, Helga resting from ten minutes stately breast stroke to and fro. She was well into her seventies, he supposed, noting the deep pathway of her neck below her several jolly chins, the large breasts reaching almost to her folded stomach.

"Don't you think such a talented kid might be frittering away valuable time here? He may, after all, have what it takes to become someone extraordinary, musically speaking."

"Only Maz can decide that." She had a faint Scandinavian lilt to her voice.

"But is he being stretched? Shouldn't he be stretched?" Jasper was regretting his choice of words as he was uttering them.

"Like a martyr you mean, or a piece of knicker elastic – until he goes ping?"

"No, just to straighten him out a little, pull him out of his fantasy world and into the real one." Jasper realised his continuation of the metaphor sounded waspish.

"He'll do that for himself, when he's ready."

"I wish I had your faith," Jasper said. "I wanted to be a musician and my parents never encouraged me – discouraged me in fact. I worry Maz will kick himself later, like me."

"Faith in the child, that's what this place is based on. Belief in the child." Helga sounded slightly bored, as if she'd had to hold this kind of conversation many times before. "But I'm not an educator, I'm just the matron. Someone who looks after the body, washes lice out of the heads, makes sure there are clean sheets. Talk to Muir, he works it out, all this. He likes talking about all this, even now . . . I have to go now, time to get the first lunch. You know it's always late, the first lunch, if I don't go over there and hurry things along."

Helga wrapped her plump old body in a black and orange kimono, and pushed her feet into a pair of flip flops. "I think your playing is marvellous, by the way." She picked up her towel and slapped her way briskly through the gate.

He felt the insistent tug of Aaron's hand. He was standing beside Jasper on the edge of the field, tugging at him as if this was his only safety, his anchor in a rough sea.

There had been a special meeting: What to do about Aaron. "Aaron . . . you musn't do this sort of thing," Helga had said to him directly after the chairman had given her permission to speak. "You put the school into danger when you do this sort of thing, as well as yourself. The school could get closed. All because of you."

Aaron had sat on the bench, pouting, face streaked with muddy tears. "Shut up, Helga, you cow !" he said, and turned his head away.

Maz said, "It's no good just going on at Aaron, we have to do something about him. Anyone can see he's unhappy, lonely . . . He needs a dad or something . . ."

Which was how Jasper came to be elected by unanimous vote as Aaron's personal friend and ombudsman, even though Jasper had protested that he was only going to be here for a couple of weeks. Aaron's sulky face had brightened immediately and he'd run over and sat next to Jasper who was sitting on the lounge floor next to Maz. And Jasper had not said no. He had compromised himself, he realised – moved, or appeared to move, from one side of the fence to the other. Any steps he took now to report back to Denise in a critical light would be interpreted in Coralford as treachery. Which is what they would be, he thought to himself.

Why had he agreed to act as temporary dad to this snotty-nosed gum-chewer whom he didn't even like that much? Why didn't he just leave the place, refuse to take sides?

Well, probably because of Charlotte, he admitted to himself. Was something going to develop between him and Charlotte? They had become friends, in an unlikely, bland sort of way. Yet Jasper had a sense of Charlotte watching him to see what he would do, which way he would jump, about the school, about her – both of them avoiding underlying feelings, underlying questions. Guilt on his part? Jealousy? He didn't want to hear about her life of failure and hardship if that was how it had been. Nor did he want to hear about happiness, fulfilment, other lovers, her child by someone else. She didn't volunteer much information and he couldn't bear to ask. When they had reached the visitors' houses at the end of that first evening in the pub, he had put his arms round her. She had disentangled herself and planted an affectionate kiss on his cheek. "Maybe another time," she had said, and pulled the door gently to behind her.

And the fact was that he had been glad. He was intrigued by her, wanted to resolve things, but so far he had not been able to connect this middle-aged woman with the real Charlotte. That terrible pang which had come to him in the swimming pool when he saw her naked body had not come to him again. Nor could he interpret what the pang meant. Jasper had become accustomed to other flesh, to his wife's flesh, to no flesh. Jasper had an image, a heart-stopping, prick-stiffening image of Charlotte, but it was not this Charlotte, it was that Charlotte, and girls he sometimes saw who looked a bit like that Charlotte used to look, behaved like that Charlotte used to behave. Sometimes he saw girls – small, dark, lively, girls with long skirts, getting onto trains carrying those big messy straw bags like Charlotte used to have. The years would spindle back and he would almost run up to them, shouting, It's me, sorry I'm late, I'll carry that. These petite, self-possessed girls were present incarnations of a life that had whirled forward out of his and Charlotte's generation, he realised that. These were the inheritors: independent, feisty, argumentative girls, casual and open. Sometimes he met such girls, but not very often. And when he did, the realisation would flood over him that these girls didn't know him, wouldn't recognise him for who he was. If he were to speak to one she would treat him with respect, not with interest, for he was grey and straight and old and a school inspector. And that's what self-control was for, remembering to act your age, remembering your station. His self-control was slipping.

Here at Coralford, the girls seemed to like him. Katie would come up and put her arms around him, saying, Hello, Jasp. She would kiss him lightly on his chin and walk arm in arm with him into second lunch, and help herself to bits of food off his plate. It unnerved Jasper, though he knew it was innocent enough. But he liked it, he needed it, this easiness, this physicality. Kids didn't normally treat inspectors in this intimate way. In fact nobody did. You separate yourself, put yourself apart when you are an inspector, he thought. Everybody "behaves" for you, but they don't trust you. He'd never quite seen it that way before. People love musicians but they don't love inspectors.

Nor was it clear what Charlotte thought of him, what she wanted of him, if anything.

Aaron was tugging at Jasper's hand again.

"Come to the dens."

"In a minute," Jasper said, wearily.

But then Maz came biking over, put a foot onto the grass to steady himself, leant over the handlebars towards Aaron and gave him a friendly dig. "Want to borrow my tent, Gumface?"

"Aren't you using it ?"

"No, I'm sharing with Leah."

Aaron raised his head. "S'pose so."

"C'mon then, I'll help you put it up." Maz turned to Jasper, "Rehearsal, Jasp, tonight after second supper – OK?" Jasper nodded. Aaron and Maz went off towards the house.

Jasper stayed watching Katie and Hiroshi who were crawling in and out of a green bivouac. It looked as if they were going to be sharing it, sleeping together bag to bag. Maz too would, it appeared, be sharing with a girl. Oh God, Jasper thought, what do you put in your report about that? – "Unsupervised inappropriate intimacy is being encouraged between boys and girls."– Was it inappropriate? How the hell did he, Jasper, who had spent quite a chunk of his childhood peering illicitly through a hole in the fence at the mysterious knickered creatures in the girls' school next door, know whether it was appropriate? He noticed Charlotte's figure on the other side of the hockey field. She was sitting on a log, writing in her notebook. He didn't go over to her. He felt his eyes smarting with tears and walked away towards the main house.

Everyone who wasn't putting up tents seemed to be painting or practising. Lessons had been suspended in the afternoons by vote of the meeting in order to prepare for the party. Muir's Birthday Committee were organising the decoration and transformation of the lounge: old sheets were draped over its many entrances with wobbling bits of paper pinned to them which said, KEEP OUT! MBC ONLY. The thump of the gram filtered through the improvised curtains. Newspaper was taped over the windows from the inside. Members of MBC came and went carrying buckets of water, trays of paint, glue, cardboard boxes, staple guns, hammers, saws, tacks. Jasper had heard that one or two enterprising kids were running a book on what the theme of the decorations was going to be, with evens on it being historical scenes covering different periods of Muir's life. He felt like an outsider again, redundant.

He walked back to his house, hands in his tracksuit pockets. He could feel the sharp edges of Denise's latest letter, the good quality, stiff paper, and the thinner, photocopied inclusion. Charlotte had passed it on to him at lunch, the envelope a bit torn and scuffed. Maybe the kids sorted the post here – none too carefully, he'd thought. He'd opened it, chucked away the envelope and stuffed the contents into his pocket, not wishing to read them in front of everybody once he realised who it was from. He felt no inclination to read them now.

He spent a while in front of his laptop once again attempting a kind of diary of his activities since arriving at the school ten days previously, jotting down impressions at the end of each day's factual account. He realised he knew almost nothing about the background of the children, or the staff for that matter. He needed to talk to more people. Now that he had been more or less accepted into the community, it had become more difficult to talk to people in this questioning, delving way, and it certainly couldn't be done notebook in hand. He sensed that people here were tired of being asked the same questions over and over again, questions which seemed to them to have self-evident answers. But he would have to try.

Outside the window the big sun dunked itself briefly behind a cloud and made its edges fluoresce in front of a darkened sky. He saved the diary to disk, erased it from the hard disk, labelled the disk with a crayon, put it in his briefcase and locked it. Then he sat on at the desk in front of the opened laptop doing nothing at all, a strange and rather unnerving experience for him. He didn't even feel as if he was thinking. He heard a bell ringing and realised that the orange balloon was quite close to the horizon and it was the second supper bell.

*   *   *

Maz was tuning his bass by the piano when Jasper arrived at the old theatre. The rest of the band hadn't arrived. Mazola von Strumm was drifting in his transporter somewhere above the big beech tree behind the theatre with the controls switched off. He had never quite got his head round earthling music, the intervals being gross compared to those on Venus. Maz was relieved not to have to play that particular part for the moment, as he wanted to pick Jasper's brains about the chord sequence to *The Girl From Ipanema*, which had been bugging him all afternoon. But Jasper seemed to want to ques-

82

tion him.

Mazola von Strumm alias Maz alias Adam Hoyle. The route to his nickname was Hoyle: Oil : Mazola : Maz and as often happens this tortuous, childish route seemed subliminally to have found a name exactly matching the wide, slightly manic smile, the open, energetic, blunt presence of the boy. Maz's mother was Venetian rather than Venusian, a mathematician, whose brilliance in the subject had enabled her to transfer to a lectureship at Cambridge when she married his father who was a classical musician. They had met when the Royal Philharmonic Orchestra, in which he played second violin, had done a season in Venice. Maz had been playing instruments since he had first climbed onto his dad's piano stool at the age of four and felt an inadvertent C minor chord caress his childish ears. His parents, delighted by his obvious gift, had put him down for Menuhin's school and sent him for piano and violin lessons.

"But when I was about ten," Maz continued, "I saw this television programme about Coralford. It was on some schools' discussion programme, and I was ill at the time, so I watched it at home. I just told Mum and Dad, 'I want to go there.'"

"They must have been a bit worried about that," Jasper said.

"Well, yeah. They kept on about it for a few nights, you know, going on about my special talent, how much I needed to learn, how pleased I'd be later on, all that sort of thing."

"But they didn't just say no?"

"I just stuck to my guns. I'm going to play music, I told them, but I'm going to go to that school. In the end they agreed."

"What do they feel about it now ?"

"Don't know really, but they're OK, my parents, they're always OK about what I want to do, they kind of, trust me." Maz was tuning the bottom E string, his ear against the bass, only seeming to half attend to Jasper's questions.

"What do you feel about your decision?"

Maz looked across at Jasper, who was sitting at the piano sounding out the notes for him. "Why are you asking me all this stuff?"

Jasper flushed a little and he could see that Maz saw him flush. "I'm thinking about myself, how I never stuck to my guns about music." Jasper's words, intended as a red herring to explain his persistent questioning, suddenly felt like the truth to him.

Maz said, " I'd rather do this sort of music, it's more . . . more . . . You learn more about stuff, how stuff works . . . chords and stuff . . ." His voice tailed off, unable to exactly express what he meant. "By the way, I wanted to ask you something, about the chords to *The Girl From Ipanema* . . . You know, the band usually plays more rock kind of stuff, the chords are more samey."

"I'll write them down for you." Jasper played the first bars tentatively.

"No, just sing them out, and we'll go through it."

After a while Jasper heard the swish of the snare drums and some cautious guitar chords and realised that the rest of the band had arrived, and weren't quite up to a piece of this complexity. He nodded at Maz. They stopped together at the end of the next eight, and swung immediately into a twelve-bar in E.

*   *   *

"So the school began to expand," Charlotte said, switching the tape on. "Who sent their kids? A school like this must have seemed so weird in the thirties."

"Folks who didn't know what else to do with the wee besoms," Muir said, "people who'd tried everything. Actually that's not the whole truth. There was a lot of debate then, about education. Not like now, how to stuff the three R's in, but more fundamental."

"How d'you mean?"

"Gawd, everything was up for the third degree between the wars – religion, the British way of life. The Soviets had taken over in Russia, Freud had discovered the subconscious mind. You couldn't turn half of Europe into a sea of corpse-infested

84

mud and shoot the Tsar and then just blame the Hun and the Bolsheviks for everything. Something was rotten on the playing fields of Eton – not to mention the mean little board schools of the East End. I wanted to scrap the whole lot. Give freedom a try. Havena quite managed it. Och weel . . ."

Muir's voice faded to a mumble. Charlotte turned the tape up a little. Muir's dog had padded into the room and laid its brindled nose across his knee. He stroked the nose absently.

"Who paid . . . for the kids to come here?"

"The parents paid. Not very much, but we had to make ends meet somehow. The staff didn't get much salary, not enough really . . . but then they didna' have to spend their time walloping kids for not knowing their nine times table. Cushy job, compared to most schools. Had to sack one or two teachers who wouldn't accept the rule of the meeting . . . Hated that, sacking people."

"Some people would say it was a bit elitist, paying for your kids to go to school," Charlotte said.

"I dare say," Muir said. "Schools are schools. All desk schools as far as I can tell, state or private, no essential difference between them. All putting the head before the heart. All putting work before play."

"That's a bit questionable isn't it," Charlotte said, "you can hardly compare the results of Eton with the alumni of some inner city state school can you?"

"True, but that's a class thing, a money thing. The state schools took their ethos from the public schools – beating, coercion, punishment. They taught one class how to punish and the other how to be punished. Overdog and underdog. You can't have the one without the other."

"But people were punished in both. Where's the difference?"

"I don't know lass. Mebbe you have to be punished in order to want to punish. It's unnatural, I believe, anger and guilt, violence. In my day they believed all that stuff was original sin. I've never understood that. Sin comes from being sinned against in childhood. Anger and violence come from punishment and frustration in childhood. We always have to complicate things. Break the will and you get wage slaves, fail to break the will and you get rebels, people seething inside, criminals. I suppose the wage slaves seethe inside as well. That doesn't happen here at Coralford. If people from here behave badly it's usually their own fault."

Muir's eyes were closing. "I've been over it all so many times. It doesn't explain everything of course, this business of childhood suppression, but it explains a lot, enough for me anyway. Nobody can understand everything. This business, Coralford . . . best I could manage."

Charlotte bent over the dog and kissed Muir's forehead. She felt a tear drip from her face onto the dog's fur.

"Put that thing off." Muir opened his eyes suddenly and gestured towards the cassette recorder. "What about this business with this little guy Aaron and this Bignold chap? Can I trust him, Bignold? Helga says *The Daily Mirror* were on the phone . . . She fobbed them off – I can't deal with all this stuff any more . . . Been so much of it, over the years. Vultures gathering, waiting for me to go . . ."

"I don't know," Charlotte said, "I don't know about Jasper. I'll talk to him."

"You like him, don't you?" Muir's eyes fixed on Charlotte, the leather round his mouth folded into a smile. "Aye lassie, but can he be trusted? A woman's heart, not a reliable instrument of measurement."

"Muir!" Charlotte grinned self-consciously. "You're such a sexist – such a naive and old-fashioned guy underneath."

"If you say so lassie." Muir stroked the dog's nose and continued to stare at Charlotte expectantly.

"We were in love at university – long time ago. Maybe we still are . . . I dunno."

"The kids like him," Muir said.

"Jealous?"

"Mebbe, a bit. Och no, I'm too old for that kind of jealousy. I'm just thinking . . . when the kids take to somebody too quickly . . . mebbe . . ."

"He's a nine-day wonder."

"Just so."

"It's because he can play the piano. He's creative, gifted. Kids like that in someone."

"Aye. Women too." Muir lowered his gaze to the dog. "Helga says he talks about "stretching kids", all that inspectorish talk coming out . . . but she likes him too . . ." Muir yawned again and closed his eyes. His head drooped sideways.

Charlotte stood up. "I'll talk to him. Trust me, at least."

Helga came into the room, brusque and bustling and removed Muir's pipe from the arm of his chair. "It's Muir's rest time. You know this man is a hundred years old. He doesn't manage these talking marathons so much any more. Come to the kitchen, Charlotte. I get you some coffee."

Notes

Helga wanted to gossip. Who was this Jasper? What did I know about him? Did I fancy him? Just a boyfriend from university days, I explained. But was he to be trusted?

Oh God, I don't know. I just don't know. Trust what? Intention? Capability? Jasper is capable. He knows the education scene from all sides. He could be a powerful ally for the school, what it needs, able to deal with all the bullshit and politics that surrounds us now. Able to talk the language. He can be an outbullshitter of bullshitters. Seen him do it in the past. Probably even better at it now! But whose side is he on? Is he on a side at all?

Oh dammit, I need Jasper on my side, by my side, on our side. I've always needed him. (Now that's an admission!) If there's to be a fight for this school, I can't see it – him on one side and me on the other . . . No, no, no.

*   *   *

At first there was a lot of noise. People putting their heads round each other's tentflaps; people leaping up to piss in the bushes; people flashing torches. When the younger kids' bedtime was called they wouldn't settle down for the noise the older ones were making and Aaron screaming and getting mad at someone who pulled one of his tent pegs out and made his little triangle sag forward with an alarming lurch. The beddies officers got tough.

"Look," Simon shouted, removing his glasses and waving them about in front of a bunch of older kids who were joking about round the remains of the campfire, "automatic 10p fine, right, for disturbing younger kids' bedtime. I don't care if you're camping out or sleeping on the fucking roof! 10p fine, Hiroshi" – pointing the finger, glasses dangling, dangerous, from the end.

"OK, OK!"

"And turn that music down . . ."

"OK."

Later Maz peeped in on Aaron, now asleep inside the little one-person tent. Contented, for him, Maz thought, seeing Aaron, an arc of sleeping bag with his blanket and toys nestling in the curve of it.

Maz surveyed the hockey field. Some of the thinner tents glowed from inside where people were talking or reading with their torches on, but everything had gone quiet. The sky tucked in round the edge of the field though you could see a faint light or two from the house through the darker mass of trees. He wriggled into the tent and worked his way out of his clothes from a sitting position. A low little tent, a modest arch tacked against the earth, held up by curved plastic rods. Leah's mum had given it her for her birthday. Not exactly what she wanted, for Leah was into clothes and highly coloured posters of the latest boy band. She had an inkling that her mum was trying to get her to be more . . . sporty, be more of a kid. She'd been a bit annoyed and disappointed. But now that they'd got the tent up – mostly Maz, who knew every-thing about tents – and were in it, she felt quite pleased.

Leah was a bit older that Maz, six months at least. He seemed still a kid to her with his daft fantasies and keeping his den, but they'd been friends since they were both little in the main house, sharing a room. For Maz's part, he was a bit in love with Katie who was older than either of them, but Katie was going with Hiroshi at the moment; she too thought

Maz was too young. Maz himself thought he was too young.

He and Leah settled down in their sleeping bags tucked against each other like double s's and talked about sex for a while.

"I'm not very bothered just yet," Maz said, "I'm happy with my hand."

They both laughed.

"I nearly did – with Steve last end of term, but neither of us had any condoms, so we were too scared. Then I went over and saw Helga. 'Leah!' she goes, you know the way she does, 'no you can't. Your mother would make mincemeat of me, she'd take you away.' Except she said minzemeat – you know, 'Your muzzer will make minzemeat off me . . .'"

Both of them giggled.

"She's quite strict, your mum, isn't she?" Maz said.

"Not exactly strict, but you know, she worries about me. She trusts me, but . . . well . . . she slept around a lot when she was a kid. Everybody used to then, apparently. Then she had me when she was only seventeen. She doesn't want me to . . ."

"Be the same."

"Exactly."

"I never talk about it with my parents," Maz said, "but I don't suppose they'd mind."

"They're quite – I dunno, your parents – they don't seem to know much about sex and stuff . . . Still, I suppose they must . . ." Leah giggled again.

"They're quite serious," Maz said. "Music and Maths, that's what they're into."

"Like you," Leah said. She wriggled closer – "Minzemeat time" – and dug a downy fist under where she thought his ribs might be.

Maz dug her right back and they began to laugh and squeak and tussle and roll about in their sleeping bags from one side of their arch to the other, the canvas giving little groans and huffing noises like a ship's sail.

"Fucking shut up, you guys," Hiroshi hissed from the next tent. Eventually, still giggling a bit, they drifted off to sleep, two question marks in the middle of a sentence.

Maz didn't really wake up through the night, but he had a sense of light, just for a second or two, on his face. He was in the middle of a dream, a dream with a rhythm to it and the rhythm broke and didn't come back. But next morning Leah said she didn't notice a thing during the night, probably a glow-worm whatever they were and shoved him over to his side of the tent while she wriggled about in her bag and dropped back to sleep. Mazola von Strumm flashed in for a mega-second or two and said "Hmmm . . ." touching his nose, wondered about Jasper, and said "Hmmn, probably not, Crimboble," as Strummians are apt to do. Maz let him zoom away, wriggled out onto the dewy grass and got dressed, shivering a little. Nobody was about but the birds had started up their racket and wispy clouds showed against the pinkish-blue dawn sky. Maz ran over to his room in the shack, got a sweater and his accoustic guitar and went down to the dens to practise a few chords and grooves. After a while a bunch of little kids trailed over in their pyjamas and sat listening. Much later, but still before breakfast, Hiroshi stumbled over from his tent, his shiny black hair tousled and wild-looking. No, he said, he hadn't heard a thing once everybody quietened down. But then, reflected MvS, surfacing again, Hiroshi wasn't an interplanetary being.

*   *   *

When Jasper got back to his house at about nine o'clock in the evening he smoothed Denise's letter out on the kitchen table and read it properly.

> Sorry to intrude again on what I'm sure is a well-earned and much needed break. Somebody (anonymously) sent me the enclosed clipping . . . We feel somewhat concerned. In view of our previous discussion, I would appreciate your opinion as to its gravity. You know what the media are like. I feel this could blow up into something rather distasteful. From all points of view we need to be prepared.
> Best wishes,
> Denise

The clipping was from *The Eliston Courier* and Jasper had seen it already. In fact the item, which had appeared the day after the hunt for Aaron, had been one of the reasons for the special meeting. It was one of the reasons why Jasper felt he shouldn't have agreed to keep an eye on Aaron, and he'd tried to explain to the meeting about how it might be interpreted.

Kevin, the maths teacher, had pointed out that *The Eliston Courier* had a new editor with a new brief – sharpen up the *EC*. He'd had the impression, talking to him in the pub, that he intended to turn the *Courier* into *The Sun* of the North-East. "How pathetic can you get?" Kevin had finished.

Helga had pointed out that Coralford could not be run according to the prejudices of the local newspaper. Everybody had said, "Hear, hear !" and Aaron had beamed with relief and nodded his head up and down frantically.

IS CORALFORD SAFE?
   A ten-year-old boy was found in bed in the cottage of a middle-aged male visitor at Coralford School after his disappearance had caused a whole-school hunt for the boy through neighbouring woods and fields. The same boy was reported as being seen wandering into the local service station in the early hours of the morning and ran off in a panic when a member of the public offered to return him to the school.
   Local residents are saying it is about time somebody in authority investigated this place. Have we got a *Lord of the Flies* situation on our doorstep? Is this another educational tragedy waiting to happen?

How rapidly things get around, Jasper was thinking, when the phone rang.

"Charlotte," Charlotte's voice said. "Wondered whether you were up for the Bottles tonight?"

"Twist my arm," Jasper said, wondering if he was up to the Bottles tonight. Always, when they sat with their drinks at the dark polished table in the corner, he wondered when she would challenge him in some way, throw down the gauntlet. "Where are you?"

"Over at Muir's, he's – well, he's a bit upset . . . Thinks the vultures are gathering already."

"The Aaron business?"

"Yes . . . And you. He's worried about you." Charlotte seemed to blurt the words out as if she'd been wanting to say them for a long time and hadn't been able to, as if she wanted to let him know that their drink at the Bottles would have a purpose other than mere reminiscence, an agenda other than the sexual possibilities that hung in the air between the two of them. "So am I."

"Not just a friendly pint then?" Jasper was surprised at the bitter edge in his own voice.

"Oh Jasp . . . I'll see you down there."

The line went dead. He could tell that she'd been crying. He took a shower and put on a clean pair of jeans and a dark-coloured shirt, the sort of thing he felt Charlotte would like, and made his way down into Eliston.

"Same as usual?" the barman said, signifying their acquaintance. The pub was almost empty and Jasper could sense the barman, underoccupied, wanting to start a conversation.

"Spot of bother up there, I see from the press."

Digging or just gossiping, Jasper wondered. He was careful what he said. "All schools have problems these days."

"Ah, you're not wrong there. In the business yourself is it?"

"After a fashion."

"Inspector, isn't it?"

Definitely digging, Jasper thought. "I do a bit for Ofsted now and then. Free-lance stuff."

"Ah, that's the way of it these days."

"I'm on holiday up here," Jasper said quickly, with a less than natural laugh. "Not my problem."

Another man had come up to the bar to order. Jasper took the opportunity to go over to a table with his drink. Charlotte was late. He trailed a forefinger across the top of his beer so that a tiny beard of froth hung from the pad. He seemed to himself to hang still for a long moment, a very long moment, nonplussed, waiting for Charlotte. He always had this odd feeling that he wouldn't recognise her, carrying the old picture in his head as he did. She was nicer than she used to be, he thought, as a person; kinder, more responsible. In the past she used frequently to be hours late when they arranged to meet somewhere. She'd turn up saying, "J, I'm sorry, you know what I'm like, come on, let's go" – perfunctory, as if she hadn't noticed that his fingers and lips were numb from waiting around in some freezing bus station or at the windy entrance to his hall of residence, not daring to go inside in case he missed her. But he'd got less nice, he thought. Had he? No, not quite so simple. He'd become nicer on the outside, nastier on the inside. He'd become more calculating, more self-interested. Becoming a family man had caused him to barricade part of himself away from the constant demands for his commitment and interest. And behind the barricade he was irritated, bored. He'd noticed himself become more dishonest in all sorts of petty ways, saying things like, "I'd love to," when people asked him to what he knew would be dull dinner parties; or "fascinating" when colleagues told him about some tedious new piece of educational research, or "really stimulating" when he was asked his opinion of yet another training course for Ofsted inspectors. He'd cultivated the kind of blandness which creates dull dinner parties, which prevents interesting or revealing conversations, turns away wrath and keeps one climbing in a middle-ranking and unexciting profession. He'd learned not to stick his neck out.

That's what you do, he thought to himself, that's the price you pay for mainstream success (hating the term mainstream even as his mind selected it). He couldn't imagine Muir ever behaving in that safe, chatty way. Or Charlotte. Or Maz come to that. Inside Jasper the poetry of wit, sarcasm, subtlety, grown weak and sour from lack of exercise, sometimes screamed up at him, demanding release, demanding a raging argument, demanding an exchange of insults with a worthy opponent. Charlotte was a worthy opponent he supposed.

Were they opponents or allies? Both. As lovers they could be both – everything they needed – to each other.

He sucked the beer off his forefinger, took a mouthful from his pint and tried to conjure up contemporary Charlotte, going over the details of her in his mind: her funny half-curly, grey hair which she wore quite short in contrast to the old shoulder length black mane; her small plumpness, her old-fashioned hip-speak, her refusal to be correct and academic about things, her directness. He liked it – there was a strength there, a refusal to jettison things that mattered to her, a humour, a lightness in contrast to the constantly changing, jargonistic, self-satisfied language that filled the mouths of his colleagues – and his own mouth too.

I'll ask her, he told himself, as soon as she comes in, before she can even say, "I'll get them," like she does. I'll blurt it out: "Come on Charlie – let's go to bed, give it a try. Nothing to be lost! Let's not think about it, just do it – now!"

The pub was beginning to fill up. The two old boys near the bar looked like farmers with huge dry-looking hands cupped around their pints of Newcastle Brown and next to them was a thinnish, bearded chap he vaguely remembered seeing before, up at the school perhaps, with whom he exchanged a perfunctory nod; three young men and a girl were sitting in a corner near the television smoking and chattering. And then Charlotte came through the door, twenty minutes late and with a hard, fixed expression on her face which drove his intended words underground immediately. He half rose to his feet to get her a drink but she waved him down and flung some bits of paper down on the table glaring at him.

"What about these? What are you up to J?"

She sat down opposite him. He saw that the effort of being nasty to him was causing tears to gather at the inner corners of her eyes and she was blinking, trying to hold them back. She clasped her hands into a fist on the table and stared down at it. Waiting. The papers curled and folded up from the shiny, damp mahogany surface. Jasper looked at the photocopies of Denise's letters and the cutting from the Eliston Gazette. He realised he was shaking.

"Quite a one with letters, aren't you, Jasp?" Her voice had a dull anger to it, sobs not far under.

"What the hell are you doing, messing about with my mail?" How insincere and feeble his protest sounded.

"Forget that," Charlotte said, picking up speed and tremolo. "Bullshit, isn't it? Tell me what's going on. What are you doing here? Ingratiating yourself with the kids, aren't you? Poking into everything, aren't you? What's your agenda?" She looked into his eyes with the heavy straight gaze he remembered from long past moods.

"I haven't one," Jasper said lamely. "I've just been put in a bit of a quandary by the Ofsted people – not what I intended. Don't know what to do about it myself . . ."

"Uh huh. . ." – a sarcastic whisper.

"I've kept wanting to talk to you about it . . ."

"Uh huh . . ."

"I really did come here out of interest, off my own bat –"

"And now you'll put it to good use?" Anger breaking up the vowels.

"Not me that wants to do that. Them."

"But your team would like the job?"

"Maybe, I'm not sure about . . ."

"OK, OK." Charlotte's voice rising to a screech. The rest of the bar seemed to have gone quiet. "What are you going to do? What do they want?"

Jasper sat very still and said nothing. He felt his eyes moving over her face as if they were fingers. A great surge of love for her, for her gutsiness, her upset-ness welled up in him. He wanted to put his bigger hands over her small fist, still clenched on the table, and say, forget all this Charl, come to bed. None of it really matters, they'll do what they do, nothing matters anymore, come to bed.

Charlotte continued to stare at him. "What do they want you to do?" she screeched.

He sat and sat, saying nothing. He couldn't remember what they wanted, how to avoid it, if it mattered, whether he'd do it.

His mind seemed to have blanked out, fixed itself on the shiny table, her hands clasped tightly there, waiting.

He heard a voice from somewhere saying, "Come on, Come on!" and remembered it would be the group watching football on the TV in the corner of the pub. Suddenly she unclenched her fist, half rose, leant over, caught hold of his shoulders with her hands and shook him. "Oh Jasper, what are you doing?"

It was the first time they had touched, since the embarrassed cheek brush after their first drink together. It was a door flying open. He almost toppled over. Charlotte began to cry, the fist wide now and holding her head up off the table while she shuddered with sobs and Jasper pulling her up and taking her out of the door, stuffing the photocopies in his pocket, the other people in the pub, gone quiet, pretending not to notice, their startled voices breaking out at his back as the door swung closed behind them.

And running. Jasper pulling Charlotte by the hand, running and stumbling, past the castle, down the hill, up the hill until they collapsed through Jasper's door, sobbing, gasping and laughing. Sobbing, gasping and laughing so much they could hardly get up the stairs and out of their clothes and into Jasper's bed which he had made all tidy again just in case.

*   *   *

Hiroshi, Katie, Leah and Maz sat in Hiroshi's tent with the flap open, playing cards by torchlight. After a while they got bored with playing rummy, which Maz kept winning.

Katie said, "My mum told me the kids used to play strip poker, when she was here."

"About a million years ago," Maz said.

"She said the boys wouldn't take their clothes off but the girls didn't mind."

"Typical," Leah said.

"The boys gambled for pocket money instead of taking their clothes off and the girls won all their pocket money."

"Er . . . what's strip poker?" Hiroshi screwed up his face and raised his eyebrows.

So the four of them started playing strip poker and pretty soon all of them were sitting more or less naked and getting cold. Maz, the best bluffer, sat in his lotus, still with his jeans on, Katie and Leah were both topless and laughing.

At one point there was a sudden flash of light from outside. "Storm coming," Katie said. But no storm came.

After a while Leah suggested they should play winner-puts-back-on-poker and gradually they all got dressed again except Hiroshi who, hopeless at bluffing, carried on losing and sat, still naked, knees up to chin and shivering but smiling in that constantly amiable way he had even when he got mad with people.

All through the game Mazola von Strumm was directing his subliminal antennae out into the surrounding night, thinking about that light. He heard the groaning of the grass as it bent under the feet of alien footsteps and then he heard the grass sigh up again and he knew the footsteps had gone. He said nothing to the others.

After Leah was asleep he wriggled out of his bag and into his jeans again, pulled his trainers onto his feet and crept out of the tent. He noted that the planet Strumm was directly over the hockey field which meant there was celestial protection. Just as well, he thought, for he noticed his heart was pounding. MvS ran round the edge of the school, checking the dens, the woods, the edge of the swimming pool. There was nobody. In the woods he gathered up some fallen bark and rubbed the soft loamy underside on his skin, knowing that it would help him stop trembling. Then he ran back to the tent and got into his bag with his clothes on next to Leah who gave a quiet moan in her sleep and snuggled up against him. But Maz von Strumm couldn't sleep. After a while he got up, crept over to the hedge behind the tent and sat in his lotus under the spangled, deep blue cap of the Northumbrian skies.

The sweet sound of the grass blades rustling their messages along the dry summer earth was amplified for him by the long wavelengths emanating from the Strumm beacons. He heard

97

the delicate stutter of rabbit's feet, the mere fleck of insect wings against the tips of stems. He fancied he even heard the tiny flup of flower petals falling against the grass.

And then the distinct thump of human feet approaching the encampment.

Maz von Strumm rose without removing his feet from the ground. "Crims!" he whispered to himself, not entirely unscared.

The man, a plumpish shadow against the night, moved swiftly from tent to tent, shone his torch a second and carried on. At Leah's tent he paused a second longer, put off the torch and just stood there. MvS sensed he was wondering about the missing body in the second sleeping bag. The beam of the torch suddenly shot thinly above the tent towards him. MvS flattened himself immediately onto the ground. The torch went off.

MvS leant his ear against the grass, heard the footfalls pick up speed, receding from the tent. He leapt up and began to run steadily after the steps, Strumm beaming strength into his legs. Once out of the darkness of the school grounds he saw the figure more clearly. A man in an anorak, he thought. By the roadside was the dark shape of a van. The man was fumbling for keys and as MvS pelted towards him he wrenched open the van door and jumped in. The ignition coughed into life, loud as a rifle crack in the surrounding silence. The lights went on and the van moved off towards Eliston. Maz von Strumm stood still, panting, staring fixedly at the lit number plate, memorising it: KPO 547C. Crummy sort of vehicle for a serious criminal, he thought, sprinting back to school under the diamonded sky. His heart was beating fast, he realised, even though Strumm was still overhead and by its singular gravitational connection with himself was lifting his feet lightly above the grass.

Leah had not stirred. Coding the number into MvS's memory (King's Pawn One, five and four don't make seven, see!) Maz crept in beside her and lay for a while pondering what was to be done. Was he to go it alone, or bring it up at the meeting?

He knew he should bring it to the meeting or tell Helga, or Muir – or Jasper. But he was attached to his role of independent boy sleuth. Maz loved doing things alone. It was a dilemma. One he would leave till the morning to resolve. Somewhere mixed in with his excitement and fear was a feeling of relief; relief that the figure running to the van had definitely not been Jasper. He could like Jasper. They could continue playing music together. And he would ask Jasp to show him that Latin-American groove he did on the keyboards. Could be adapted for bass guitar he felt sure. The rhythm of it eased him into sleep, cuddled up against Leah to re-warm himself.

The next morning Hiroshi called him over, all bug-eyed and tousled. "About that light. Better bring it up," he said.

"No need for a special meeting," Maz said, giving himself sleuthing time. "We'll put it on the agenda for Saturday."

.

CHAPTER EIGHT

The bed felt cold and slightly damp, but Charlotte's body felt hot, almost burning against his. She had put the light off and the room was dark but for the faint glow of a streetlight through the window. Arms tightly round each other they lay without moving. Jasper found himself thinking not so much of what Charlotte had felt like in the past, but of the feel of his wife, Kay. She was the sort of woman who in middle age had become angular, rangy. Her waist had merged into her almost masculine haunches and her breasts had seemed to retreat and flatten against her chest. Charlotte, by contrast, was small and a little plump though her upper back, which he now ran his hands along, was unexpectedly flat, her waist narrow; her buttocks flared out, felt fleshy. Jasper had been to bed with just two women in his life. It is easier to go to bed with an ex-lover, so people said – how could he know? But it was true that though Charlotte's body felt strange, he felt comfortable with her – safe, knowing she would be kind with him in spite of everything. Comfort, the thought of his wife, had made the urgency he had felt running up the hill drain away. He had become detached, unphysical. His hands moving over Charlotte's back were someone else's hands. He noted the taut skin of her back without emotion. Her soft belly pressed against his but he felt nothing, understood nothing. His hands continued mechanically, as if out of politeness, respect, up and down her back until he realised after a while that she was not responding in any way to his touch. She was inert. Hot. She clung to him but didn't move.

"Are you OK?" he muttered putting a hand on her short hair. His hand felt her bend and lift her head but she didn't speak. He felt round and discovered her face was wet, a strange woman's tearful face beneath his hand. At his touch she start- ed to shake and was soon sobbing. He held on to her. Not knowing what else he should do he carried on stroking her hair. "It's OK, it's OK. What is it? What's the matter?"

"It's . . . been . . . so long since . . . You know I've never stopped . . . Always been with me . . . all this time . . ."

"It's OK." His head was stabbing.

Her sobbing increased, continued, subsided, stopped. She lay sniffing, snuffling and heaving in his arms. Perversely, inexplicably he started to feel desperately horny again. He was aware he should not be – he should be cuddling her, saving the sex till later, another time maybe, looking after her, talking more, getting to know her. His erection, embarrassing him, pressed itself against her belly. She seemed to tense herself clear of it.

A sharply focussed mental picture of Charlotte from the past had stabbed into his mind – her long black hair against the pillow, Charlotte spreadeagled, naked, while he stood by the bed looking down at her, knowing she wanted him, would do anything with him, for him.

Charlotte didn't speak or move. He put his hands up and felt her lips, moved his fingers across to where tendrils of her short hair turned around her ears, felt the new, yielding flesh of her neck.

"I'm still me, I'm no different, I don't feel any different, not to myself," she murmured against his ear. Still snuffling she pressed her lips to his cheek.

He freed an arm, put the bedside light on and sat on the edge of the bed looking down at her in the dull light. Her eyes, yes, he remembered those dark blue, forthright eyes, and her teeth, the way her upper front teeth overlapped each other, just slightly, saving her from mere conventional prettiness. He knelt towards her and took his hands down her whole body with its new curves and folds, down over her full breasts, the slight mound of her stomach, the black bush which now had three coarse white hairs in it, on down over her thighs. Below the knee her legs were the same as they'd always been, full calves tapering into the same slim ankles. And her feet. He remembered her feet. He held her left foot in the palm of his hand and kissed each of the perfectly formed toenails.

Charlotte's feet – small, bunionless, cornless, the five toes forming a perfect geometrical arc. He traced a finger along the bone towards her ankle and found it there – an unnatural smoothness of skin – a scar, a circular white patch the size of an old sixpence.

They had been in her flat and she had been teaching him how to toss pancakes. They had fed sweet lemony forkfuls into each other's mouths, licking the syrup from each other's lips and laughing – they were always laughing. He'd tossed the last pancake but it had fallen on the floor. He'd stood the pan back on the lit ring in his hurry to scrape up the pancake and Charlotte had leapt forward to grab the pan off the ring and a gobbet of scalding fat had splashed onto her bare foot. He'd filled a bowl with cold water while she hopped and groaned and he'd tenderly dunked her foot in the water for a while and then slid his hands up from her foot to her thigh . . . to her crotch and made love to her right there, one foot in the bowl of water, Charlie laughing, going, "Goddammit J . . . I'm injured," steadying herself with her good foot against the wall . . . She'd had a blister on her foot for days, hadn't been able to wear her favourite flat shoes with the straps across the front . . .

"Shouldn't cook with bare feet," Charlotte said. She sat up smiling her twisted smile and gazed at him where he sat, naked, cradling her foot.

She put her hands over his ears, moved his head up level with hers and kissed him. He kissed her back; a long, slow, kiss, his tongue exploring her teeth, the roof of her mouth, the valley under her tongue. The tips of their tongues teased each other, made rings around each other, played together as they always had.

"Oh Charlie . . . Charlie . . ." He pulled her to the edge of the bed, knelt before her, shameless of his hard erection and sank himself into her wet, soft interior, plugged himself into the essential Charlotte, ageless, eternally his, who now lived in a plump, sweet little house with a grey thatch. They moved together clinging on to each other and moaning, flesh gliding easily between them, oiled and full. He held himself back – a

102

dark, terse pleasure to hold himself back, be in readiness, let the dam build – until at last as he felt he could hold himself no longer, she lay back across the bed and he felt her tighten and pulse around him. He let himself go into his final thrusts, shuddering and fierce, a flooding. The orgasm snaked up over his chest, poured round him, opened out into a huge jazzy chord. A solid bass figure vibrated along his spine. A pure, thin melody horned its way, leisurely, around the inside of his head above the waning chord. He heard his own harsh exhalation, left his body for a while and hovered above, looking down on himself and Charlotte: Adam and Eve, Rodin's lovers, Hardy's country tumblers amongst the hay, Charlotte and Jasper . . .

She put her arms up and pulled him down onto her breast. He sank into it as a feather sinks to rest in warm, still air. He was aware of his tears as well as drops of sweat falling onto her skin. He felt her arms circling him.

As Jasper slept, he dreamed of flying and walking across water, of driving his car across huge open plains, Charlotte flying alongside him, a bird of fortune, two birds, migrating south across a flat, blue sea and the sky-sound of an alto-sax playing.

And Charlotte slept a little, woke a little, slept a little. Each time she woke she looked at Jasper in the half-light and a surge of exultation and relief filled her. She even spoke in a quiet voice to the sleeping figure beside her. "I still love you. Do you know that, J? I love you again." It reminded her of when her boy had been born, how all through those early nights of motherhood she woke and snoozed, woke and snoozed. And each time she woke she looked across at the baby and felt a great wild rush of happiness and satisfaction as if nothing else could matter so much as this wonderful new self she'd acquired, created.

She stretched her back along the length of Jasper's back and drifted off again.

*   *   *

He woke up. A dim square of sky was pulling the sun up from behind the roofs of Eliston, a mottled square – blue, white, pink. No-one else in the bed, he realised. His consciousness focussed on noises, careful steps trying not to creak on the steep stairs, the echoing sound of water in the kettle. He raised his head and squinted at the clock. Five. He remembered how Charlotte used to make tea in the early hours and bring it back to bed. Maybe she got up early anyway these days. Jasper threw the cover back, stood up and looked out of the window. He felt wide awake, the pleasant chill of earliness pimpling his skin but the day's heat already promising. A milk float trundled past the window and clanked round the corner towards the school. Summer, he thought. Naked with Charlotte on summer mornings and nobody else about. He went downstairs, energetic, revelling in nakedness.

Charlotte was standing with her back to him wearing his dark shirt and stretching up for mugs from the shelf. He went up behind her, pushed his arms up under his shirt and clasped them over her belly.

"Charlie," he kept singing, "Charlie, Charlie."

"Let me make the tea, pest-bollocks," Charlotte said at last, turning to finger his bare chest. She looked him straight in the eye, a long, exploring look.

"Took you a long time to get back. What kept you?"

"Traffic was terrible. Stuck in Bromley. Thirty-year traffic jam, stuck on the by-pass . . ."

". . . and you'd only popped out for some milk."

They exploded into laughter, staggering about the room, clutching on to each other, honking, crying with laughter. Charlotte wrapped his shirt tightly round her, hugging herself and cackling. She leant against him, kissing the top of his head. He could feel the hiccup of her laughter.

"Go to bed and I'll bring the tea up," he said.

She climbed the stairs ahead of him still giggling.

CHAPTER NINE

They went to the Coffee Pot for a late breakfast. Jasper noticed for the first time the way the late morning sun made the stern, stony, grey exteriors of the Eliston houses look creamy and soft. The citizens of Eliston passed by, greeting them and smiling. They walked hand in hand. In the Coffee Pot they both ordered bacon and eggs.

Charlotte sipped her coffee, hands around the cup, elbows on the table, looking over at him, relaxed. Middle-age suited her.

"Do you know what I want?" Jasper said, "I want to finish eating my breakfast here with you, Charlie, sitting just where you are, and then what I want is for us to go and get in my car, my nice smooth BMW, and drive off somewhere. Anywhere – Scotland, Spain, Italy, Worksop, Scunthorpe – I don't care. I want you to tell me, slowly over months and months, what you were doing all that time I was out fetching the milk."

She smiled in that way of hers, crookedly, lips pressed together, listening.

"I want to be completely irresponsible," he continued, "I don't even want to tell anyone we're going . . . Let's do it! Come on Charlie, eat up. Let's do it!"

Charlotte piled apricot jam from a small jar on to her last mouthful of toast and crunched it slowly.

"You think I haven't changed, don't you? You think I'll do it – do anything – and I nearly will . . . but I can't." Her face went serious. "One running-away is enough."

Jasper's stomach clenched into a knot. They hadn't really spoken about his running away, that treacherous letter from Bromley thirty years ago which now, by a circuitous post had been returned to sender, as it had to be – this tortoise post which had plopped through the door of the Coffee Pot in Eliston and crawling towards his English breakfast, making him feel sick.

105

Why had he ever left Charlotte? He had never really understood. He knew in theory at least that he must have somehow needed to leave her. He'd never wanted to examine it, had somehow dug it in under the dross of his professional and domestic life, persuading himself that he had been a different person then, young and irresponsible, not like the solid citizen he had become, persuading himself that Charlotte had been just a youthful affair, his first, a student fling – what young men did when they got away from home, a rite of passage. Did he really want to leave Charlie, marry Kay, just to appease his parents? Had he really been so docile, so malleable? He stared over at Charlotte. She was sipping her coffee again, gazing back at him, waiting for his response. His thoughts tumbled over themselves, panicking for answers. Why? Fear? Fear of what? Fear of freedom? Of happiness? What clichés! Fear of being dominated, that was more likely. For wasn't he under Charlie's thumb in those days, wasn't she forcing him to be free? Wasn't she pressing him out of the mould into the great wild world with her thumb – with her logic, her long hair, with her kisses, her sexy love-making, the way she challenged everything he said and did? He had been running away from the wild, running back to the safety of tradition and tedium, everything he'd known before he met her. This nagging, inside him. Life wasn't simple and perfect and happy. One always had to pay for things – that was his upbringing, the way his parents talked – "he'll pay for it in the end," "people always get their just deserts," "you make your bed and . . ." So he'd started paying in advance. It had been nerves, sheer nerves. He hadn't had the nerve for it, hadn't had the nerve to spend a lifetime with Charlotte.

He stared at her small soft hands, ringless, folded on the table, thumbs tucked away. He'd loved the feel of her hands on him. How mad people are, he thought. He'd contracted to spend a life with a woman he didn't even love, who was kind and pleasant but boring and unsexy, who didn't, it appears, even love him, because that didn't call for so much nerve, so that something wild in him – his deep self, musician, lover –

couldn't get the upper hand. How could Charlotte, coming from Coralford, really understand that fear?

She was pouring more coffee from the cafetière that, amazingly, was part of the Coffee Pot's catering arrangements. He loved the way she moved her hands, the careful way she poured, head on one side, a libation.

"It's OK, J," she was saying, putting the milk jug down and stroking his stubbly cheek across the table with the back of her hand. "I don't want to rake over all that, it's finished. We'd never have managed a lifetime together – not how we were then. We'd have died of starvation, or music, or sex . . ." She giggled, her gift still – or burden –to know what he was thinking. "All I'm saying is we can't just run away now."

It was true, he thought. When he was twenty-one he couldn't have survived Charlotte – Charlotte who travelled with the power of this island in her sails. He had to leave, be part of the mainland where you learned to be cautious and smooth-tongued, learned to grapple with tedious things, learned to bargain, plot, equivocate, compromise . . .

"We're needed here – it's down to us," Charlotte was saying. "Down to you. Muir's too old now and there's nobody else there who knows how to deal with. . . you lot. We have to stick around and sort it."

"But not today, not now."

"It means . . ."

"I don't want to talk about schools and education and classrooms and kids and discipline. Not just now. I've been putting up with that fucking stuff since I was five years old – and I hated it even then." He shrugged and smiled at her to offset the unexpected force of his words.

"You like it here though, don't you? You've come alive. I've seen you with the kids, with Maz and the band. You're in your element. You see now, don't you? At Coralford it's –"

"– different. I know, I know that." Jasper remembered the nights they used to spend talking, debating. "Why J?" she'd say. "Why?" Her favourite word. The hours they talked. He leant over and took the coffee cup out of Charlotte's hands and

107

put it carefully on its white saucer. He took hold of both her hands across the table. They felt cool and small. "Later we'll talk about all that. Let's go somewhere today, just today."

She was smiling and squeezing his hands. "We'll go to Hadrian's Wall, it's near here – just for the day. But you'll have to tell Aaron."

"Oh God ! He'll want to come."

Charlotte and Jasper walked back to the school. Jasper was reliving the music of his orgasm, re-inventing the tune. He would work in that bass, that climbing, foxy phrase, adding a romantic piano, syncopated, loitering above the beat. Chords were sounding in his head. And a tom-tom, he thought, a simple, driving beat. The rhythm of their feet up the hill seemed to add percussion. His hands tingled, ached for the piano keys, but he'd wait, hold it in his head till nightfall, develop the ideas as they walked Hadrian's wall, sun beating down, Charlie still wearing his shirt.

*   *   *

Helga's ritual on Sunday morning was to drive Muir down to Eliston for the papers. She'd help him in and out of the car, hand him his stick. Muir enjoyed tottering from the car park to the Coffee Pot under his own steam. He'd tap on the glass door with his spare hand and two waitresses would hurry over, one holding the door open, the other settling him at his table over in the smoking area. "Good morning, Mr Muir. Lovely day." – even if it wasn't. He'd tamp his pipe and nod to the locals, sipping his coffee and waiting for Helga to bring the papers and read them to him.

This morning Helga glanced at the front page of *The Eliston Sunday Courier* and took the papers straight to the car. She thought it would be better to deal with these headlines when they got back home.

"I forgot my glasses," she told Muir.

Muir just said "Aye." One of the problems of being so old was that even your wife treated you like a child. "Aye," he repeated, letting her believe he hadn't noticed her putting her glasses in her bag. On top of that there was the way the waitresses were being especially nice – "All right today, are we Mr Muir?" – and then chatting in the corner in a half whisper, looking over at him. Old age is a bugger, he thought. You canna budge from the seat without a hand, but you understand everything better than you've ever done, backwards and forwards, inside and outside.

"We'll mebbe get back then," he said to Helga.

"As you like." Helga took a moment to finish her coffee and helped him up.

As they swung into the school drive, he caught sight of Charlotte with the Inspector talking to Aaron. Then at the far end of the drive he saw two men he didn't know from Adam, one with a square bag slung over his shoulder – a camera he supposed. They looked over as the car passed, stepped forward, appeared to change their minds and stepped back again. Muir felt extremely weary suddenly. As Helga helped him out of the car he said, "I'll see the papers in a while."

She nodded, took him in and settled him back in his chair. "There's – "

"I know. It'll keep a wee while."

Helga put the pile of papers on the table over by the television, the big, fat Observer and the thinner, local paper underneath. "When you're ready." She laid her glasses on top of the papers. Muir would have liked to have a talk with Charlotte on her own. Find out what she'd got out of that inspector laddie. Nothing gets any better, he thought, bored and miserable. Gawd, nothing changes!

"We need to make some decisions," Helga said, "about when you go. You know I can't run this place on my own."

Muir hated making decisions. Decisions, he felt, should manage themselves.

He and Helga had talked about it many times, of course, Helga in her brisk way, anxious to have something planned, somebody in mind, Muir, cautious and instinctive, vague, feeling that something, somebody would appear to make clear

109

what they should do, if anything.

"You know, sometimes I think you believe in angels, in machines that fly down from the sky," Helga said. "The longer you leave it, the harder it will get."

"Aye." His neck was itching, he felt tired. "After the birthday, mebbe."

He knew Helga had something in mind and he thought he knew what it was.

CHAPTER TEN

Aaron was waiting, sitting in the doorway of Jasper's house, bottom lip jutting, restlessly pushing the buttons on a bright green computer game he had just received in the post from his mother. He pulled himself up by putting his arms round Jasper's legs. Charlotte stepped back.

"Jathp, where've you been?" He sounded like an aggrieved housewife whose husband is late for dinner.

"Aaron, that's none of your business," Charlotte intervened.

"Shut up! I'm asking Jathp."

"Don't talk to Charlotte like – "

"Shut up yourself," said Charlotte to Aaron.

"OK, Aaron." Jasper felt as if he had just crashlanded. "What did you want?"

"Wondered what you were doing . . . jutht wanted to see you . . ." Aaron's voice trickled back to its normal, only slightly demanding tone.

One of the pleasures of being an inspector is that you don't have to deal with kids, Jasper thought. You deal in kids, but not with kids. Sometimes you see kids, but always at one remove. Inspectors see teachers dealing with kids but they don't, mustn't, intervene; they watch carefully how the teacher manages it, taking notes so they can tell the teacher how to do it better next time, but they never have to do it better next time themselves. Anyway, inspectors rarely see kids behaving like this, such kids are secreted away beforehand or are simply so overawed by the solemn, suited presence of the inspector that they behave themselves.

"What are you doing today, Jathp?"

Too late to play the inspector now. He'd forgotten the lines, the appropriate pose, stepped through the proscenium arch and mingled in among the crowd where his dour magic had immediately dispersed. He picked Aaron up. Aaron wrapped his sticky legs around Jasper's waist and clung on with them.

111

"Charlotte and I are going out today, Aaron. Sorry mate, you're going to have to amuse yourself."

"Where? Where are you going?"

Charlotte's eyes smiled into Jasper's above Aaron's scruffy brown hair, in which Jasper felt sure he could see a tangle centred on a wodge of pink gum. She was grinning and shrugging.

"Haven't you got things to do, Aaron? Aren't you on Muir's Birthday Committee? Haven't you got jobs to do?"

"No, course not. I'm helping with the jumble sale, tomorrow. Nothing to do today. Jathp, where . . ."

Charlotte continued to shrug and smile.

"Aren't you grounded?"

"Finished. Only grounded for three days."

"No lessons?"

"Don't go to Hithtory and English. Only go to Art and Maths."

So Charlotte had carefully removed the gum with her hairbrush and taken him over to tell Jane and get his anorak while Jasper got some sandwiches together, and here they were, the three of them, purring along the hilly little roads away from Eliston with Aaron, quiet and content on the back seat and Jasper had decided he didn't really mind. He'd imagined them making love in some old Roman fort, lying in the grass, his head in Charlotte's lap afterwards while they talked and talked. But he didn't mind. He put Fairport Convention on the stereo to please Charlotte, though he'd have preferred Miles Davis, but he didn't mind. He was happy – yes, happy. The high hedges and stone walls ran into the past behind them. Every so often they crossed one of those pleated stone bridges which seemed to be a feature of Northumbria, usually where the road lurched round at ninety degrees or so, but the BMW would swing round smoothly. He felt they were buzzing through summer – pastureland, cows, sheep, white hedge blossoms, the faint smell of tar from the hot road – like bees, dragonflies. Aaron had drifted off to sleep. Charlotte kissed the side of Jasper's face, he put out a hand and stroked her knee.

"He'll moan like hell when we've walked up a few steps," Charlotte said. "It's quite strenuous walking, Hadrian's Wall."

But she was wrong. Aaron sprang and pranced up the steep stone steps without complaining, ran ahead of them along the wide, grassed-over wall, tumbled and skipped on the fields between, as if energised by his inclusion in the trip. They stopped to eat their sandwiches in a small wood growing precariously on a ledge above a steep, rough cliff. Below them a stretch of water in the sun, its surface broken here and there by clumps of twigs where water birds nested. They threw twigs down, watching as they plopped and floated on the shining water far below. They tried to work out which side was Scotland and which England.

"This your first visit?" Charlotte asked Aaron. "We used to come here quite a lot when I was here. We had this history teacher and he had a van. He used to bring the whole history class and we'd tromp about all day and play games of prisoners round the mile castles."

Jasper felt Charlotte was really talking to him, explaining about her childhood.

"So you must know which side England is."

"I'm pretty sure when you look over the lake you're looking towards Scotland. But we didn't use to worry too much about stuff like that. Who needs to know?"

"Hadrian did, I suppose."

"Hadrian's dead."

"Never been before," Aaron said. "They did go once, but I had a mump so I didn't go."

"You have quite a few mumps, don't you?" Charlotte said.

"Shut up." Aaron had gone a bit red. ". . . Actually, you know my mum?"

"Yeah . . ."

"Well, she sent me here because of mumps and stuff. They kept kicking me out."

Jasper noticed how similar they sounded, Aaron and Charlotte. Their slang, their style of speaking. Coming from Coralford was like coming from, say, the west of England, there was always a trace of accent, a style. He noted how easily she brought Aaron out of himself.

"Of your other school?"

"Whenever I had a hairy or a mump they'd give me a detention and then I'd run out of the school and then they'd kick me out."

"What do they do here?"

"Nothing much. If I do something dangerous they bring me up in the meeting."

"Dangerous?"

"Well, like if I run out of school."

"What does your dad think of your new school?" Jasper asked, conscious of the formality of his own tone compared with theirs.

"I don't have a dad. Well, I suppose I do – somewhere," Aaron said vaguely. "Let's go."

He went to the edge of the cliff again and flung down a curl of orange peel. It floated towards a tiny nest in the middle of the lake and disappeared behind it. Aaron ran into the wood and came out with a pile of stones. He leant out over the cliff and flung them rhythmically into the lake, counting. Jasper itched to pull him back, but Charlotte put a hand on his arm. "He'll be all right." In between stones, Aaron turned and looked at Jasper and Charlotte, as if waiting for them to come and grab him back. There were eleven stones. "His age," Charlotte murmured.

After the last stone arced and fell Aaron turned again and ran back to them. He touched Jasper's arm. "Let's go on now. I'm bored of that now. I get silly when I'm bored. That's what my mum says."

"What else does your mum say ?" Charlotte asked.

"Oh, stuff. I told her about the rabbit, and – "

"Rabbit?"

"About when I tried to kill the rabbit . . . and . . ."

"When was that?" Charlotte sat down again on a hump of stones which, according to a peeling wooden noticeboard, had been a Roman footsoldier's sleeping quarters. Jasper put down the day bag again. Aaron was standing next to Charlotte swishing a stick through the thin grass.

"When I first came here . . . my mum – well she's a sort of, vegan and stuff, she went all funny – about the rabbit. I had to make her some jasmine tea – she likes me to make tea for her."

"In the hockey field was it?" Charlotte asked, "I remember that. Some kids used to chase rabbits in the hockey field."

"Over by the fence."

"You actually managed to catch one?"

"Nearly. With a thnare. My grandad showed me how to make thnares. You make them with a peeth of wire, and then when they run through the wire, they get caught."

"But it got away."

"Kevin came and let it go."

"The guy who takes you for maths?"

"He got some wire cutters."

"Get brought up?"

"Yeah. They voted to give me extra poc?"

"I suppose that was Muir's proposal," Charlotte said.

"Yeah, Leah wanted me to get banned the hockey field 'cos she's a vegan as well, but everyone voted for Muir's proposal and Leah's jutht a bitch."

"So how much extra poc did you get ?"

"20p."

"Not much."

"And Wendy said she'd take me rabbit-hunting up by the woods."

"And did she?"

"She would've but I didn't want to go." Aaron chucked the stick down, "I was going to let the rabbit go anyway. Come on." He ran ahead, zigzagging across the grass.

"What do you make of that?" Jasper asked Charlotte.

"Typical Muir. He has this policy of rewarding certain kids for their misdeeds. The ones he thinks are a bit disturbed. About showing you're on the side of the child."

"Does it work ?"

115

"Dunno. Guess so. In the long run."

"Takes a while to decimate the rabbit population I suppose."

"People hunt rabbits all the time up here," Charlotte said, "the local lads, the farmers. It's what they do."

"When you talk to Aaron," Jasper said, "it's as if you're both the same age, counting out your pocket money or something. There's no distance."

"We're both from the same stable. It's quite hard for anyone who wasn't here to pick up on."

"Doesn't there need to be some distance, some authority?"

Jasper could see Aaron ahead of them, sitting on a gate, his arms and legs waving in the air as he balanced above the rocky ground. He suppressed the wish to shout at him to get down before he fell and hurt himself. Strange, he thought, how this nervousness had overtaken him again, now that he wasn't in the school, this feeling that he had to keep control, be responsible.

"I think you have to stop theorising about it," Charlotte said, "just be natural. Of course you have to be in authority sometimes." They were level with the gate now. Charlotte grabbed Aaron and swung him down to the ground. The sun had gone behind a black cloud. The vast sky stretching over the fields and the lake and the wall, over Scotland and England, seemed to be closing in, tightening. "Time we started walking back."

Jasper walked behind. He liked the look of Charlotte from behind, the way she walked quite fast but seemed nevertheless to saunter. He could sense the movement of her buttocks beneath his shirt which came down over her jeans almost to her knees, except for the sides where the shirt flaps curved up over her hips. He let the chords back into his thoughts, playing with the tempo, the sax melody arching over, and all the time the vision of Charlotte, removing his shirt, her jeans, the thought of running his hands over her again.

Charlotte drove the car back. She enjoyed driving and once she got used to it the power and smoothness of the BMW compared to her own modest little Panda made her feel elated and capable. Thin strands of mist lay above the ground beside the road. Dusk seemed to roll in towards them. She stopped for a herd of cattle that were being driven across the road back to their barn. By the time they got back to Eliston, a thin, transparent moon had already stationed itself above the town. They had missed school supper.

"We could get fish and chips," Charlotte said. "Best fish and chips in the country." She pulled into the centre of town and stopped the car, waiting for Aaron and Jasper to fetch their supper, insisting that they waited till they got back to Jasper's house before they unwrapped the paper bundles. She found plates, warmed them in hot water and they sat round the kitchen table and ate.

"I'll take you over to the school," Charlotte said. "Story time."

"Can't I sleep here?" Aaron said, predictably.

"No, not this time."

"Are you sleeping here?"

"Yes," Charlotte said.

"In Jasper's bed?"

"Yes."

"Thought so." Aaron leapt towards the door. "Race you."

Jasper cleared up the plates and chip wrappers. The thought of being alone with Charlotte at last excited him. He was dying to make love to her, talk to her, stroke her, find out everything about her. He realised he knew almost nothing about her. All their evenings in the Dirty Bottles had been devoted to him – how he felt, what he did, what he should do, or the school, the situation, the department.

When you've wronged someone, as he had Charlotte, he thought, there's a reticence, an indelicacy about asking questions like, "How've you been getting on . . . ?"

Charlotte returned alone. She was carrying a newspaper. "End of brief honeymoon." She shrugged her shoulders and tipped her head, lips tight, spreading the newspaper out on the kitchen table. They both leant over it, Jasper stroking the nape of Charlotte's neck, feeling the hair on his own neck rising. The photograph took up a quarter of the front page, above it the thick black headline. You could see where the picture

117

had been touched up round the edges, the outline of the tent clarified so that the setting was unmistakable. The kids didn't need much retouching – Maz in his lotus, bare-chested but wearing his jeans, Katie with no top either, her plump teenage breasts the focus of the picture. Leah, thinner and smaller, bare-topped and squinting at her hand of cards, and Hiroshi, grinning his contented grin, hugging himself, full-frontal and totally nude. A white square had been printed over his genitalia. It was clear that gambling was in progress for by each cardplayer was a small pile of stones which obviously served as chips. Hiroshi's pile was smaller than anyone else's.

The headline read: "STRIP POKER AT CORALFORD SCHOOL."

> Our reporter was shocked to find boys and girls in the nude at Coralford School, apparently taking part in a midnight game of strip poker out in the grounds.
> This paper has also learned that an Ofsted inspector is currently in residence at the school . . .

Charlotte flipped through the paper to the opinion page.

> *The Courier* says it is time the government took its responsibilities to children seriously and closed Coralford School . . .

Charlotte had straightened up and was standing back from Jasper looking at him.

Jasper no longer had any doubts about which side he was on. "Ok," he said, "we fight."

"How?"

"By politics and blackmail and rule-bending and truth-economy, as these battles are always won."

"No barricades."

"No barricades."

"No sit-ins."

"No sit-ins"

"Damn!" Charlotte said.

"And now, can we go to bed?" He let his finger run down her face, over her tight-clenched lips.

Charlotte threw her arms around him. He disentangled himself, caught hold of her hand and pulled her up the stairs.

I sit in the van some days, look out for them by the drive, in the town. Or go up the tree, take the camera. They rush about, arse about, laughing, joking. Biking. Skateboarding. Having the time of their lives. Not a thing they have to do – bastards! One day I'll grab one, beat the shit out of the rich little fucker. I take pictures in the dark. I walk about the grounds, over the field.

Died, the old man – long time ago – I don't remember. Found him in bed. Two days he didn't shout out at me; then I went in. Left him there, day or two, mouth open, eyes open. Police came, took him away.

I burned all his stuff – clothes, bed. Made a bonfire of it out the back. Neighbours watching, standing about. Nobody said a word. Nobody came round, only from the smoke-house, bringing his work things, three days' wages. If you want anything . . . all they said. No, I said, nothing. Shut the door on them. Found the money in the wardrobe bottom – two thousand in fivers. Bought the van. Enlarger. Never spent a spare penny on me. Mean, terrible, old bugger, dad. Fist like a rock off Whinnick beach.

Turned his bedroom into a darkroom.

I live in the darkroom, watch the faces, the bare bodies, the girls' tits, float up at me out of the tank. With my pincers, I move them about, wait for them to show up.

PART THREE

CHAPTER ELEVEN

The meeting was held in the dining room since the lounge was still being decorated for Muir's birthday, still secret, still out of bounds. People sat on tables, stood on the benches round the edge of the room.

There was a group of visitors waiting by the back door for permission to come in. Simon went out to tell them they were not allowed in, since this was a special meeting and they were reporters. The cameras clicked at him as he went back inside.

"The thing is," Maz said, "I was going to bring it up at the next general meeting, it didn't seem that urgent. I mean, you often get down-townies wandering around the place."

Tamara's hand was up. "I saw a man in the tree."

Lots of hands went up. "There's always guys climbing the tree – looking over . . ."

"Not at midnight," Helga said. "Anyway, you should all have been in bed. Just because you're camping out it doesn't mean there's no bedtime rule."

Muir's hand was waving. "There's no point in crying over spilt milk. Maz had better tell us what he knows. Spill the beans, laddie." He leaned over towards Maz.

"What d'you mean, Muir?" Maz knew what he meant.

"I mean this is no game. Tell us what you saw."

"A man in an anorak getting into a crummy old van – a white one I think."

"Is that all?"

Maz took a resigned breath and scrolled MvS's head for his most precious piece of information. "King to pawn one, five and four don't make seven, see."

The meeting groaned. "Come on Maz, for God's sake . . ."

"Er . . . KPO 547C . . . See?"

Hiroshi, the secretary, wrote the number down.

"So what?" Katie said.

"Jasper," said the chairman.

"That number should be passed on to the police," Jasper said. "And may I suggest you stop camping out for the moment – an invitation for more indiscreet pictures – specially with our visitors outside." He gestured through the windows where the reporters could be seen standing about, peering through the dining room windows, photographing the guinea pigs, the dens, a couple of little kids who were late for the meeting.

Helga looked over at Jasper. "We need to know what you inspector people are going to do about it."

The meeting went silent, everyone looking at him.

Jasper gazed round the room: Maz, still knitting, the girl chairing the meeting, Hiroshi cross-legged writing in the meeting book, Muir tamping his pipe. Just the same as the first meeting. His heart flicked over. He had changed, sitting on the floor with his arm round Charlotte, Aaron, still chewing, propped up against the grubby knees of his tracksuit. He looked just like the rest of them. And he felt like the rest of them, a sea-change in him. He was one of them now. He heard himself talking in a low charged voice breaking with emotion.

"Everything's changed for me, coming here. I didn't know a thing before I came here . . . I can hardly remember what it's like, being an inspector person." A laugh from the meeting. "I'm going to do everything I can – everything I used to be good at – dealing with them, working the system . . . if I still can. You'd better . . . leave them to me. And you – you must just carry on the same, getting Muir's party ready, doing all the things you do. No concessions – except the tents." He didn't explain to them how he felt about the kids in the tents, so exposed, so vulnerable – any nutter could . . . He just said, "You see, if they can show the kids aren't safe, then that's a good reason to close the school. I can't do anything about that, but – I'll do everything I can, with Charlotte, to stop them . . . Witness for the defence . . ."

He heard them cheering and felt Charlotte's hand pressing his shoulder. Not aware of himself he was walking over to the piano, which had been pushed into the dining room, and he was playing an encore, he didn't even know what, a stomping riff over a boogie bass and everyone was clapping in rhythm and cheering and Maz was putting in a sort of descant on the treble keys, foot pounding, hair on end, everyone grinning, the air electric with their energy.

The chairman took a while to bring the meeting back to order and close it. Then the kids went off to pack up the tents and the grown-ups went over to Muir's to talk strategy, walking past the reporters, cameras going as they called out, "Give us a smile, Muir," as if he were royalty in trouble. Muir watched Charlotte and Jasper walking slowly ahead of him as Helga helped him along. Happiness. They seemed happy. He trusted happiness.

*   *   *

The Eliston Courier office was above the Sweetbox in Market Street. Charlotte and Jasper sat in a little waiting room. Jasper was wearing his suit and a clean white shirt. It reminded him of his trip to Newcastle which seemed like another century to him now. Charlotte had put on a dress and high heels to keep him company. Nothing but a couple of *Country Life* magazines on a glass-topped table and a coffee machine against the wall. Jasper sent his card in to the editor, and very soon they were admitted to his office. Two girls sat word-processing at screens in one corner.

"Ronald Porter." The editor offered them each in turn a handshake and pulled two plastic chairs to his desk which was cluttered with printouts and paper cups. He eased his lanky frame back behind the desk and sat down, blinking at them through his glasses, looking frazzled and slightly embarrassed. A man of perhaps forty, according to Muir a recent appointment to what had been a small circulation local paper reporting on village fêtes, planning applications and petty crime. This new man had not been to visit the school in person since his appointment some three months before.

"What can I do . . . ?"

"The picture," Jasper said, "on yesterday's front page. Who

125

took it?"

The editor went a little pink, tapped a pencil for a while. "To be perfectly honest with you . . . we're not completely sure. May I ask who . . . ?"

"You have my card," Jasper said.

"You're the one who – the inspector who is – ?"

"That's right." Jasper's voice was professional, firm. "Naturally it's good to know that the local press is vigilant about this kind of thing. Your sources would be most helpful to us in investigating the matter further. Are we talking about someone who works at the school perhaps, even one of the older pupils?"

The editor blinked again, continued tapping. "I somehow don't think so." His Northumbrian accent was faint, but there, blunting the authority of his position, making you like him a little more. A man who went off to college, got a very average degree and came back, Jasper thought, encouraging himself to feel superior. "We've been sent a number of pictures since I've been here. Anonymously. And I have a feeling that a lot of them came from the same . . . er . . . chap. We've mostly chosen not to print them."

"I see," Jasper said. He sounded faintly disapproving, as if the paper should have been keeping an eye on the school and had failed in its duty.

"Well, most of them were nothing special – the sort of thing you expect. Children jumping in the pool with no clothes on, girls and boys walking about with their arms round each other. One of them was a man, I remember, member of staff I suppose, by the side of the pool, starkers. All in long shot, you couldn't make out much of what was going on." He shrugged, put down the pencil and opened his hands.

"I see. Not enough . . . er . . . physical detail, I suppose."

"I do run a newspaper," the editor cut in, "I'm not here for . . ."

"Fun."

"Quite."

"So if you'd been sent something more . . . page three-ish . . .

126

before, you'd have printed it?"

The editor was not abashed. "Yes and no. You see the public perception has changed. There was a time when all that sort of thing wouldn't have – I mean, education – it's news these days."

"I see."

The editor offered them a sheepish conspiratorial grin. "Look, we don't like this anonymous business, but, frankly . . . this one was too good to miss . . . I mean, as I said . . . I have a newspaper to run."

How people like to let other people know they run things, Jasper thought, recognising the feeling in himself. But really it was only worth admitting to running something that was worth running. "How do you suppose he – or she – got the shot?" he asked.

"Oh, just a flash in the dark." He laughed at his own wit.

"A close-up? Or did you . . ?"

"He'd have enlarged it in a darkroom, no doubt."

"So if it isn't a member of staff or one of the pupils, we may be dealing with an intruder here, a peeping Tom, maybe a paedo –"

"It is not my business to –"

"But it is mine," Jasper cut in, "as you rightly point out. We could be dealing with a threat to the children far more dangerous than whether they are playing strip poker or not. You say you've received pictures from this source before, but you've no idea who it is?"

"I –"

"This is a small community . . . er . . . Ronald. People usually know things. Does he post them in?"

"They're delivered by hand . . . We find them when we get in in the morning, usually."

"And you've no idea who he is?"

"No. Now sir, –" the editor's tone suddenly changed "– may we enquire what Ofsted has in mind for the school? I believe you've been here for some time, been, familiarising yourself with the place, been," he smiled, "getting to know the children.

You must be aware that –"

"I must stress to you –" Jasper's voice was cool "– that Ofsted has the matter under control. There will be an inspection, then there will be a report, then there will be a decision taken as to the future of the school. That is all we can say for the moment. Meanwhile –" Jasper stared hard at the editor "– I must ask you to do what you can to find out who this mysterious photographer is. Could be a matter of life and death."

He got up and put the plastic chair back against the wall. Charlotte, who had sat silently throughout, watching Jasper work, got up and did the same. The editor half rose. Jasper waved him down. The muted clicking of the computer keys, which Jasper now realised had stopped during the interview, began again.

"J, you're brilliant at this stuff." Charlotte hugged him when they were out in the street.

"I've served my apprenticeship," Jasper said, "but it doesn't mean much. It won't stop them, or make them say who it was."

"Do you think they know who it was?"

"I'd be very surprised if they didn't have a good idea. Now we'll go and see the police – make a complaint and give them the registration number. The great thing is to take the offensive." He pushed his arm through Charlotte's. "I feel as if I've come back from the dead."

"I know."

"But all this is preliminary stuff." His mind was racing. "The key to all this is Denise. I must phone Denise, arrange to meet her, get her on our side."

"On our side! – Isn't she the enemy?"

"Not exactly. Civil servants have no fixed loyalties. I'll explain it all to you after we've seen the police."

They threaded their way up Market Street, Charlotte hurrying to keep up with Jasper's determined steps. I always used to be the pace-setter, the organiser, she thought. It cramped his style. And she decided she would never tell him about how she had rung up the school to ask about Muir's health and how Helga had said, "There's this inspector coming – such a funny name – Jasper Bignold." And Charlotte's stomach had given that lurch, which it hadn't done for ages. She'd arranged to do the article, and had her hair cut, and booked the other visitors' house and bought a couple of new tops and driven up from London, thinking, "What the hell, I'll just do it."

*   *   *

Mazola von Strumm sat with his thumbs and index fingers pressed against his temples. He was listening for advice, for guidance. He was thinking in that amplified way that those with Venusian fluid in their veins can think – in colours and sounds and at least seven dimensions. He was thinking van. He was thinking white van. He was thinking recent talk of vans. What crummy white vans did. They chased people. People like Aaron. They had to be filled up with petrol. Maybe they always filled up at the same service station because there weren't very many and because that service station was probably cheaper and a mean man, which he probably was, would want to save those few pence. And maybe he filled up at the same time – at night, because a mean man like him wouldn't show himself much in the daytime. Bit of a long shot, Crimbly, but you had to start somewhere.

He went off to find Aaron, who as he expected was hanging around at the end of the drive hoping to catch sight of Jasp and Charlotte, who were not there, because, as MvS knew, they were in town at the newspaper offices.

Aaron looked at him and his face lightened a little. "Hi Maz. Going to the chip shop at all?"

"Could be, could be. Got any money?"

"A bit." Aaron dug in his jeans pocket and fished out fifty pence.

"Come on then, I've got enough for myself."

"The guy who chased you," MvS said when they were about level with the castle, "what did he look like?"

"Horrible. He had this raggly beard. He was thkinny."

"And he had a crummy white van?"

"Yeth, white."

MvS and Aaron got their chips, put lots of salt and vinegar on and walked back up the hill eating them. MvS loved the way the salt and vinegar felt almost painful on his lips while he was munching the soft sweetish chips. The faint burble of the stream could be heard through the hedgerow. "Let's go across the field," he said to Aaron, but Aaron refused in that half-sulky way he had and MvS didn't insist because his penetrating mind understood how scared Aaron was. And he didn't mind going the longer way round companionably munching his chips along with Aaron while he was making plans for later which were both exciting and terrifying.

CHAPTER TWELVE

They were lying naked on Jasper's bed. A pattern of afternoon sun slanted across them round the edges of the thin cotton curtains which were drawn to. A muted peachy light filled the room.

"You think it's the ideas behind the place they're bothered about," Jasper was saying, "but that isn't the way it works."

"What makes you think that?" Charlotte said. "These people are really scared of freedom for kids. Full of jealousy because they never had a moment to themselves all day long when they were at school. It's a case of the bullied bullying. The imposed-on imposing."

"You might be right about individuals," Jasper said patiently, "but departments don't work like that."

Charlotte stopped pushing her fingers through his hair, which curled against the tender, pale skin of her breasts. "So, come on. How do they work then?"

"Don't stop," Jasper said. He moved his ear slightly so he could hear her heart beating. She stroked his hair some more and kissed his head.

"I'm not arguing, I just want to understand."

"OK. I'm trying to get it right, it's quite a complicated thing." He felt distracted by the rhythmic thud of her heart and moved his ear again. "Institutions have a generalised mistrust of things that are not under their control. One aspect of that is, of course, that places with ideas which don't fit in with their brief sometimes feel dangerous."

"Well, isn't that what I said? Institutions fear freedom."

"An organisation, a department, doesn't subscribe to, or object to, vague philosophical ideas like freedom. That's politicians' rhetoric. Civil servants don't have time for that sort of thing. They are just a collection of people organised in a particular hierarchical way."

"What particular way?"

131

"It's like a series of checks and balances, like an old fashioned watch, each person concerned with his own role, his own tick. That way the whole machine works, grindingly perhaps, but reasonably decently. If some high-up politician starts acting according to some personal philosophy or phobia – fear of freedom, let's say – by the time all the cogs have activated themselves in order to maintain their position or if possible improve it, the top man's phobia will be extremely compromised, will be the least important thing."

"Like a car . . . someone starts the car and then the machine takes over with its transmission and gears."

"Kind of." Jasper had the feeling he himself was being driven into a cul-de-sac.

"And if some nutty guy tries to start up the car with his peeping Tom pictures?"

"Then he won't get the key to the machine. He doesn't get a licence."

"Oh come on, Jasp. He's going to be driving the car straight through the kids' freedom – well, your department will do it for him."

"Not exactly. Government vehicles are slow and ponderous. The ancient family saloon. He might be able to start the vehicle, he'd never be able to send it off at speed."

Charlotte was lightly drumming her fingers on his chest. "But he might start the machine in a certain direction and it would just lumber on of its own accord."

"True, but that would lead to all sorts of manoeuvring to make sure everyone didn't end up in the ditch."

"Ah." Charlotte heaved herself up the bed so that Jasper's head was on her stomach. "Isn't this idea of yours out of date? You're describing the past; when people had job security. Everything changed slowly, and you couldn't get rid of people then. Haven't we had an education revolution, everything up for grabs, weakest to the wall?"

"That makes people near the top even more cautious. The last thing they want to do is get attached to some new, short-lived directive and end up losing their jobs. What I'm trying to

132

tell you is that if they close Coralford, it will be out of caution, not out of conviction. It isn't influential enough to be closed out of conviction."

He stroked her thigh, moving his fingers gently up towards her bush of black hair.

"Caution?"

"They will close it in case something happens here that may cost them their jobs."

"An accident to a kid or something?"

"Yes. Something happens here, the press are on to it, the media demand action."

"Precisely what's happening."

"Except that there hasn't been an accident."

"Sex and nudity is better than an accident, isn't it?"

"I'm not sure if it is anymore," Jasper said. "I'm just not sure. Fifteen-year-olds are on the pill these days, confidentially, from their GP. It's a nice little scandal for the press, but I'm not sure Ofsted or Social Services could sustain a case against the school unless an adult, a teacher say, were involved."

"Or an inspector – you! They'd make it up if necessary. Aren't we full circle? Aren't I right in essence? The nutter with the camera has freedom phobia, points the finger, *The Sun* directs the finger at the DfEE, involving you as the rogue inspector if necessary, they move in to protect their jobs, sack you, close the school. Bit like Hitler really. Totalitarian," Charlotte said, leaping a few rungs up the argument.

"Precisely. The department doesn't want to be seen as a collective dictator. In the end it is safer for them to be seen as a defender of freedom than as a mouthpiece for some little Hitler. Especially if they are defending an irrelevant little institution in the middle of nowhere."

"Are you sure?"

"No, I'm not sure, but I'm going to try to make sure."

Charlotte squeezed his shoulders, "Via Denise?"

"Exactly."

"What's she like, Denise?" Charlotte was stroking his hair again, fingers caressing his ears, making him shiver.

"Full of jargon. A very competent operator who likes things to go her way and usually sees to it that they do. But she's intelligent and sort of OK underneath. Heart in the right place. She is capable of seeing a point of view. We've worked together quite a lot and she trusts me."

"And the press?"

"We must encourage the press towards a more succulent victim."

"Our poor little peeping Tom."

"The dangerous crypto-paedophile. Exactly, him."

"Poor bugger," Charlotte said.

"Beside the point," Jasper said. "You can't make an omelette without breaking eggs."

"The mills of the Inspectorate grind exceeding nasty." Charlotte grinned down at him. "God, J, I could never have worked out all this."

Jasper pushed his head up and kissed her nose. "That's because you went to the wrong school, my dear. I have some experience of grinding the mills of the Inspectorate."

"And will you grind yourself out of a job?"

"Hope so, when I'm ready. Fed up with being a cog."

"Poor coggie. What will you do?"

He sat up. "Dunno . . . Something with you." He was stroking her face, looking at her. "I love talking to you, Charlie. I've had nobody to talk to, really talk to, all this time. A good sharp discussion with an uncluttered mind – you don't know how much I've missed that."

"Come on, J, that can't be true. Nobody?"

"Well, it's nearly true. Nobody talks ideas much anymore. So many things you can't say because it's not fashionable, not PC. Nobody wants to get to the bottom of anything – all these buzzwords which are never investigated: "self-esteem", "under-achieving", "evaluation", "vocational" and so on. How can you talk about under-achievement or over-achievement when achievement itself is so subjective? I'm an under-achiever."

"No you're not," Charlotte murmured into his hair.

"Yes I am. All I've achieved is status. Another of those damned words. Getting the bass line to *Mood Indigo* right – now that's an achievement."

Charlotte laughed. "What do kids make of all this rabbit?"

"I don't suppose they understand a word of it, but then nobody asks them." He kissed her nipples slowly one after the other. "Enough of that . . ."

Later, Jasper phoned Denise and invited her to dinner in Newcastle. On Charlotte's advice he had chosen a chic little vegetarian restaurant down by the river. "My treat," he explained.

"We do have departmental business to discuss," Denise said. "I don't see why . . ."

"I know that. I'd like to talk things over very informally – off-site as it were. I'd like to invite you to dinner, simply that."

Charlotte stroked his thigh with her bare foot.

"That's awfully kind of you, Jasper, thanks for that, but –"

"No buts. Shall we say Wednesday?"

"Well, if you're absolutely sure."

He gave her the address of the restaurant, arranged to meet her there at eight-thirty and put down the phone. "It's important in these things to be the one who pays the piper."

"Doesn't Denise know that?"

"Yes, that's why she demurred, and she'll still try to pay I expect, but I've won the first round."

*　　　*　　　*

MvS strolled into the service station and looked around the shelves. The man behind the counter watched him suspiciously, said nothing but followed him with his eyes as he sauntered around the shop, picking up a bag of crisps, a can of coke from the cold box, putting them back again. All this time MvS was trying to make up his mind how to approach him, his steely mental antennae feeling towards the man's mind, the way he thought. At last he selected an old-fashioned Mars Bar from the display by the side of the till and pushed his money down into the plastic dip. The man slid the money through and pushed his change back to him.

"Saw you in the paper, didn't I? Have some fun up there, don't you?"

MvS hadn't expected that response. "Yeah, well, it's . . . OK. Actually – I've been sent by Mr Muir."

"Mr Muir. Oh yes, I know Mr Muir and Mrs Muir. Come up here for a fill-up, every week, regular as clockwork."

"He asked me to ask you – a boy came up here the other night, maybe you read about it in the paper. . ."

"Certainly did. He was up here, the reporter, asking all sorts of silly questions."

"Mr Muir wanted to thank you – and the man in the van, who tried to bring him back. You see he's . . . a bit of a disturbed boy and . . . But Mr Muir didn't know . . . how to find the man and he just thought . . ."

MvS's hair was combed back. Quite tidy and polite, the man thought, for up there.

"You'll be meaning the one with the beard, with the white van. Don't know him really, lives over Whinnick way, they say. Usually comes in of a Thursday afternoon at half past four to fill up, or sometimes late at night. Couldn't tell you more than that. If Mr Muir would like to send up a letter, I'd pass it on to him next time he's in."

MvS gave the man his most charming smile. "That's awfully kind of you – I'll let Mr Muir know . . ."

"Watch that gambling now – never gamble with a woman." The man laughed at his own joke and MvS did his best with a little embarrassed giggle, lowering his head. He could see that the man would have liked to know more, all about the camping and the girls and everything else. He backed out, waving, glancing at the calendar hanging up behind the counter depicting a bare-chested girl with large tits sitting astride a motor bike. MvS struggled to understand the mentality of earthlings, their obsessions.

Thursday afternoon, he thought, running back down into

Eliston, counting his foot thuds and skipping every third paving stone for luck. I'll get up here straight after band rehearsal. Once again he wondered if he should let someone know – Hiroshi, Jasp? MvS works alone – he sang it aloud, skipping over the slab on "alone", making a kind of dance song. Hip-hop, doodly-bop! MvS works . . . alone!

CHAPTER THIRTEEN

To his right one of those blazing skies you only seem to get as you're driving along, the light ahead shading through the lightly tinted screen. And you'd like to stop, get out, stretch your legs and watch this fiery counterpane of illuminated clouds floating slowly towards some vast bed of night behind the hills, but you can't because you are on the A1 and must keep your eyes on the road, following the cars and trucks ahead. Phrases only fit for sentimental popsongs floated on their trite tunes across his mind, "Sunset over Eliston but sunrise in my heart . . ." he hummed and smiled to himself. Heart, start – a new start. He'd been a dutiful once a week man, now he was a wild three times a day man again. Fifty-two years old and a three times a day man. He sang out the piano accompaniment as best he could given that a voice couldn't make chords.

As the lights of Newcastle approached he pushed a cassette of Art Tatum into the stereo, turned it low and tried to concentrate his thoughts on education again. Where was the crux of it all? Nobody knows. Ego-battles, it was all mixed up with ego-battles he decided.

For the first time in years he thought about Jackie Wallace. You don't remember pupils' names after a time, but he'd never forgotten that one. His first job, Yarborough, a newish comprehensive in Plaistow. "You've got to stamp your authority on them," the headmaster had said, "right from the start. Don't let them get away with a thing. Pick on someone, doesn't matter who, let them see you're the boss." He understood from his own grammar school days that this was sound advice. Easier in those days of course, with the cane, though actually he had never had to use the cane.

He'd picked on Jackie Wallace, the roughest, toughest, most ignorant kid in the class. Wallace had done nothing wrong that day, but he'd found an excuse and belted him hard on the side of the face, in front of the whole class, watching the tears quickly blinked back in the lad's eyes. He hadn't felt good about it, and even worse about the slight erection he felt at the time, a dark pulse of excitement that made his face flush also.

You could say that his entire career was built on the firm foundation of the flat of his hand contacting the rather fleshy cheek and far from clean ear of Jackie Wallace, who lived in a high-rise block and whose concentration span during lessons was about thirty seconds, but who had built a functioning motorbike from bits and pieces on the old waste ground behind the flats. Jackie Wallace disappeared for a while and surfaced inside Maidstone Gaol whereas Jasper, having taken him on, having no further trouble with discipline, was able to give his latent skills as a teacher full rein. Fifteen years later he was head of a medium-sized comprehensive in Walthamstow and by the time the education changes started to come in in the nineties, he had already moved into the calmer and more prestigious ambiance of the Inspectorate.

Jackie Wallace was himself a bully, a puncher of smaller kids, a molester of girls, a leader of gangs. Jasper had chosen his victim carefully. No, not his victim – his partner. His partner in a historic ritual, well-known to both of them, that had to be gone through before Jackie could submit to authority without losing status and Jasper could have a peaceable, productive day and a successful career. It was the equivalent of two mafia bosses shaking hands and sharing out the territory.

And Jackie learnt a smattering of those things which Jasper decided he should learn – and very minimal they were.

Jasper, the decisive, bearing the accumulated prestige of all those lives he had shaped like a mass-producer of pots – a curve of algebra here, a handle on geography there, a plateful of spellings: a successful teacher, pummelling, dragging, stretching, moulding . . . Looking back, it seemed that the tight, locking feeling in his jaw had occurred first the day he hit Jackie Wallace, a physical acknowledgement of the sense he'd had of knuckling down, getting to grips with the reality of his chosen profession. Underneath there was always a soft whoosh of sadness like a silk scarf touching your neck – a feeling he had always associated with Charlotte.

And it was still the same. No corporal punishment but the principle was the same – establish your authority. He remembered being in a school quite recently and overhearing a teacher verbally berating a child for coming in late because she had needed to go to the toilet. A long diatribe in front of the class – why had she not gone during break, had she a weak bladder in which case she must bring a letter from her doctor, did she understand how much she had disrupted the class by her selfish behaviour . . . yes, she'd better sit down quickly and start her work before she was put on report, which because of her magnanimous nature, she, the teacher, would refrain from doing on this one occasion . . . And when the school was inspected, it was clear that this was the most successful teacher, got the best results, appeared, at least when being formally inspected, to be kind and thoughtful with the students, really cared, was listened to, taught a good lesson to an attentive class.

But at Coralford they seemed to have circumvented the ego struggle, nobody challenged anybody's power. They simply co-existed. Even in the meeting they were good-natured, seemed not to resent the winners, not to lord it over the losers. How was it done? How had Muir with his conventionial, kirk-going Presbyterian background managed it? Was it extraordinarily simple – you stop trying to win, trying to teach, just let the kids be, wait for them to ask? It seemed to work at Coralford but Jasper couldn't see how it would work at Yarborough Comprehensive. But in that case, what were they trying to achieve at Yarborough Comprehensive? Academic excellence! Or was it more sinister than that? Wasn't Yarborough Comprehensive inadvertently teaching survival skills at a deep level, what you needed on the factory floor, the parade ground, the football terrace? The love of boredom, the philosophy of kill-or-be-killed, the herd instinct? But the factory floor's swept clean, the parade ground's empty and that leaves the football terrace to burn off the excess . . .

Jasper parked the car and went into the restaurant. He was wearing his casual clothes, the dark shirt and no tie. He wanted Denise to be the one who felt slightly out of place in her navy suit and pearl earrings. It was ten past eight. He had decided to get there first, be at the table, relaxed, glass in hand, olives and crudités in situ on its pitch pine, unclothed surface.

Denise was punctual, wearing the tailored black dress he remembered from drinks evenings in the departmental lounge. The pearl earrings were slightly larger and pinker, matched with a necklace which curved modestly over the high-necked dress and under its turndown collar. He rose, bussed her clean delicately-fragranced cheek and helped her out of her pink linen collarless jacket. It was a warm evening and even Denise looked faintly flushed. A good sign, Jasper thought. Then he realised that the flush was because he had invited her to dinner, creating a slightly unnerving intimacy between them even though she knew they were here to talk business.

"I do hope I'm not late." It was her habit to set scenes, not to be orchestrated into them.

"No," Jasper said, "I was early." He poured her a glass of wine.

"I'm not sure I . . . "

"Just a small glass . . . it's rather good. Do me the honour – I'm feeling a lot better. A little celebration."

How perfectly groomed she was. Her slightly raised eyebrow plucked, brushed, between the palest hint of eyeshadow and her smooth, matt forehead.

"My divorce. I just feel over the whole thing; ready to get on with my life, rebuild." His introduction was planned, increasing the intimacy of the evening: a declaration of bache-lordom, an impression that he was "in the marketplace." He had guessed that this would cause her a small frisson but would also alarm her a little, unsure of his intention, anxious to keep him at bay if need be. Her anxiety would make her more amenable to compromise in other directions, a kind of

141

compensation.

She lifted her glass by the stem and sipped it, her eyes wary, "I'm pleased for you."

"I don't know how familiar you are with the food here – all vegetarian or vegan – but quite delicious."

"How nice." She lifted her spectacles on their chain and looked at the menu which was handwritten in black, art school script.

"Or there's more on the board." He indicated the same script, now white, which filled the blackboard over by the bar. Denise let her glasses fall and peered over at it.

"The chickpea terrine with orange and bilberry sauce is an awfully good starter," Jasper murmured. Just a hint of irony.

"Why not." Denise took her glasses from round her neck and put them on the table. The syllables came out clipped and firm. He suspected they disguised a sigh of irritation and relief.

It wasn't till half way through the speciality of the maison (Roti de Noisettes Blanches with a Rosemary and Carrot Sauce) that he began to talk about the school. Denise had allowed herself a second glass of wine. ("Absolutely my last, I'm driving.") Her fork, carefully scooping up crumbling mouthfuls of nut roast, had slowed considerably. He could tell she'd had enough.

"What should we do, do you think, about Coralford?" Jasper said.

Denise took the opportunity to put her fork down, dabbing at her mouth with a deep purple napkin. She attempted to gain the initiative: "What should we do? I think I outlined the Department's concerns last time we met, Jasper. Everything that has happened since and been reported, quite extensively, in the press, simply underlines the Department's good sense. The fact that you were there to witness these events means that we can proceed to the inspection with the outcome in little doubt. You will be able to confirm the lack of appropriate supervision and guidance."

"There are one or two problems with that scenario," Jasper

said. Denise's smooth brow adopted a polite furrow of attention. "You see, this place, Coralford, is, in fact, exceptionally
successful and very important. It shouldn't be closed."

Her face decorated itself with a strained half-smile. Jasper
surged on with his prepared speech.

"On the contrary, we should give it every encouragement to
remain open. Secondly, the man who took that picture, as far
as I can determine, is a peeping Tom and would-be paedophile.
We may be giving ourselves a great deal of grief if we appear
to associate ourselves with this extremely undesirable person
and at the same time bring all the liberal protesters and
freeschoolers of yesteryear out of the woodwork." He leaned
back in his wicker chair and gazed at her, hand cupping his
chin.

Denise flicked some imaginary crumbs off her sleeve with
the purple napkin. Her eyes opened and closed rapidly a few
times as if blinking her brain into gear. She leant forward in
another bid to take the initiative. "Those people don't have any
credibility these days, unless they are already on board. The
others are ineffectual and disorganised, as you'd expect."

"Look at me Denise," Jasper said boldly.

She stopped blinking and stared into his eyes speculatively,
with a tiny flick of her red tongue.

"You and I know the reality. The Minister doesn't. The
Minister never sets foot in a school without carefully signalling the event weeks before. Inspectors are the same. But
you and I, Denise, were teachers for, what, fifteen, twenty
years? We know the realities. We know that even the best
school isn't that good and the worst ones are diabolical. We
know that a good twenty per cent of pupils don't learn much
and most of the other eighty per cent forget what they do learn
the minute they leave. We know that in most schools there's
persistent bullying and truanting which we can't eradicate –
not only by kids but by teachers too. It's one of those things we
all know but won't admit. Schools, by and large, are not the
best places for children to be in. If they are not over-disciplined
and rigid then they are a shambles. That's how it works."

Denise folded her napkin and put it next to her plate. "Of course I hear what you say. However, we have a much better system being put into place now." She took a deep, energising breath. "We're getting there. There are some very positive initiatives going on in schools. Standards are being raised, pupils are beginning to achieve. We're on target."

"With respect, both you and I know that fundamental things have changed very little and can't change." He told her about Jackie Wallace.

"Corporal punishment is a thing of the past."

"And now we have whole-school policies of containment, sanctions, suspensions, exclusions – all intended to keep the child quiet, in its place, on task and doing as it is told. This is not natural to children and can only be done by intimidation and bribery. Teacher authority is still the principle." He told her about the girl who went to the toilet.

"That teacher did the right thing," Denise said. "You did the right thing. If there is no discipline, nobody learns anything. Learning is crucial. Discipline is crucial. It's how civilisation progresses. I believe in what we do, what we have to do."

"Civilisation progressing. Hmm." Jasper left a deliberate pause. "If I met Jackie Wallace now," Jasper said, "he wouldn't know his ten times table from his left elbow, he wouldn't be able to spell "cat", but he'd know how to bully and fight people weaker than himself, because that is the lesson I taught him."

"He was already like that."

"Yes, and I reinforced it."

Denise leant forward again and spoke in a harsher voice. "Listen to me, Jasper. What about the people it did work for? You don't judge the education system by the likes of Jackie Wallace. You may have persuaded yourself that education doesn't matter, that kids are better off playing about, not learning unless they feel like it, but that wouldn't have worked for Jackie Wallace and it won't work for most kids. They need guiding. They need boundaries. You can't judge everyone by yourself. You come from a wealthy family that nurtured you, saw to it you got to grammar school, university, believed in you, wanted the best for you. And you were no doubt clever, talented. You'd have been all right anywhere. But if you don't have those things then school is your only hope."

Jasper could hear a kind of desperation in Denise's voice. He kept quiet.

"It may not be at all apparent to look at me now, but I didn't have those privileges. My father was a foundry worker, couldn't keep a job, drank and swore and used his fists on my mother and me. I was a late reader because there weren't any books in our house." ("Ow rouse" – a distinct Northern accent had crept into her voice.) "How do you think I got out of it? Oh yeah, I got smacked a time or two at school – by the same teacher who made it clear to me that the only way forward was work, work, work, study, study, study, and yes, I passed my eleven plus and got to grammar school." She gave a small rasping laugh. "My father thought I'd betrayed the family traditions – gone all stuck up and snooty. But here I am." Her eyes bored into him aggressively. "You wouldn't guess, would you Jasper, that I was brought up in a home with a privy out the back and a square of newsprint for loo paper?" She gulped the rest of her wine and poured herself some mineral water. "Firmness matters Jasper. And the Jackie Wallaces of this world are not going to be better off, and nor is anyone else, if you let them run riot."

Jasper took a deep breath. Neither of them spoke. He marvelled at her poise, her impeccability in the light of what she had said. She was, he thought for the first time, a beautiful woman; in her fifties but with scarcely a wrinkle, her figure trim, with formidable pluck and intelligence, even a sort of hard grace. A woman who had forged her own success with an iron will, relentless self-discipline; a woman with no children, no lovers, he felt sure. Charlotte in reverse.

"Denise." He leaned forward and took her hands. They felt dry and cold. She stared at the hands lying in his."Were you happy as a child?"

"I don't think happiness came into it." She slid her hands from under his and examined them as if they needed washing.

145

Then she took her napkin and carefully wiped the corners of her eyes without disturbing her make-up.

"Don't you think that matters, that a child is happy?"

"Of course it matters. But an adult who can't read isn't happy. A child out of control isn't happy."

"Do unhappy children learn to read better?"

"Of course not. It's more difficult for an unhappy child to learn as we all know. "

"But you did. So did I. Is that what you're saying?"

"Precisely. We had no choice. We learned what we had to learn. Happiness is an optional extra, if you're lucky."

"Let me ask you something else: do unhappy children grow into happy adults?"

She looked up. "You're asking me if I'm happy?"

He had not expected her to personalise the conversation so readily, as if she wanted something deeper between them, wanted to move below the arid professionalism she always displayed, move towards a more satisfying exchange.

"Sort of." He waited.

She blinked rapidly for a while, "I – there are certain . . . satisfactions, a job well done . . ." She blinked some more. "I don't think I'm particularly happy."

"Because you never learned what happiness was?" Jasper spoke as he supposed therapists speak.

"I'm sure that has a lot to do with it."

"So should we be teaching happiness? Should that be on the core curriculum?"

"I don't think it has occurred to anyone. How would you train happiness teachers?" A tiny spark had come into Denise's moist eyes. He sensed she was beginning to enjoy the conversation. They were no longer quite adversaries – more conspirators. What he wanted.

"Standard Attainment Tests in happiness – level three – the pupil is able to smile independently, responds well to appropriate stimuli such as the bell for the beginning of break, chocolate bars, has some difficulty in laughing aloud – I like it Jasper."

146

"The school report – 'Plays well.' Muir said happiness is the absence of fear, something like that."

Denise said, "I've never heard you speak like this before, Jasper. I always assumed you were – well, you know, a typical inspector. A conversion on the road to Damascus?"

"Not a conversion exactly, more – I dunno – a coming back to my senses – literally. Denise, we don't know anything about kids living in a natural environment. They're different – peaceable, intelligent." He spoke forcefully. "These kids at Coralford . . . the last blue whales living in the environment a blue whale should have. You and I are being expected to let out the water. We are not going to do it Denise."

She stared at him, flicking her red tongue. "Lord of the Flies re-assessed . . ."

". . . in the light of compelling factual evidence. Golding's was a fantasy, the fantasy of a repressed public-school product. How could he imagine how free children might behave?"

"Basically, you are saying we have a vendetta against this place because we didn't go there ourselves."

"Maybe vendetta is too strong a word. I'm saying our experience of childhood means we simply don't understand its importance. We tend to assume childhood should be sacrificed to adulthood, because that's what happened to us. We seem to think children are savages we have to tame. You know, I've discovered something – it's not places like Coralford which create savages, it's the rest of the education system. Remember it's Golding's regimented choirboys who initiate the savagery. Coralford is important evidence about childhood, about human-ness. It's about original goodness if you like, a cause for optimism."

There was a long silence.

"The noble savage revisited."

"If you like."

"And if some ghastly accident occurs because the children are not supervised?"

"Accidents can happen anywhere. These are sensible kids, they know how to look after themselves. They even look after

147

each other."

Another long silence.

"What do you want me to do?"

"Not a great deal. Keep them off my back while I sort it out. Make sure I get the contract for the inspection and write a memo to the Minister saying it is very important to make no move until after my team's report. Be on my side. Get a bit of positive spin going in the press. Trust me. I haven't gone native, just seen the other side of the moon – it isn't so dark after all."

She pressed her lips together in a thin smile. "And if I feel I can't manage that?"

Jasper knew he'd won. "I shall leave the service and make a damned nuisance of myself, including organising all those ineffectual liberals." He smiled back. "And I'll dig up a few skeletons – those inspections we've collaborated on, all the compromises we made." He put his hands over hers again briefly. "I have great respect for you, Denise." He gestured towards the sweet trolley. "And now we're going to have a big creamy, fruity, fattening pudding,"

"I don't usually . . ."

"I know, and it shows. But tonight you're going to have what-ever takes your fancy. It's a happiness lesson."

And she laughed, she actually laughed. Jasper couldn't recall ever hearing her laugh before. It was a laugh which made him able to believe in her background, a bold shout of a laugh.

He saw Denise to her car. She turned and looked at him a second too long before getting in. She looked vulnerable. He knew he had to make sure. He put an arm round her and pressed his lips to her cheek. She went to speak and he put a finger against her mouth. "No, don't say, 'Thanks for that'."

"I wasn't . . . ," she protested, laughing again.

"I'll take you to see the place when this is sorted. We'll make a day of it, there are some nice little fish restaurants along the coast up there."

He watched her drive away. He was pleased with the way it

had gone but he felt like a bastard nevertheless. He liked her so much better now. If it weren't for Charlotte, he thought, he wouldn't have been averse, not at all averse . . . and when he saw her again he would find a way to tell her that, tell her about Charlotte.

CHAPTER FOURTEEN

Charlotte had second supper and went over to the hockey field with Aaron tagging behind.

"When's Jathp coming back?"

"Not till late tonight. You'll be in bed by then."

"Maz is trading me his den."

"What for?"

"Two weeks poc and my old Gameboy."

"Not bad. Well, you'd better show it to me and then I've got to go and see Muir."

Charlotte looked at the neat mosaic Maz had made with stones and shells and bits of brick and sat on the outer wall round the dens for a while as Aaron busied himself writing his name on a piece of wood and fixing it outside his entrance. Yesterday there had been another photograph which had made the front page of a few nationals, along with the first. It showed Hiroshi and Katie in a close embrace lying in their tent. This had brought a few more reporters, who hung about on the edge of the grounds, and occasionally were caught inside the school itself and politely asked to leave by older kids or staff. One had even been discovered in the lounge, carrying in a cardboard box full of paints like a kind of disguise. Some of the younger kids had been excited by the attention, offering to pose for pictures in exchange for money or sweets, but by now they too were fed up with the intruders. So far the papers had mostly confined themselves to reportage. Charlotte realised she should finish her article quickly and offer it to *The Guardian* rather than the little alternative journal that had commissioned it. But already *The Guardian*'s education correspondent had been on the phone to Muir to arrange an interview and no doubt they would use that instead.

"See you later," she called to Aaron and walked over to Muir's cottage.

Muir was watching Channel Four news, but fumbled for the off button on the remote when she came in.

"Were we on again?"

"Aye. Some Tory back bencher calling for action. Archive footage of the school – bare bums in the swimming pool."

"Muir –" she kissed his forehead and put the tape recorder on "– how do you feel?"

"Weary. You know I'd like to die feeling I'd moved things on a wee bit. Worried too. That chap snooping round the place. What do I do about that? Now the kids can't even camp in our own grounds without mebbe being in danger." Muir eased off his glasses, wiped his eyes and carefully put them back on again.

"Jasper's having dinner with the HMI woman," Charlotte said. "He seems confident he can get them on our side."

"Aye."

"Muir, I want to finish this article, and . . . you've written lots of stuff yourself and people write about you, you tell your little stories, your examples, jokes, try to shock people a bit . . ."

"That's the way of it." He nodded and smiled his leathery smile.

"I want to get a bit deeper. Why you, Muir? Why you? Your background, impoverished, repressed – so unlikely. Why? You must have thought about it."

"I have. Oh aye, I've done some thinking about it . . ."

"And?"

"Failure. Failure and chance."

"Explain."

"I was a failure at everything. I couldna pass exams, couldna discipline the kids, couldna teach them anything. And I got the job in Kirkstone. Heidmaister! A wee success! Don't let them get the better of you, I thought to myself, Make them toe the line. Impose your authority. I was about to leather this kid. I looked at him, standing there – now here's the element of chance – he happened to be a kid who looked exactly like I'd looked at his age – I saw myself – a gangling, underfed lad wi' carroty hair and big feet holding his hand out, bending his fingers up so it wouldna hurt so much. I was about to leather myself."

151

Charlotte went to speak, but Muir raised his hand.

"Now, I'd been leathered like that, but more to the point, I leathered myself all the time, in my dreams, in my thoughts, for being such a failure. And now I was holding out my hand to be leathered again, wanting it, expecting it. And I thought, I'm not going to give you what you want, you scrawny little bastard. I put down the tawse and looked at the kid and he looked back at me, as if we were both looking in a mirror. 'Stand up!' I said. 'Stand up for yourself.' The kid tried to straighten his shoulders and he couldna, he was too scared. I put down the tawse and put my hands on his shoulders – my shoulders – and I said, 'You've done nothing wrong. Understand? You've done nothing wrong.'

"'No sir,' he said, and he walked away. I watched him and I saw him put up his head and straighten up. He went out the gates of the school and I heard him whistling. I put my own head up and tried it – whistling. The other bairns had gone home. I walked round the classroom for half an hour. I whistled *Annie Laurie* and *Alexander's Ragtime Band* and *The Marseillaise*. And I went back home and I wrote on a big piece of paper, 'Every time you beat a bairn you're beating yourself.'"

"But a lot of teachers would have got really angry, when they heard the lad whistling – as if he was ungrateful." Charlotte could imagine them running out, grabbing the kid back: Don't you dare whistle at me!

"Aye. But mebbe it was because this boy was a damn good whistler. And it reminded me I was a damn good whistler too and I hadna whistled for a long time."

"What if he'd been a bad whistler?"

"Children are not bad whistlers, unless you force them to whistle. That's the point – children whistle as naturally as birds do."

"I don't think it's an explanation," Charlotte said (she had never been able to whistle), "but it's a new story."

"Well it was the beginning. After that I stopped trying to be the boss, I began to enjoy myself and once I began to enjoy myself it became obvious what an absurd thing schooling was,

152

teachers making themselves miserable trying to stop kids being themselves, enjoying themselves."

"And it's still happening."

"Aye, that's the devil of it."

"So, the most important thing is happiness. Coralford is based on the idea of happiness."

"I've thought about that a lot lately," Muir said, reaching for his pipe, "and I'm not sure. Happiness is too vague a word. We can't define it. There are kids here who are happy, who leave happy. But some don't. You can't make other people happy. You can't make yourself happy. Happiness is a butterfly, fickle, promiscuous. But you can see it and feel it land on you. Happiness is harmless, has no sting in its tail. This place, the idea of it, is harmless. That's the most I can say."

"Not a very ambitious claim," Charlotte said. "The absence of a bad schooling, a negative claim. Is that all?"

Muir shifted around in his chair trying to get comfortable. "When you're a hundred years old, you'd expect to have a perspective, but you don't. What is happiness? What is harm? If my skin would stop itching then I'd be happy, but if my skin wasn't itching, mebbe I'd make more demands – a woman, a whisky, a sunset. Every move we make we harm somebody, something, squash a beetle, invade a fly's airspace, move an arm a flea might have jumped onto and had a feed . . ."

Charlotte said, "That idea leads to doing nothing. And maybe that's a problem with this place – not enough happens. I sometimes think everybody needs deadlines. Coercion has its benefits – you get things done, because you have to. Freedom can be a bit vacant – nothing to react against, nothing to tip you off your perch. You sit there balancing, do nothing, achieve nothing. Neurosis energises – don't you think?"

Muir looked up from the contemplation of his empty pipe, and reached for his baccy. "Aye, there's truth in that. But it's a destructive energy, energy trying to get rid of itself. People who're driven by some demon trying to get out."

"Could be an angel."

"Aye. But angels are usually happy staying where they are."

153

"So you were never . . . driven?"

"Can't say I was. It's exhausting, trying to get others to do what you want – specially children. I was driven to stop wearing myself out."

Charlotte changed tack. "If I'd gone to public school or grammar school would I be rich, famous, well-married? Who can tell?"

"Was that what you wanted?"

"I don't know what I would have wanted."

"Some people who came here are rich, famous and well-married," Muir said. "An accident of fate, family connections, individual personality."

"You don't think schools control that?"

"Dunno lassie. I wonder what school helped to make . . . Margaret Thatcher or the Yorkshire Ripper . . . Ian Paisley . . . Adolf Hitler . . . We didn't spawn any of them, thank God."

"I think that's a good enough ending for the article." Charlotte switched off the tape. Muir began to ask her some searching questions about Jasper. Were they serious about each other? Was Jasper intending to stay in the inspectorate? How did Charlotte think he was getting on with the kids now?

Notes

I think Muir has some plan about Jasper – amazing! A brilliant idea in my opinion. Wouldn't it be great?

Trouble with Muir, he tells these funny apocryphal stories and you never get any further. And yet, thinking about the whistling story, I think there's meaning there – an argument of sorts – a simple logic there: if a child whistles, listen to the whistling, don't tell yourself he should be doing algebra.

Oh, and I remember happiness landing on me. I'd have been about fifteen and it was the end of term party. There used to be this custom. The people who were leaving would stand in the middle of the lounge and all the others would link arms in a big circle around them and sing Auld Lang Syne. And then everybody hugged and kissed the leavers and then the gram went back on. And the butterfly had landed on me and folded its delicate blue wings. Fluttered off again when Jasper left, but I always knew it was there somewhere, waiting to land again.

CHAPTER FIFTEEN

I've put the tea caddy back on the shelf, square on, where he always kept it. No damn tea. I've had to put on my fatigues and boots and go over to the shop. Can't stand that shop. She looks at me, stiff and severe, "Good morning Robert," turns away. Everybody turns away. I hate this place, Whinnick. Crappy little bungalow up against the grey sea. Have to keep it the same. Exactly the same. Everything tidy like he had it. If I didn't keep it tidy my head would spill over like the sea, swamp the house, grey waves everywhere on the grey lino.

The darkroom is my place.

I take my boots off by the outside door, put them on the left of the porch, go in the house with my stocking feet, make my tea with one tea bag in the white teacup which hangs on the hook inside the cupboard on the left above the sink. Won't go in the darkroom today. Must go inland, in the van, get away from the breakers. Take the van up the hill, to the school. Watch them go in and out the driveway shouting and laughing. Not for long they won't! Reporters there now, after the pictures. My pictures! I've cut them out of the Sun, put them above my bed. Nobody comes here.

Savage today. Tea not there first thing? One of my savage days. Waves pounding on the whinstone like his ghost at the front door. Sea fret today and a mist out there, but still the damn trippers, women in shorts, brats yelling and running back from the spray. Got to get inland today. What can I do but drive and stand, drive and walk, drive and sit? Half an hour I can fill washing my cup and sweeping the floor with his old broom, mopping it clean. For nobody.

Drive to Newcastle today, get my film, developer. Nobody knows me there.

Locked everything up. Leave this bungalow, the lane, the chapel, the allotments, the stone walls, no gardens and all

155

the layers of grey houses up the hill to the bare fields. Nothing there for me. Nobody I speak to. Savage today. I could grab that little kid with the yellow anorak screaming by the harbour, chuck him down against the rocks, let the sea quieten the little runt.

The van won't start first time like it should. I throttle it again. Nothing! Fucking useless thing! Sea air makes everything damp. Go back to that poxy bungalow, take my boots off again, leave them in the porch, unlock the door, find the WD40 from the shelf behind the door on the left, put my boots back on again. Back at the van, lift the bonnet, spray all around, get in and try it again, leave the van running and run back to the house, off with the boots again and put the WD40 back on the shelf, boots back on and lock everything up again. Better to leave the WD40 in the van, but I can't. The WD40 is kept on the shelf to the left of the door.

Savage today, but I don't let it show. I smile to a couple who ask me which way for the castle. "Bit misty out at sea, but it'll clear," I say. I watch them going along the grass path, through the gate. The wind takes her hair across his face. They laugh and she ties a red scarf round her head.

Savage all right. Coaches coming in and out of Whinnick through that ridiculous stone arch in the middle of nowhere and I have to wait to get through myself.

Should I go up there again tonight? Take more pictures? But they'll be watching out now and reporters on the prowl. I daren't go there today, not too close.

Through the stone arch, down the tight little lanes, all dull and muddy from the rain last night. There'll be sun again today blistering the van where the salt's come for the paintwork. Nothing's any good.

Fist – that's life, a fucking fist! And if you open your hand some bastard will spit on it. She left, mum did. Took off. Left me with that dodgy bugger. Sit here sometime, up in the van, think about it. Not much of a life so far and not going to get any better. Sky and land all around and nobody in it for me. Nothing in it for me. Sunrises and sunsets and birds and grass and getting up and going to bed and driving around. Not part of it. I go up that tree and I hate that tree. I could burn that tree down to the ground and that would be something to see – a tree on fire. Whinnick – I hate the place. "What a charming spot!" the tourists say in their posh voices. And they buy kippers and sail off in their pleasure boats. The birds scream mournful and the waves crash on the dead shore. Everything shits on me. Grey waves in my head and birds screaming. I need action. I need a voice. A voice to tell me what to do.

∗   ∗   ∗

The band is shaping up. They've got a half-hour set together which will be performed during the party. Maz seemed uncharacteristically tense though, Jasper thought. That usually unhurried, strolling bass which kept the whole band relaxed and swinging seemed uneven, frenetic. Jasper, marking the barlines of *Georgia* with nice clumpy chords and then breaking into his florid solo, did his best to lean back on the beat but felt Maz always anticipating him a fraction. "Keep it steady," he called over as they moved into the middle section. Still two days to the show and already he's nervous, he thought, glancing over at Maz. His face was pale and intense below the short, stiff hair. "Maz, keep it steady."

Maz looked round with a start. "Sorry Jasp." He seemed to pull himself back into focus, into the stride of the music.

They got through the ten numbers on the set list, including the bass and piano solos. Jasper wanted to do another run through before they finished but Maz said, "Can't do it now, got to go somewhere. Same time tomorrow?" And that was decided. Charlotte had come into the back of the theatre; Jasper moved over to kiss her. Just then the tea bell went and the rest of the band disappeared in the direction of the house.

"I thought we'd go over and see Muir," Charlotte said, "put him in the picture about Denise, and then go for a walk. Want

157

to show you my childhood haunts." She smiled and squeezed his hand.

"OK." He wanted to spend every moment with her – it didn't matter how or where, as long as he could reach over and touch her skin, slide his hand across her firm straight back.

MvS surfaced as soon as the rehearsal ended. He borrowed some of Simon's gel again and combed his hair back, got into some clean jeans and set off downtown at a brisk Strummian trot. But all the time something nagging, an undercurrent of fear as if Strumm's protective beams had gone off line. Some kind of interference humming – not a groove, not Strumm, more like the fearful bleeping of a trapped bird, a repeated chirp, Don't do it, don't do it. The bleep of Maz. Sensible. Cautious. Oh all right! MvS steered his running feet in a perfect semi-circle and jogged back to the school, found an envelope, pencil and paper in his top drawer, scribbled the note and sealed it, turned back again, grabbed his Walkman and his Swiss army knife, then back down town dropping the note through Jasper's door on the way.

Down through town and up to the service station in time to the pounding rhythm coming from Radio Northumbria and the sensitive thoughts filtering off Strumm. It was four fifteen. He dropped the earphones round his neck and walked into the shop. There was a small queue: someone paying for petrol and a woman buying cigarettes and chocolate. The man looked up when Maz's turn came, recognising him. "Hello young fellow." A little too heartily. "Not you again."

"The man in the white van . . . I wondered . . ."

"Not here yet. Always punctual, set your watch by him. He'll be here at half-past four, no doubt about it. I can give him Mr Muir's letter, happy to."

MvS understood the man's need to be involved, have a role, but he said as lightly as he could, "It's fine. I'm happy to wait for him. I'll wait over by the pumps."

"As you wish," the man said, a trifle more stiffly.

MvS waited by the wall at the back of the pumps, along from the air machine, fixing his earphones over his head once more, trying to ride on the music while patiently eyeing the cars in and out – a red Ford, and a big blue space wagon with a pile of kids in it, a fat man in a Jeep who spat on the ground and spent ages in the shop before coming out with a big bundle of chocolate bars. MvSs mouth watered uncontrollably. A white Escort van came into the forecourt, KP4 . . . It was four thirty precisely. A bearded man wearing army fatigues got out and filled the tank. MvS waited until he went into the shop to pay and then went over to the van, taking the opportunity to glance inside. There was a camera, a Canon, on the front seat and a few loose boxes of film. The bearded man came out of the shop looking round the forecourt. MvS guessed the shop man had said something to him. He waited by the van, earphones round his neck but something pounding inside him heavier than music.

*   *   *

There he is! Bigger than the other one. Not running. Not scared. Full of himself. I recognise him right away. Got his hair gelled back now. Quite the little ponce. He's waiting for me; one on his own. "Mr Muir wanted to thank you . . ." *Some crap like that. Thank me! He's full of it.*

"I believe you're going to Whinnick." *I look at him.* "The man in the shop said."

"Did he now."

"I wondered if you'd give me a lift." *Playing into my hands.*

"Sure," *I say,* "jump in." *I'd like to wipe the bumptious smile off his face but I bide my time.* "Fishing?" *But I know he isn't, he hasn't got the tackle.*

"No, just taking a look."

"Shouldn't you be in school?"

"I'm doing a project." *As if he's just thought of it.* "You know . . . those birds . . . those nests on the cliffs there. A project on birds."

I'm right on to it. "Kittiwakes," *I say.* "I've got some good pictures. I'll show you."

159

"You're a photographer?" He's looking at the camera on the seat next to him.

I say, "Do your seat belt up."

We turn off by the war memorial, over the broken bridge and back down the lanes. Crummy little brat. I test him out. "Didn't I see you in that picture in the papers? You get up to some stuff at that school, don't you?"

"Sometimes. How would you take a picture like that? I mean at night like that?"

Fishing all right. "Just a flash, I shouldn't doubt."

He says nothing, looking out the window. We drive under the old arch into Whinnick. I park the van in front of the house. The sea's in. Spotting with rain. "Come in," I say, "I'll get the bird pictures for you, see if I can find some lemonade." He doesn't look too keen but he says, "Thank you, that would be nice." Self-possessed little fucker. I say to him, very firm, "Take your boots off will you." He stands in the porch like he's not sure whether to run off. He's gone a bit pale. But he sits down on the step, takes his trainers off and steps inside. I take him through the kitchen into the lounge. "Sit down on that settee," I say. "Make yourself at home." I smile and give a bit of a laugh but it doesn't turn out right. He perches on the edge of the sofa.

"Wait there." I go into the darkroom. All the time I'm saying stuff to keep him there. "Won't be a minute . . . Just looking through my prints . . . Let me see now . . ." I'm thinking quickly, taking bulbs out, putting them in my pockets, taking down pictures, the two big blow-ups I did, off the wall. He's got up. I hear him moving around the room, snooping no doubt. "Sit down," I shout. "Won't be long. I've just found them." I stand there in the darkroom with the pictures. Truth is I daren't go out, face him with them. Have to remind myself he's just some cheeky little kid, deserves a good hiding for getting up to all that mischief. Kids should do as they're told. Shouldn't answer back. I can deal with this little kid. I burst out of the darkroom with the two prints in my hand. He's standing up, quite still, close to the

160

*door back into the kitchen, keeping an exit for himself. I hold
the two pictures close to my chest. "Sit down," I say, "let me
show you." He squares his shoulders, walks over to the settee in his stocking feet and sits down. Waits, squints up at
me.*

*I lay the two pictures on the floor facing him side by side.
I stand facing him, quite close. "That what you want?"*

*He looks up. Plucky little bastard. "Thought so. Why? Why
do you come snooping round the school, doing stuff like
that?"*

*That makes me savage. I want to shout, Who do you think
you're talking to, you toffee-nosed brat? But I don't, I bide
my time, he's in the wrong place. I say, "Come on, come on,
I'll show you, lots more where those come from." He stands
up, follows me over to the dark room, stands there. He's looking jittery now. That gives me courage. I step aside and give
him one almighty shove into the darkroom and pull the door
closed with a bang. The Yale snaps shut and I turn the dead-
lock for good measure. He yells, "What the fuck are you
doing!" I say nothing to that filth. He pounds the door. I
wait and he pounds. When the pounding stops, I say,
"That'll do you no good at all. You want to mind your man-
ners. Just sit there, be still and behave yourself."*

"What do you want?" He sounds scared.

*"Never mind what I want. Just watch how you speak to
me. Wait to be spoken to. I'll decide what to do with you in
my own good time."*

*Everything goes quiet behind the door. I wait. I go into the
porch, put my boots on and walk round the outside of the
bungalow, past the darkroom window, checking. Little bastard won't get out of there in a hurry. I've put a big sheet of
board across outside, over the glass, fixed it with six-inch
nails. I take my boots off and go back into the house, get my
cup off its hook and make a cup of tea.*

Silence.

*I feel savage but calm, drinking my tea. I look at my
watch. Half past five and coming on to bloody rain. Big*

black clouds. Best of the light gone already. But he won't know about any of that in there. I've filled and felted every crack. Deepest night in there. I lean back and wait and after a while I drift off a bit.

•

CHAPTER SIXTEEN

Muir was sitting in the kitchen watching Helga as she moved about, flip flop, flip flop, clearing the table, stacking the pots by the sink. She'd always done more than her share of the chores and now she did them all. She didn't want to take on the whole thing, she'd told him again, when he went, and it needed to be sorted out. Muir was not surprised at her suggestion. He wished things would surprise him more. Jasper, she'd said, Jasper and Charlotte, with that spur of the moment intuition that Muir couldn't help attributing to women.

"But I thought you said he –"

"That was at first. He's with Charlotte now, she'll help him to understand. He's the right one. And he knows how to deal with the people," she'd gestured vaguely. "out there. We need that nowadays."

"Mebbe we don't need anyone to be in charge."

"We need someone in charge who doesn't need to be in charge."

Muir was sometimes amazed at Helga's perspicacity. He'd got used to thinking of her carrying piles of bed linen about, nagging the kids to wash their hair, clean their teeth, in the kitchen organising the meals, settling him into bed, easing him out of bed. He'd forgotten how intelligent she was.

Muir's mind ambled across his century, to be completed in two days time. The advantage of having a leader who takes a back seat, is that it stops you having a leader who shoulders his way to the front, takes over. Well, unless he was totally inept. Jasper didn't seem inept. He fitted in. Aye, Muir admitted to himself, inspector or not, he rather liked the laddie. His thoughts ambled on. Had he ever heard a boy whistling or was it just one of his apocryphal stories? He wasn't sure. Well, it was true, whether it happened or not. He'd learned to watch and listen in the darkness. Wait for the dawn chorus. Not ambling, rambling. He was rambling again, dozing and ram-

163

bling. He didn't like making decisions, preferred to wait for nature, chirping out, softly whistling its harmony. But he must decide now. Would Jasper Bignold be able to listen and wait? Mebbe not . . . but Charlotte would, and the kids. Could Jasper whistle? He could play the piano so he must be able to whistle.

He watched through the kitchen window as Jasper and Charlotte walked hand in hand up the path towards him. He would put it to them, he decided. He had some difficulty remembering what it was like to be in love. Yet it was the love he sensed between these two which made him sure it would be OK. A safeguard, a guarantee of balance between this man from the outside who would have the energy, the sense of discovery to do the job, and Charlotte who understood from the inside, but for whom being at the school without Jasper would simply be a repetition.

"Of course, there's very little money in it," Muir started in his usual oblique style, "but a bit of fame by the look of the way things are going."

There was purpose to this way of putting things – a notion that if Jasper wasn't bright enough to get the point, to respond in some original way, then Muir would be able to withdraw the offer without having quite made it in the first place.

Jasper glanced at Charlotte not certain he'd grasped the point, unable to believe he'd grasped the point. She winked and Helga smiled and nodded. He remembered he had thought about it. It was after that time he played the piano in the meeting, after his speech committing himself to support the school, as he was playing a phrase had crept into the rhythm, *I belong here, I belong here . . . I live here, I love here . . .* But he had not imagined that Muir would have, could have understood the depth of his conversion.

He sat there silent, unable to reply, drumming his fingers and running a hand through the back of his hair until Muir was forced to speak again, sounding quavery and anxious.

"Well, laddie?"

Jasper said, "I'm not sure it would be any good without Charlotte."

"We had in mind the two of you," Muir said.

Jasper looked at Charlotte again and she smiled back. It occurred to him that she must have known about it already, maybe she and Helga set it up. Charlotte taking the lead again, but he didn't seem to care.

"I'm up for it," Charlotte said.

Jasper recovered his tongue, "I have to have my own piano – that school piano is hell . . ."

"The offer includes the piano," Helga said. "We need all three of you – Charlotte, the piano and yourself."

She poured four small glasses of whisky and passed them round the table. "We'll talk about it more after the party. There's a lot to be talked about. And we'll need to bring it to the meeting."

Jasper and Charlotte sat at the table, hands clasped, across from Muir and Helga, Muir knarled and folded, head bent sideways, waiting; Helga leaning forward resting her large breasts comfortably on her arms which lay along the edge of the table. Nobody spoke for a while.

Charlotte loosed his hand and stood up holding her glass. "Actually, we just came to let you know that Jasper's talked to the DfEE people. He thinks they'll maintain a neutral position, not be swayed by all this stuff going on in the press."

Muir nodded, "Good." He knew there would be many more battles. He wasn't sorry that he wouldn't have to fight them.

Jasper wanted to cry, put his arms round Charlotte and cry, in the way that you cry after something terrible hasn't happened, after you come first in the egg and spoon race, after you make love for the first time – cry with relief and excitement.

Charlotte and Helga went into the other room, leaving Muir and Jasper alone in the kitchen.

"Och, it was Helga's idea," Muir said, "but I knew she was right the moment she mentioned it. She likes you. And the kids don't seem to mind you either."

"What about Helga? What's she going to do?"

"Helga'll carry on doing what she always does. But she doesn't want to do it on her own." Contemplating Helga without him, carrying on, gave Muir an insecure, empty feeling. He had not visualised his own absence in quite that way before. He took a sip of scotch and replaced the glass on the table.

"But you, Muir, what do you think?"

Muir rubbed the side of his nose, feeling the skin loose against the bone. How do you leave painlessly, decently, he wondered. Bernard Shaw had managed it, and Bertie Russell, and the man who used to bring the groceries on Monday mornings who, it was said, just sat down in his armchair, closed his eyes and went. An effort of will perhaps, dying. He finished his scotch and contemplated Jasper for a while, his grey curly hair, which seemed to have got longer, the easy way he sat at the table. He was trying to imagine Jasper, Charlotte and Helga carrying on, and him somewhere else – nowhere else, he reminded himself. He moved his hand to his face again and wiped his eye. "A question of balance. I don't know. You and Charlotte between you have a balance. I can see you're happy with each other. And you're a creative kind of chap. With a bit of luck you won't need to go stamping about running things, manipulating people. It's not so easy, knowing what to do for the best." He let his hand fall back on the table. "Everything's a gamble except death." Muir forced himself not to drift off into deeper thoughts of death. "When I first started I only had a vague general idea – not what I'd do, what I'd stop doing. I stopped beating them, stopped bullying them, stopped telling them what to do. I made an important discovery – free kids are much more agreeable than unfree kids. I started liking the little besoms." Aye, he'd miss the kids. No, he remembered, he wouldn't miss them. "They did the rest, set things up for themselves. Och, the adults helped a bit but they had most of the ideas. The kids will show you the way. Question of letting them."

"Not a leading role for a teacher then?"

Muir forced his thin shoulders back against the hardbacked chair and scratched his arm. "I've often wondered about the word 'role'. 'Playing a role', 'acting as a role model.' A teacher shouldn't be an actor, except for fun – just play your piano and keep the rest of the world off our backs. Oh, and sack the occasional teacher who thinks he's got a leading role. You'll need to avoid missionaries."

Jasper was mostly playing devil's advocate. He enjoyed Muir's gifted demolition of education-speak. "What about teaching itself – lessons? That must have some importance surely?"

"Aye, kids enjoy a good teacher. At the same time one mustn't ram things down the throat. Most kids go to lessons here, as you know, but if they don't we conclude they've got better things to do, for the moment. They come when they're ready."

Jasper persisted in his advocacy, "What about the ones who fall through the net?"

"Gawd, how much education jargon is founded on blood sports! Public school legacy mebbe. Cold-blood sports in this case. The problem is to get rid of the net; get back in the water. Dive, jump, splash, swim. Awfu' crowded in the net, you canna get your breath. Poor wee fish, wriggling, squirming, gasping. Back in their element, the ones who got away – how I like to think of Coralford."

Jasper corrected his metaphor. "I meant trapeze artists, not fish."

"Och aye."

"Little tightrope walkers, one foot in front of the other, looking neither to left or right . . . high fliers . . ."

"Aye." Muir gave a sigh.

"Sex," Jasper persisted. "What do I do about sex?"

"At a certain age most kids are more interested in sex than lessons. I always like to see that. Healthy." Muir yawned. He wished he didn't have to keep repeating himself, these same old witticisms – not wit really, just truth. Wit is the simple truth the rest of the world doesn't seem to have the wit to understand.

"And the pregnancies?"

"Och, we don't get many of those. Fewer than elsewhere, I'm told. Musn't withhold the facts of life from kids, or the facts of contraception."

167

"Culture?" Jasper was only half-playing. He did wonder about the passing on of culture.

"Ach, Kultur . . ." Muir put on his German accent, only a vowel away from his Scots. "When I hear the word culture I reach for my pipe, I ken there's going to be a tedious conversation. Are art galleries compulsory for adults? Do we imprison adults and force them to read books?"

The question was rhetorical. Jasper studied Muir's brown eyes in their sagging pouches and reflected that they'd seen an entire century: Ypres, the Russian revolution, the Wall Street crash, the hunger marches, the Holocaust, Hiroshima, Vietnam. He wondered why he'd mentioned culture.

Muir closed his eyes and opened them again. He seemed to have caught the drift of Jasper's thoughts. "Mebbe compulsory book-learning leads to compulsive book-burning. Better to burn the syllabus. I don't know much about culture."

Jasper leant forward and asked a serious question. "Why me?"

Muir offered his faintly cunning smile. "There are lots of chappies who'd jump at taking this place over. Chappies with bees in their bonnets – Buddhism or vegetarianism, or animal rights or new-age Christianity. You don't seem to have any bees except that jazz of yours. Och weel – not my favourite music, I like a good plain melody myself, but a relatively harmless bee." He stared over at Jasper, "What d'ye say laddie?"

"Of course I'll do it," Jasper said, staring back.

"Aye." Muir fidgeted on his chair. "Give me a hand into the other room."

Jasper went round the table and helped Muir to his feet. The clasp of Muir's hand on his arm felt like a handshake and an embrace.

*   *   *

Charlotte took him all round the school, showing him where she had played, where she had cut her knee on a stone, where she had first kissed a boy, which rooms she had slept in. He imagined her as a child here, dunking her feet in the stream, blackberrying, bringing points up at the meeting, becoming the chairwoman, the secretary, decorating the lounge for end of term, building dens, camping in the field with her childhood sweethearts.

"Were you an Aaron or a Maz? A Katie?"

"I was an obnoxious little know-all when I first got here. I'd been top of the class at my primary school, always being patted on the head, told how clever I was. I began to believe it."

"So why didn't they just leave you there, being clever – your parents?"

"We had this teacher, Miss Sparks. One day someone hid the board rubber and no one would own up. So she kept us all in for half an hour after school until someone owned up."

"And did they?"

Charlotte smiled. "I think it was about the only really brave thing I've ever done. I owned up."

"You'd hidden the board rubber?" Jasper ruffled her grey hair.

"No, of course not. I was a goody-goody. I was teacher's pet."

"So . . . ?"

"Because I was teacher's pet, I knew I wouldn't get anything worse than a telling-off. It was the only way to get out of there. And I knew it was a way to make the other kids like me. I was a devious little brat. I don't think Miss Sparks believed me. I guess she was pretty keen to get out of there as well."

"And . . . ?"

"When my dad heard about it, he was furious. It reminded him of the Germans in France, he said. Same principle. So he looked around for a different sort of school . . ."

They sat down on the front lawn. Jasper heard himself speaking almost formally, like an old-fashioned poet – *'Come live with me and be my . . .'*

"Will you come here and live with me . . . ? Not just to help run the school. You know I love you, I've always loved you. Whatever happens with the school I want us to be together."

Charlotte sat hugging her knees. Her mind was full of their past, full of Manchester. "My fingers were in love with you. And my knees and my toes and my nipples."

Jasper sat beside her, head bowed, saying nothing.

"That last week before you left I knew something was wrong. I tried to talk to you, to get you to talk to me, but . . . you wouldn't. The last day I set eyes on you we made love. Your head was on my pillow. I tried to look at you and you turned your head away. So I knew. I knew. And you got up and made tea to avoid my eyes. You forget lots of stuff, but that image, you screwing up your face and turning away your eyes, I've always carried it with me."

When she saw he was sobbing, Charlotte put her arms around Jasper's hunched shoulders. Why am I talking about this, she wondered, upsetting him and myself, yet it has to be said aloud between us. Now – not erupting out of some future argument like a buried demon waiting to destroy us.

Jasper wiped his face with a handkerchief and looked at Charlotte sitting on the grass.

"What did you do after I left?"

"I was in a bad way for a while. Every day I woke up and wanted to kick the furniture. It's hard to remember the feeling now – irritable, impatient, scared – heartbroken I suppose."

Jasper stroked her back. "I'm sorry, I'm so sorry."

"Then I just worked and worked. I got my degree and went back to London. Got caught up in all that stuff that was going on in the early seventies – wholefood, squats, anti-apartheid, the free schools movement. This place, Coralford was a passport in those days: the fount of wisdom. I got into writing stuff about it for these little radical journals – *Undercurrents*, *New Left Review*, went round giving talks about the school. Remember those days? *Alternative London*, self-sufficiency, macrobiotics."

"Not my world," Jasper said.

"Then I had my baby, my boy, split up from his father, sent him to Coralford. I didn't stay with anyone that long. Never quite got over you, I suppose. Don't quite know why." A pause.

170

"All in the fingers." She smiled, walking her fingers across his shoulders. "I haven't told you I called the boy Jasper. Nobody knew why except me – and his dad, he was good about that . . ."

Jasper looked at her, astonished. (His own firstborn had been named Jonathan Charles after his wife's father.) His name, Jasper, attached to her child, maintaining their connection for her over all their long separation. He murmured his own name with a new respect – Jas-per. He felt humbled before his excellent name, proud to own it, to pass it on.

"Lets go back to the house."

The sky had clouded over and light specks of rain began to fall on them. As they hurried back there was a flash of lightning and thunder sounded across the hills behind Eliston. Spots of rain began to plop on the hot, dry pavement.

Maz's envelope was on the mat: "Gone to find van man – Whinnick I think – KPO 547C. Back soon (I hope!) – Maz."

"Oh God," Jasper groaned.

Charlotte was reading over his arm. "Typical Maz, playing the boy detective again. And he'll find him as well, if I know Maz."

Jasper felt his jaw clenching again. "What now? Can't just sit here hoping nothing bad's going to happen."

"Won't the police have the address? They should have checked him out by now."

"We'll go to the police station first," Jasper said. "In the car, it's going to pelt down."

Charlotte grabbed one of Jasper's sweaters and they ran through the rain to the car.

Eliston police station was combined with the county court, an intimidating red brick Victorian building in a side street. The woman in the police station was plump and friendly. She didn't hurry. "You made a complaint already you say. When was that?"

"Two days ago."

"Can't find a note of it." She fished out a form under the desk. "Perhaps you'd like to just fill in another of these." She caught the look of anger and despair on Jasper's face. "No, you wouldn't, would you. Just a minute." She took the registration number from them and disappeared behind a screen. They could hear her arguing.

"Well, why wasn't it followed up?" and a laconic local voice answering, "Nothing to follow up. We've all been up there in our time, peering over the wall, looking at the lasses in the pool. Nothing to it."

"A complaint's a complaint."

"Aye. Well, it's got mislaid."

"It's serious. You've seen the pictures in the papers?"

"Oh aye, I've seen them. Who's going to say it were him?"

"Friend of yours?"

"Give over!"

Her voice lowered. "Well, what will I tell them.?"

"It'll take twenty-four hours – that's what you can tell them."

"What's your computer for?"

"It can't be done today."

The woman came back, pink-faced. "How long has the child been missing, sir?" She fished out a different form. "We'll investigate the matter as soon as –"

The flat of Jasper's hand thwacked down on the shiny plastic counter. "Get someone over there – before you get yourelves into serious trouble."

She stepped back in alarm. "I'll do what I can to –"

Charlotte tugged at Jasper's arm. "Come on, we're wasting time. I know the way to Whinnick."

*   *   *

MvS had gone, transported in an instant to the starry heaven which Maz could no longer see or feel, could not even imagine. After the first panic had subsided he felt his way along to a corner, slid his back down it and sat. He waited for his eyes to become accustomed to the dark, for faint shapes to emerge, make sense, but nothing emerged, nothing made sense. He curled his legs into lotus and made his eyes work round in a circle – a darkness so complete that even when he closed his eyes he saw only the most intense black. It closed around him, made him the tiniest speck of soot in a chimney. He kept his eyes closed to make the blackness seem more normal and felt his arms and legs, cautiously moved his hands out to the edge of himself and out along the floor. Some kind of lino, he guessed, cold and slightly bobbly. He knelt up and ran his hands along the wall – bobbly too, but different, the grain of wallpaper with a raised pattern on it. His fingertips met a paper edge, lifted over it and felt its smooth surface. He felt along and found the round protrusions of tacks at the corners. A print he guessed, he had put his prints on the wall. Maybe more prints of them, in the tent. Maz put both hands flat on the wall and made his way cautiously round the room side-ways. There was no word, no sound from the other side of the door. He had the feeling that if he made a noise again the voice would come again, shout at him, threaten him. He preferred the silence. This was a window he thought, deeply set in the wall, for he could feel a flat shelf, maybe two handspans going in from the wall. But if it was a window, it had something fixed against it, a felt cover attached all around its edge. His fingers hooked round the overlapped material, contacting the harder substance of the frame. He tugged but nothing happened. His fingers delved all round the edge – no catch. A window that didn't open and must be boarded over on the outside as well, judging by the fact that not a pinprick of light showed.

It would still be light outside, people walking past, kids play-ing along the shore. He put his ear to the window. He could hear the faint boff and suck of waves, voices in the distance, a plane. Then a deep roll of sound swelling in, echoing away. Thunder. There must be lightning out over the sea. Maz loved lightning. And now the steady thrum of rain on the roof of the house.

Along the third wall a wide surface with things on it – trays, an enlarger (he guessed, feeling up over its odd angular shapes); then a sink, one of those old pot sinks. Higher up the wall more shelves with packets and boxes and plastic containers. Darkrooms do have lights, Maz thought, they have special safe lights; enlargers have lights. The room itself will have a light. He felt around for sockets, found switches, pressed them down. Nothing. On the fourth wall a heavy curtain and behind it what must be the door, but felted over so it took him what seemed like minutes to distinguish door from frame. A lot of tacks holding it in place. The switch on this wall did nothing either. He got his Swiss Army Knife out of his jeans pocket and fumbled out a blade. Guiding it with his other hand under the edge of the felt he loosened a tack and put his face level with the wall. After an uncountable amount of time a thin strip of light registered itself on his eye and with it a great and immediate need to be free, to have light, to feel the rain pouring down on him and to look up at the sky, the great, wide Northumbrian sky, any sky. He thumped on the door with his foot and shouted, "Let me out, you bastard!"

"I don't want any of that lip," the voice responded immediately. It seemed to Maz to be just the other side of the door.

"Let me out !!"

"You'll stay there and learn to behave."

There was satisfaction in the voice. "Do you hear me?"

It wanted a response. Maz realised he should not respond.

He sank down into a corner and wondered what he should do. He felt tears trickling down his face, put his hands over his wet face and his face between his knees to hide the darkness.

CHAPTER SEVENTEEN

Even the powerful wipers of the BMW could scarcely cope with the deluge. They seemed enclosed in a world of rain. At the bottom of hills on the winding lanes the car threw up sheets of water around itself. "Slow down, J," Charlotte said. "We'll get lost. These lanes are tricky."

Jasper felt irritated, but he slowed the car down to thirty. "I didn't think Maz was capable of being so stupid, so irresponsible. God knows what sort of madman we're dealing with."

"Maz likes doing things on his own. He's that kind of kid. Feels immortal – you do at that age."

"Yeah. Well he couldn't be more wrong. How did he find out where the guy lives I wonder? How can Maz know what the police don't know – what we don't know?"

"Perhaps the police do know. Won't say."

"Perhaps Maz knew all along. Didn't say."

"No," Charlotte said. "Maz can be reckless, but he would have told the meeting the truth."

"Well, he didn't tell the meeting he meant to rush off with some bloody child-abuser." Jasper stopped the car at a small crossroads. "Which way now?"

"Straight over I think. No wait, I'm not sure."

"Oh God," Jasper groaned. "Come on, Charlie."

"They always put the signposts where you can't see them."

"I'll go." Jasper pulled the handbrake on hard.

But Charlotte was already out of the car running through the rain, head ducked. Jasper kept the wipers going and stared out miserably over the green, stone-pocked countryside as it blurred and cleared, blurred and cleared. He should have found out about the guy before. Never mind Denise. Never mind the police. Get the priorities right. Damn! Damn!!

Charlotte got back in. "Straight on." Blinking water from her eyes, pushing her wet hair back.

"Two miles. You go through this ancient stone arch in the

middle of nowhere, then about a mile after that you're in Whinnick."

"What is Whinnick?" Jasper said. "I mean, town? Village? How are we supposed to find Maz in Whinnick?" He sounded irritable to himself. He was irritable. "This wasn't a good idea, Charlie. We should have insisted that the police got on to it."

Charlotte put her hand on his arm. "J, stop this. Stop blaming yourself. You couldn't predict that Maz was going to act like a prat. He may not even be in danger. Whinnick's a tiny place – sea, pub, smokehouse and a few dozen houses. We'll find him."

"Thing is," Jasper persisted, "if Maz knew how to suss it out, why didn't we? We didn't use our heads, didn't think it through. We haven't even let anybody know where we are. We're being even more irresponsible than Maz – if that's possible."

"Maz might be back at school by now, not a scratch on him," Charlotte said.

"No, he's with that fucking peeping Tom, somewhere here in Whinnick." Jasper struck his forehead with his fist. "But where?" He drove through the elegant old arch without slowing down, scarcely seeming to notice it.

"Slow down. We're coming into Whinnick."

The rain had eased. An eerie, greenish light over the sea and an intermittent flashing in the distance – a lighthouse along the coast somewhere. A tiny harbour, semi-circular concrete with a gap in it. Beyond, the sea foaming and crashing, spurting over the top of the grey concrete and sluicing down into the semi-circle. A few boats upended or leaning on their keels on the shore side.

"Now what?" Jasper stopped the car where their road formed the vertical of the T – more like a Y – sea and harbour ahead and a thin coast road running obliquely to left and right.

"Easier to find the van than the house," Charlotte said. "Not many garages here, I bet. Let's think about it."

"I'm trying to."

"We'll go to the right, looking in any side streets and gateways – there's not much of it. If we don't find anything we'll go back the other way. If we still draw a blank we'll go in the pub – ask a few questions." Charlotte realised she was taking over again. "What do you think?"

"If you say so." Jasper eased off the brake and turned right. "Makes as much sense as anything else."

This is the test, Charlotte was thinking, how you operate together in a crisis, when nobody feels too pleased with themselves and you're scared. This is the test. She felt a peculiar sense of guilt, as if it was somehow her fault Jasper was feeling irritable, as if she had somehow led him into this situation, moved him into her sphere which had failed to live up to its promise.

They drove slowly along. A black cloud was moving along with them in front of pink clouds, pulling the light from the sky, dousing it behind the hills. Jasper switched on the headlights. A few cars parked along the verges of the road, a van with a sign saying Whinnick Smokehouse on it standing in the courtyard of its own premises. In front of The Jolly Fisherman with its garish painted sign, an old Ford Sierra and a brand new yellow Fiat with its slick modish curves. The houses, small semis and pebbledashed bungalows led to a square of modest grey dwellings with a small playing field and children's play park on the sea side. The road ended there and a footpath continued along the cliffs. Ahead of them they could see allotments and fields sloping up a green heugh. The dark shapes of cows huddled round a distant tree. Nobody about. Waves crashing. The rain had almost stopped. They got out of the car and stood looking back towards Whinnick. A couple of birds swooped in off the fields, scooped over their heads and out towards the dim outlines of the shore.

"The other way," Jasper said.

*　　*　　*

Maz sat in the corner listening and thinking. He heard no sound from inside the house except what he thought might be

177

the rhythmic snore of somebody sleeping. The sound of rain on the roof lessened to a faint pattering and finally stopped. He could hear a dripping sound outside as if water from the gutter was falling onto a bucket. Like you get up here, he thought, heavy but soon over.

Either you try to get out by crashing through the window or by crashing through the door. You won't crash out without something to crash out with. There might be something in here. A camera tripod? But where? And if he hears you and gets mad what will he do? What will he do anyway? What does he want? Maz's mind, in a corner, was working better. His panic had subsided, his misery ebbed away. His thoughts took on an energetic rhythm tuned in to the crash of the waves which seemed to have got closer, seemed to be crashing against the house itself. He thought back. This man, he gave him a name – Kingspawn – had made it up as he went along. Must have, because how could he know Maz would turn up at the service station, how could he know Maz would ask for a lift, get in the van, come here? He'd come into the darkroom, hurrying, thinking quickly, taking out the bulbs, stuffing them into the big pockets in the legs of his fatigues. So he wouldn't remember everything. There might be matches, a tripod, a torch, a candle . . . If you couldn't see out you couldn't see in, so if he could somehow find a light he could see what was here, know what he should do.

He worked his way along the surface of the floor around him again with the flat of his hands. Then, putting one foot carefully in front of the other he left the shelter of the walls and tried to go across the open space in the middle of the room. It felt as if you'd never get to the other side. His toe touched something, the leg of something. He felt up the leg. A stool, quite tall, he thought, with a round seat, bars in the shape of an H strengthening the legs. He kept one hand on the stool and stretched the other out to find the surface. Then he lifted the stool and fetched it nearer. Maz climbed carefully on to the stool and stood up. He put his hand up and felt the ceiling, probably a foot or so above his head. Holding on to a shelf with one hand, he flatted the other over the shelves above the surface – boxes and plastic bottles on the first, on the second, flat boxes – paper. On the third shelf objects he couldn't identify – small objects. Lenses perhaps, a pebble from the beach? Heavy, but not heavy enough. And then a big one, a stone he thought, irregular, with holes you could fit your thumb and finger into. He could picture the grey stone, the holes where fossils had once been, a whiter interior smoothed by sea and sand. It was holding a pile of papers in place. He hefted it in his hand. It would break a window but not a door or a board outside a window. He needed a battering ram, something like a tripod. Putting it back on the shelf he heard it clunk against something metallic, heard the thing topple on to the shelf, sensed it rolling, tried to grab it, grabbed air instead. Then the sharp crack of metal against pot sink and the thing rolling to a stop. The stool wobbled and he clung on to the shelf, steadying himself. It had sounded like a gunshot, echoing in the still, close darkness. He counted to a hundred. Nothing happened. No sound from inside. The sea continued its comforting rhythm. He sensed the breathing on the other side of the door continue undisturbed.

Maz felt for the big stone again, picked it up and manoeuvred himself to a sitting position on the stool and let his feet back down onto the floor. Still holding the stone he felt his way to the sink, put the stone down on the surface next to it and with both hands felt around inside the sink, the wetness on his hands a reminder of the rain-soaked textures and colours of the world outside. His fingers closed around the thing, delicate and slim, which widened towards a thicker circumference at one end. He twisted that end. A thin beam of white light shot through the darkness.

*   *   *

Charlotte said, "I'm just remembering what it's like on the other side: a few houses along the front and then a sort of track goes up behind. And there's several lots of little houses and bungalows with tracks and gardens between them, allotments. A jumble of stuff. Might be quite hard to find the van. We're just passing the pub now."

"Pub first?"

"Exactly." They were back, Charlotte thought, together again. Test over.

They parked by the Fiat. The rain had stopped completely but it was dark. A fierce salt breeze caught them as they got out of the car. The sweater Charlotte had grabbed felt damp and cold. She shivered and drew in a breath as the wind gusted through it. Jasper took her arm, they bent towards the wind and went through the door of the pub, forcing it back onto its latch behind them.

"Chilly evening," the lady behind the bar greeted them. It was a small room. Three old men sat on stools up at the bar, one wearing a fisherman's sweater and woollen hat. At a table to their left a young couple with a rucksack drinking beer.

"Best to buy a drink first," Charlotte murmured.

"An evening for two whiskies," Jasper said.

"I'd say so. Anything in it."

"Neat," Charlotte said.

Jasper turned to the landlay. "Two neat whiskies. Malt perhaps."

"Just got here?"

"Actually we've just driven over from Eliston." Jasper put a five pound note on the bar. "Got a bit lost." He pocketed his change.

"On holiday?" the man in the woollen hat asked.

"Visiting friends. Actually we came here to look up a friend, we should have come on a better day, when you could see where you were going, 'cos we don't really know where he lives. Along the front somewhere I think."

"Drives a white van, Ford Escort," Charlotte said quickly. "Bearded chap."

"That'll likely be Robert Jarvis," the landlady said. "Number two, Fore Street."

"Yes, Robert," Jasper said. "That's the chap."

"Can't be him," the man in the hat chipped in,. "Hasn't got

any friends, him."

"Walter!" The landlady frowned at him, glanced at Charlotte and Jasper. "He likes his joke."

"Seemed a nice enough chap to us," Jasper said. "We don't know much about him."

"Aye, he's all right really. On his own there since his dad died." The landlady began to tell them how Robert's dad had worked in the smokehouse for thirty years, but Robert couldn't get a job. How his mother had walked out on them when Robert was seven, how Robert had bought the van, how his father's funeral had been a bit of a paltry affair, how . . .

"We really must go . . . Can't leave it too late."

The landlady placed two more Glenfiddichs in front of them, "From Walter . . . before you go . . ."

"We really can't –"

"Thank you. Most kind of you," Charlotte cut in. "Down it in one Jasper. What they do up here." She swallowed her whisky back and pulled him to the door. "Thank you for the help, and the whisky."

"Aye, number two, can't miss it. Right on the front. You'll see the van outside."

*   *   *

He shone the torch round the room. Much smaller than he'd thought. There was a tripod propped under the surface, a heavy-looking metal one. You could probably bash a way out of the window with that, but by the time you'd done that he'd be there behind you – battering you.

Maz sat in the corner again and played the torch round in circles. The man, Kingspawn, was the big problem and the solution. He must get Kingspawn to open the door and then find a way past him. He had the stone, the torch and the Swiss Army Knife and he was fast. If you'd shut someone up in a room, Maz thought, you'd want to know what they were doing. If he kept totally quiet, Kingspawn would eventually open the door to see what was going on. But that could take days, days

181

of no food and . . . Maz stood up, holding the torch, went over to the sink and quietly peed in it. He smelt the warm smell of his pee, ran the tap, listening to the sound of the water trickling into the sink. There was water, but he would get weaker and weaker. And it was stuffy. Not much ventilation in here. Suffocating. Panic started to rise in him again, but he forced it back under. Then again, Kingspawn worked on impulse, driven by something he, Maz, would never understand and maybe Kingspawn didn't understand either. He might decide just to leave him here to die, might be too scared of what he'd done to open the door. He must make him mad enough to open that door, and soon. And he must be ready for him.

Maz took out his knife again, opened a blade and slid it between two pins in the felt on the door, working them loose. Three or four tacks sprang away from the wood quite easily. The felt was tacked across in strips. He tugged and a whole section came away leaving a rectangle of door bare, the felt hanging down, still full of tacks, on the hinge side. He stood, listened, waited. Nothing. He knew he must keep the torch in his pocket for later, knife in one hand, stone in the other, be prepared to keep changing over as his arm got tired. He picked up the stone from beside the sink, hefted it in his right hand, clenched the fingers of his left hand round the knife. Now!

He began to bang on the wood with the stone. Rhythmically, insistently. Bang! Bang! Bang! Bang!

"Stop that! Stop that at once!"

Bang! Bang! Bang! Bang!

"I said stop that! Did you hear me? Stop it at once!"

Maz carried on, changing hands every twenty strokes so as not to lose the rhythm.

"Stop it!!!" The voice rose to a scream. He could hear the boards creaking as Kingspawn paced about the room. "Stop it!!!" He knew the voice was right against the door. "You'll get the thrashing of your life when I come in."

Bang! Bang! Maz tensed his fingers round the knife. He had a rough plan. As Kingspawn pushed open the door he would wait behind it. He'd let him get in, looking around in the darkness, and Maz would be out, the door slammed behind him. Reversal. Kingspawn in the dark. He'd have to drop the stone to slam the door. The knife just an insurance.

Kingspawn was pacing again. Maz was sure he could hear the rasp of his breath.

Bang! Bang! Bang! Bang!

A harsh shriek of pain and anger from the other side of the door. And then a kicking and banging from both sides, as if the two of them were engaged in a vicious fight through the medium of the wood. "You wait, you just wait!" the voice is screeching.

* * *

Can't stand this noise, this banging. My head screaming, get him, get at him. I kick and scream at the door. He won't stop. I rush to get the key off the table. I push the key in the lock. But I can't turn it. I can't turn the key. Fingers won't turn the key. I see him in there, lying on the bed. Face gone dark. Stubble on his chin. Eyes always staring, mouth open, cheeks drawn in. Last breath has gone. "Stay there, fucking bastard, stay there!" I scream. I pull out the key. I hear the banging, it doesn't stop. I run, grab my boots from the step, run to the van.

* * *

Maz heard the back door of the house slam. He continued to bang. He heard the engine of the van cough and start. He continued to bang. He heard the van drive away. He stopped banging and put the stone down. He took the torch out of his pocket and put it on the surface by the enlarger so that its beam shone towards the window. With his knife he picked and slashed at the felt, pulled at it with his hands until he could see the dim, dull reflection of a boy in the glass. He put the knife back in his pocket, picked up the heavy tripod and smashed it against the glass.

*　　*　　*

"It's only two minutes down the hill," Charlotte said. "Better to leave the car here."

Jasper opened the boot and found a spanner, put it in the pocket of his coat. "Come on then."

They walked past the harbour. The wind had fallen, but you could still see the waves, white-crested against the dark harbour wall.

"No van," Charlotte whispered. They looked at number two. No lights. It looked deserted. One of the two front windows had been boarded up, but the board had come loose, flapping now as a gust of wind caught it.

"Anybody there?" Jasper banged on the front door with its tiny diamond pane of frosted glass. It looked like one of those front doors that didn't get used. "Let's go round the back." They walked up the track at the side of the bungalow and pushed through the iron gate into the tiny, stone-walled back garden. A neatly trimmed lawn, a small shed, padlocked, and nothing more. A wooden porch jutted over the back door. Jasper tapped on the door. "Anybody at home?"

But Charlotte was pulling on his arm, pointing. "Those are Maz's."

Jasper looked down at the orange and black trainers, neatly aligned, at the side of the porch. His mouth went dry. He rattled on the knob, put his shoulder against the door. "We won't break in here in a hurry."

"Try the broken board." Charlotte went to pick up Maz's trainers and then decided against it. They hurried round to the front. Jasper tried to lever up the board, grabbing it with both hands where it was loose, trying to tug it away from the windowframe towards him.

"Maybe we should go back to the pub and call the police," Charlotte said.

"Fuck the police!" The board came away suddenly and Jasper staggered and caught his balance. He stacked the board

184

against the house and looked in through the broken window pane in the lower part of the window. "Left the bloody torch in the car. Can't see a thing. There's this." He handed Charlotte some Walkman earphones dangling by their lead which had hooked itself round the broken window. He was shaking his head. "You're right, let's go up to the pub. I can't get through this window." He pressed his fingers hard into his forehead. Charlotte stood looking at the earphones. She pushed her hand into Jasper's and they turned back towards the pub.

"Wait!" a voice shouted behind them. They turned back again. A dark figure was running from the direction of Dunstanburgh Castle, along the path which skirted the edge of the shore. They ran towards it. And the figure, small, bare-foot, muddy and with blood on its face, fumbled through the gate and fell into Charlotte's arms.

*   *   *

Maz cuddled up with Charlotte in the back of the car, saying only, "What time is it?"

"Half past nine."

"Not even beddies yet."

"I wouldn't worry about beddies," Charlotte said. "They'll understand."

"I just thought it was much later."

"Want to tell us what happened?"

Maz shook his head against her shoulder. He was shivering. "Later?"

He moved his head up and down.

As they got into Eliston Jasper said, "I'm afraid we need to go to the police. In fact we need to go now. Presumably that guy's on the loose somewhere." He stopped the car. "What do you think, Maz? Can you face it?"

Maz's shoulders shrugged up and down against Charlotte's sweater. She and Jasper looked at each other.

"It's OK," Maz said, "I'm OK now."

He disentangled himself from Charlotte and leaned back in

the seat.

In the light slanting in from the street Charlotte could see that the coagulated blood on his face originated from a jagged cut on his cheek. His hands, too, were scratched and bloody, and there was a smear of blood on the seat where his feet had been tucked up.

"Isn't a doctor more important?"

"The police will get a doctor more quickly than we can," Jasper said. "We've got to show them the evidence or the bastards won't take it seriously."

"Did that guy do those cuts?" Charlotte asked.

"No. Did it on the window getting out."

The same policewoman was at the desk. Her friendly smile froze in mid-motion. "Oh –!"

"I warned you," Jasper said. Now that Maz was safe he could feel the anger coursing through him again. "If you'll stay here with Maz," he said to Charlotte, "I'll go up and let the school know what's happened," and to the policewoman, "Make sure this boy gets medical treatment. I don't want to have to make yet another complaint."

"Of course we will." She pouted her lips and looked at him, mock-reproachful. She came round the counter and shepherded Maz and Charlotte through a door which she unlocked. "Come on now, it's all right. We'll soon get something sorted out . . ."

Jasper wanted to hit her though none of it was exactly her fault.

He got back in the car, fished around in the dash compartment, found the small notepad he kept there and wrote two identical notes to the editor of *The Eliston Courier* referring him to the police. He put one of the notes in his pocket. Then he wrapped the other one round his professional card, walked down the road to the *Courier* Office and pushed it through the letter box.

He walked up to the school. Jasper needed to walk. His nerve-ends jangled and he was seething with rage, which, though he directed it towards the man in the white van, the

186

police, the press, was actually much more general – rage at the incompetence and nastiness of reality – the way things were. Grown men went around taking salacious pictures, abducting children for God knows what nefarious reason, and the press would capitalise on it, the rest of the world read it, get off on it, hounding the guy responsible, as if only tacky dramas, violent episodes in the lives of other people could bring them to life, satisfy their craving for revenge, excitement, blood. And he wasn't much different himself. If he could catch this poor, sad fucker in the van who hadn't got a mother or a father or a friend in the world, the way he felt at the moment, he would string him up. He'd string him up for being what he and thousands of people who should know better had helped him to be – vengeful and puritanical, repressed and sex-starved. Repression and control. Insidious, deadly, turning us into hateful, foul-tempered, uncreative savages.

He turned the corner into the school drive A late reporter in the shadow of a damp bush stepped forward to intercept Jasper. "What –?"

Jasper was prepared for him. He got the piece of paper out of his pocket, pushed it into the reporter's hand and strode on into the school. He felt as if he were coming home after long wandering in an alien wasteland populated by demons and dragons.

He found Simon, who was the beddies officer, and gave him a brief explanation of Maz's absence, not going into detail. He would tell Muir and Helga about it tomorrow. No point in bothering them tonight, Muir would probably be in bed.

Maz was safe. That was what mattered, he told himself as he walked back down to the police station, placated somehow by the ambiance of the school: Simon cheerfully swearing to the younger kids to get the fuck into bed, the carriage kids sitting chatting on a bench on the front lawn, Hiroshi and Katie cuddled up on a sofa in the lounge reading a magazine together. Sensible there, so much more sensible than things were on the mainland.

187

CHAPTER EIGHTEEN

On the run now. Can't go back. Drive in and out the lanes, along the coast, park up behind the dunes, other side of the golf course, past Embleton. What's left behind? Don't know. The brat in the darkroom? Him? Banging? The police? Don't know.

Lie down in the back of the van, coat round me. Rain again in the night, lashing round the van, rocking it. Roar of the sea. I'm hungry. Dawn comes up. Drive onto the A1, drive north, to the transport cafe, park behind the big trucks, away from the road. Bacon, sausage and eggs. No taste to it. See a police car park on the other side. I drive out of there. Back south, turn off the main road. Down the lanes again round Seahouses. Park away from the petrol station and take the can in.

"Run out?" he says to me. For a minute I don't understand.

"Yup," I say after a bit. "Thirsty, those old Volvos." Buy two packs of ham sandwiches, meat pie. Put them in my pockets. Pick up the can by the pumps.

And I drive. South, east, west, north. Drive and stand, drive and sit, drive and sleep. Cold and hard in the back of the van. Wash my face in the streams.

Why? Don't know why. Teach him a lesson, that's all. Wouldn't really hurt him – would I? That why I ran off? So I wouldn't hurt him? Don't know. Thought it was him for a minute, my dad. Banging. Banging. Thought he'd come back. Let me out, let me out. Scared me. Saturday morning, drove back to the transport cafe, got the paper. I'm in there, Robert Jarvis, with that picture of me – took it myself, idiot, didn't I. Photo, van registration number. Don't approach. Might be armed. Might be dangerous. That other picture again, smaller, next to the photo of me.

I drive down the lanes. Go with the can for petrol. Cut my beard, best I can, with my penknife in the car mirror.

I am not armed. I am not dangerous – am I?
Lonely.
And fucking angry.

*   *   *

Saturday morning. Sunny again, the ground dried out, awareness of people coming out of the house, playing football on the hockey field, stretching their arms and legs into the warmth. The dens are dry again but bear the scars of the storm. Maz's carefully built mosaic is covered with dried mud and the rain has loosened the stones. Something else for Aaron to have a mump about, but his mum has arrived and taken him and Tamara down to the Coffee Pot for cakes and lemonade. "Who would you like to bring?" she'd asked, and Aaron had looked around for Maz, but Maz was being photographed and interviewed again, so he decided on Tamara. His mum had got her hair done in those little plaits that black people have and she was wearing a long purple dress with no sleeves. Aaron felt half proud and half ashamed of the way she was so pretty and not like someone's mum at all.

Muir's party tonight and the visitors are trickling in. Charlotte has moved into Jasper's house so that her son, Jasper, his girlfriend and two other ex-Coralforders can have her visitors' house. The two Jasper's have grinned at each other and shaken hands. Young Jasper has given his mother a hug – "See you later" – and gone over to the school with his friends. Tall, thin, hair cut close to his scalp. Only the tilted smile, Jasper thought, connected him to Charlotte. She would have told him why he was called Jasper no doubt, and that accounted for the warm but slightly quizzical look.

Jasper watched the four of them stopping at the end of the drive where a uniformed policeman was checking their connection with the school. There had been two policemen, one at each entrance, since yesterday, along with the reporters, whose ranks had swelled again since this morning's news. They made a kind of cordon sanitaire round the school,

189

approaching every adult who entered.

The Maz story had filled most of the front page of *The Eliston Courier* under the headline, LOCAL MAN ABDUCTS CHILD FROM CORALFORD SCHOOL (*Lord of the Flies* had been forgotten). There was a picture of the house in Whinnick with its broken window, a crowd standing about outside – neighbours, trippers; plucky, smiling Maz with a large sticking plaster on his cheek; a photo of Robert Jarvis (unemployed), a smaller inset version of the strip-poker and an interview with the landlady of the Jolly Fisherman, an amplified description of her part in the events of Thursday night.

The story had made the nationals too: OFSTED INSPECTOR IN RESCUE DRAMA – *The Mirror*; STRIP-POKER BOY ABDUCTED BY PERVERT – *The Sun*. *The Guardian*, on an inside page, had the headline, PROTECTING CHILDREN'S FREEDOM and a picture of the local bobby checking somebody's credentials. It was obviously posed, since the visitor in question was Graham the history teacher. Kids skateboarding in the background and behind that Helga helping Muir into the front door of the house. The article began: "The free-est school in the world is surrounded by strict security since a thirteen year old pupil was abducted by a local man with a grudge. 'Nice to have the law on our side for a change,' quips Muir, Coralford's headmaster, about to celebrate his hundredth birthday . . ." and then an interview with Maz: "I had to run in bare feet because he'd made me take my shoes off . . . I don't know why he abducted me, he seemed to want to punish me about something . . . I don't think he likes the way we enjoy ourselves here . . . I was pretty scared at first, but I just concentrated on getting out . . . I thought he'd come and attack me when I started banging but he just ran off." Then a paragraph on the school and how it had just been the focus of adverse publicity because of the abductor's photographs.

On the correspondence page they had printed a letter from Denise Roxborough, HMI, distancing the department from criticism of the school: "The department has no intention of discouraging diversity and choice . . . valuable and long established experimental school . . . would be inspected as a normal part of the Ofsted progamme . . ."

And Coralford had made the leader columns too: a mention of Muir's birthday celebrations, its coincidence with recent bad publicity, Britain's most controversial but possibly most important contribution to the twentieth century education debate, a reminder to editors to check their sources before publishing scurrilous photographs illegally obtained.

The Independent also flagged a retrospective article on the school to appear in next Tuesday's paper.

"Not mine, unfortunately," Charlotte said. "Still, not a bad little crop for one morning's reading."

"Thanks to Maz."

"And you. Denise's letter was . . . timely."

Strange, Jasper thought, to be sitting here in this cottage with Charlotte, discussing the papers over breakfast like a long-married couple. They had woken up, chest to back in Jasper's bed, kissed and cuddled, joked, showered and while Jasper went to fetch the papers and more milk, Charlotte had made coffee, sliced bread for toast and laid the table. What had been a dull, claustrophobic ritual to him in the past, now felt like an enchanting extension of their lovemaking.

Something to do with the eyes, he thought. He hadn't wanted to meet Kay's eyes across the table at this intimate, vulnerable moment, when you had to find a way to stop your hungry, neglected soul, loosened by sleep, from slipping out of your eyes and signalling your internal abdication. So you raised your protective newspaper, clenching yourself together for the day, saying from behind your flimsy screen, "Probably be a bit late back tonight . . ." Not that you had a mistress – just another meeting or a round of drinks in some pub – something to relieve the obscurely threatening mixture of boredom and unease you felt at home, where you were never quite yourself. And she'd felt the same, had done something about it, more robust in defence of herself than he. Both of them must have felt the same at breakfast, she relieved to see the back of the paper across the table instead of his untenanted eyes, a blip of

191

anticipation when he'd said he'd be out that night and she could phone Don later in the morning and make arrangements.

His eyes met Charlotte's above the toast and jam-pots.

They cleared the table and laid the papers out, bending over them side by side, quoting bits to each other.

"How about this from *The Sun*? – 'Maz, a thirteen-year-old musical prodigy, says, referring to the notorious strip-poker picture, "I like to relax with a game of cards, but it's just a bit of fun. Most of the time we work very hard at Coralford. Boys and girls respect each other here. I think this peeping Tom must have had a very bad childhood, not like us here."' – Doesn't sound like Maz talking."

"It's the editor talking," Jasper said, "the editor changing his tune. There's a load of stuff about Jarvis and his van: 'He was always a disturbed boy,' (his old schoolteacher), 'A crime waiting to happen,' (his next-door neighbour), 'He left his father to die in the back room,' (another neighbour), 'Van sighted on Holy Island,' (a holidaymaker)."

Charlotte folded up the papers and piled them at the other end of the table. She poured more coffee.

"It's worked out exactly as you said."

"Yeah. But I don't feel that good about it."

"Because of Maz."

"Yes, that, and, I dunno, the stupidity, the fickleness of it all. We're being manipulated by fools. Nothing feels constant out there. Even the Ofsted turnaround . . . I'm glad of course, but . . . to be governed by such a malleable, unprincipled lot . . ."

"I've never had any illusions about it in the first place, so I suppose I just feel gleeful that we're calling the tune for a change."

"I'm uneasy. We've still got our friend – what does Maz call him? – Kingspawn – touring the area. I don't for a moment think he's in Holy Island."

"Why not?"

"He wouldn't trap himself like that – Holy Island gets cut off from the mainland when the tide's in. He'd be a sitting duck."

"Where do you think he is then?"

"People with obsessions return to them. That's what I think."

"With the local force out there, defending us?"

"He won't come down the front drive," Jasper said. He started washing up the breakfast dishes.

Charlotte wrapped herself round him from behind. "I love you."

CHAPTER NINETEEN

Jasper felt like an insider. No longer the stranger waiting anxiously in the lobby. At the same time he was aware that a lot of the faces were familiar to everyone but him – young people who'd recently left and were still spiritually bound to the place. The older kids came up to them, hugged them, joked with them, took them off to the carriages, to their rooms in the house. A few people splashing about in the pool in the last of the day's sunshine.

Most of the visitors hanging around in front of the house waiting for the lounge to open and reveal its surprises are older – ex-pupils meeting each other after a long gap who stand chatting in little groups. Parents. A few people from downtown. Elderly people who had been pupils in the distant past, ex-members of staff.

A lot of cars are parked in the hockey field; and there are tents – parents' tents, visitors' tents. At the front drive a little queue of cars has built up while the policeman interviews the occupants. Reporters angle their lenses for a shot or two. The policeman has acquired an assistant from MBC – Leah. She has a list, is nodding, Yes, OK, Yes, OK, and calling hallo to people, embracing them through the open windows of the cars. Aaron appears with a wobbling tray – a cup of tea and biscuits for the policeman who says, "Thankyou, sonny," and pats his head. Aaron grimaces and runs off.

The back drive is easier, people on foot, a few friends from downtown, people on bikes.

Once in the grounds the visitors spread around, can be seen sitting outside the tents or on the front lawn. MBC are going in and out round the curtain over the lounge door with mops and dusters, packets of balloons.

Maz brought his parents over to meet Jasper. They were anxious to thank him and Charlotte for the rescue. Maz's mum still has a slight Italian accent, wears a smart well-cut skirt and top, Maz's dad somewhat older with the same thick, straight hair as his son, but longer, combed back and anchoring itself round his ears. Jasper explained for the tenth time that Maz rescued himself, he and Charlotte simply gave him a lift home. Maz's mum stroked her son's hair protectively, smiling. Jasper and Maz's dad compared notes on how they'd managed to avoid being interviewed by the press.

Charlotte seems to know everybody, wanders about embracing people, drags Jasper over to meet Elsa, her old music teacher, a small, incredibly wizened lady, who is to play a duet with Maz's father. Jane gathers her up with a few other elderly visitors and takes them all to her room for coffee.

"One last run through our solos," Maz said to Jasper, and to his parents, "Jasp's joining the band tonight."

"Great. We look forward to hearing you."

Jasper was pleased to get out of the way, not to have to be introduced yet again – the man from Ofsted who . . .

Maz, too, who had enjoyed his brief fame at first, and had thrown himself wholeheartedly into being interviewed, had grown tired of it, tired of repeating himself, tired of saying, yes he was all right, no, he didn't think he'd need counselling, yes, he'd definitely recognise the man again. Finally he'd said in a loud voice to all and sundry:

"Look, Muir's birthday party now – OK? – We're concentrating on that!"

"Are you really OK?" Jasper asked as they were tuning up.

"Don't you start Jasp," Maz said, exasperated. "I am OK. Let's play."

And Jasper could tell he was OK, back on form, relaxed. Both of them reclined into the music with relief, back where they belonged, recognising each other again.

Just as they were finishing the second number they became aware of a different beat, a pounding, coming over from the house.

"The gram," Maz said. "The lounge is open. About time."

The lobby had been transformed into a kind of gateway

195

made, Jasper supposed, of painted cardboard. Across the arch of the gateway, the words "CORALFORD 2099" – one hundred years in the future. In the lounge itself a trompe l'oeil. The exterior of the school had been brought inside – on one wall the swimming pool with a bunch of naked girls and boys diving into the rippling green painted across the base of the scene which covered the entire wall. On the adjacent wall the Coralford band was depicted playing in the middle of the hockey field, brass instruments lifted, a snowstorm of notes drifting across the sky, surrounded by tents and people lying in the grass. The third wall encompassed the gate into the lobby and the real outside.

The rest of that wall had been painted as the exterior wall of the school grounds with the big beech looming above it.

Beyond that, in the distance, could be seen the tops of futuristic buildings: domes, towers, triangular shapes in bold metallic colours. On the last wall, the stairs curved up as usual. Standing and sitting on the stairs and about the lounge were papier-mâché figures, clearly derived from the present occupants, Helga and Jane, Maz sitting on a real bike, Aaron with a pink expanse of gum stretched between his fingers. Under the stairs real foliage had been arranged and a young papier-mâché child looking like Tamara was crawling out from beneath it.

Jasper glanced upwards. Muir's face, covering the entire ceiling, smiled down at him, one eye closed in a wink.

Helga brought Muir through the gate and helped him get settled in his chair in the corner. The decorations truly gave an effect of space. An old man on his island in the sun, waves lapping or storming against the shore. The music was turned down a few decibels as a mark of respect and a little knot of visitors gathered round him.

"Where are the big kids?" Jasper asked.

"Most of them'll be getting changed," Maz said. "The visitors'll be down the pub, half of them. Just like end of term parties. Nothing gets going till about nine o'clock."

Jasper looked round for Charlotte. She had changed into her

dress and high heels and was standing with a group he hadn't met. Her contemporaries from school he supposed. He had a moment's flashback to his first days here, how uncomfortable, disapproving and alone he'd felt. Being an outsider makes you disapproving, he thought – redundant, embarrassed.

Aaron, who'd been walking round the lounge with his mum, looking at the decorations, pulled her over to meet him, "This is Jathp – he's my friend."

"Aaron's never stopped talking about you," his mum said. She was young and beautiful, new-agey, Jasper thought to himself, three studs on the rim of one ear and one in the left nostril. But with a forlorn, isolated look about her. He got the feeling that Aaron was too much for her, overpowered her with his clinging presence. He sensed that she would like to be here on her own, re-make her own childhood here. Aaron tugged her into the middle of the floor and they jigged about to the music. She gave Jasper a fleeting apologetic smile, a slight shrug of the shoulders.

Soon after nine the older girls began appearing, some of them almost unrecognisable in the finery which they had been making in the sewing room for most of the term. Katie made up, with hair piled on top of her head and wearing an ankle-length blue silk dress; Leah in a pair of skin-tight white trousers and big, baggy striped top, platform shoes, hair sprayed in bright colours and lacquered. The boys too had changed; Maz wore dark green trousers and a sweater he'd knitted, Hiroshi a brightly patterned Japanese garment which hung loosely around his legs.

The music was turned up. The big kids moved in among the smaller kids and began to dance.

"Come on, J," Charlotte said.

"You know I can't dance." But he moved about opposite her while she bopped away energetically like a teenager. When the track finished he put his arms around her. "You look great. You should have told me about all this dressing up, I'd have put my suit on."

"I looked round for you, but you were rehearsing. You"ll do

fine as you are."

The music started up again. More people were drifting in and the floor had got crowded, Aaron still clinging to his mum, Maz dancing with an elderly visitor, Hiroshi waltzing about with one of the papier-mâché figures, Simon and Katie in a wild, whirling recreation of what Jasper took to be jitterbug. He kept his arms round Charlotte, drifting round and round the edge of the room, past the swimming pool, the hockey field, the painted band. Colours swam and turned around him.

"You're dancing, really dancing," Charlotte whispered, pressing herself against his sweating body.

"Am I?" He felt himself grinning, the rhythm of some hot popular tune (was this Hip Hop, he wondered) taking his legs, moving them in tempo.

Then the music stopped and MBC came around with plate-fuls of food – sandwiches, sausage rolls, sliced-up cucumber, pieces of melon – and edged people through the arch. "We have to put the chairs out for the floor show."

Jasper and Charlotte wandered out of the open door of the brightly coloured lounge. It had turned dark – a clear, warm night, nourished by the two hot dry days that had followed Thursday's storm. Their eyes adjusted, picked out the silhouettes of heads and shoulders round the bonfire in the hockey field, the glowing tents, the small coloured lights strung along the front of the house.

The two policemen had taken a break from sentry duty now and were standing in the lobby, helmets off, chatting to the two waitresses from the Coffee Pot, waiting for the floor show to start. A few people smoking, their cigarettes tiny reflections of the star-filled sky. Jasper looked around the real outside, the black shapes of the outbuildings, the sombre outline of the big beech tree against the distant glow of streetlamps beyond. They would live here together, he and Charlotte. Their grown-up kids would visit them from time to time. He would grow old here like Muir, if he was lucky, his days punctuated by school meetings, end of term parties, bonfires, children arriving, settling in and leaving. Probably he'd sell that featureless house in Bromley which seemed impossibly alien and far away, buy a little cottage, somewhere to get away to in the holidays.

There were shouts and laughter coming from the darkness over by the wall. He felt uneasy suddenly, something nagging in the back of his mind. But it was Young Jasper and his friends, he realised; they'd been taking turns from the swing on the big beech. They emerged now out of the dark and came towards the lobby.

The school bell was clanging. "Floor show, floor show!" somebody was shouting.

Everyone crowded back into the lounge. MBC had put out benches and chairs in rows which soon filled. Other people sat on the floor in front or stood at the back, leaning against the decorations.

"We're last," Maz said to Jasper. The rest of the band stood in a little group at the front and to the side. Whatever his worry was, Jasper let it slip away. He squatted next to Charlotte at the front and gave himself up to the moment, to the buzz of excitement and expectation around him.

There were a number of spots in the floor show. First Hiroshi's play about Muir's early life, funny, full of Ochs, Ayes and Gawds.

"The tawse story," Charlotte said.

Muir was played by Hiroshi himself, rolling his r's and flourishing his tawse, but the story was mostly mimed, with a minimum of props – a plaited leather riding-crop as tawse and a few chairs. Two of the smallest children played the tawse buriers.

"Everybody knows it," Charlotte murmured, but to Jasper the story was new. He heard the voices of the kids joining in around him with the epitaph,

"Tawse, tawse, rest in peace."

The sketch ended with a Coralford joke – Muir stretches himself on two chairs and sleeps, wakes up, puts his finger to his temple in an exaggerated Japanese gesture of thought, returns to the grave, mimes digging up the tawse, sits down and begins unravelling it: "Waste not, want not, och aye, this is a good bit of leather after all." Hiroshi takes off Muir's great square boots which he has been clomping about in and begins to re-thread them with strips of tawse leather. Everybody cheers, the lights go out for a second and come on again for Hiroshi and his cast to bow to the audience.

"Muir's reputation for Scottish thrift," Charlotte explained to Jasper.

"Got that," he smiled and squeezed her hand.

Next came a tumbling act from more little kids culminating in an unsteady pyramid with Tamara precariously balanced on the top and then leaping into Simon's outstretched arms.

At a signal from Maz his father moved shyly to the front, tuning up his violin, fixing the rest under his chin, whilst Elsa gathered her pleated skirt under her and sat at the piano. They played the adagio movement of one of Mozart's piano and violin sonatas. Jasper was surprised at the choice – so lyrical, delicate and unshowy. Jasper glanced at Maz. Was it an ordeal here, he wondered, having your parent perform? Maz looked a little flushed, but seemed lost in the cadences of the music. When the piece ended and the big cheer and shouts for an encore exploded all around him, Maz grinned and shouted with the rest. For an encore they played an unannounced short piece which Jasper guessed from the strange modal harmonies would be Bartok.

Charlotte helped Elsa back to her seat as Jasper got up and the band took their places at the front. They kicked off with *Sweet Georgia Brown*, a nice, crisp middle-tempo number, followed by a Latin-American piece. Next Maz and Jasper did their first duet. Jasper glimpsed Maz's parents sitting at the front with Charlotte, all three faces beaming with pride and love. And then he was lost in the music, aware only of the bond between himself and Maz, a line of steady heartbeats under the syncopated swirls of notes that were dropping, floating, fizzing from his own fingers, rolling along on Maz's beat till it took over time itself, took out time, made the present everything. The end of the set was a stomping, clapping, audience-participation affair with Katie fetched up from the floor to sing with the band. This was impromptu – Jasper hadn't realised Katie could sing. Nor did he know the number she sang, but Maz hissed, "I'll lead in Jasp. Come in when you can, it's dead simple, in G." Katie sang in a surprisingly deep, raunchy voice, and Jasper concentrated on filling in round the heavy beat of some rock number, that was, as he soon realised, essentially an up-tempo blues. He grinned over at Charlotte, shrugged his shoulders, pounded on the keys.

The lights flashed off and back on again, and they all waved and bowed as the crowd roared. Charlotte rushed over and kissed him. "That was great, great!"

Everyone stood about in the lounge for a while, chatting in groups and waiting for the next thing to happen.

"I often wish I could improvise," Maz's father said to Jasper. "I have to learn everything by heart."

"Question of where you start from, I suppose," Jasper said. "I never had any formal musical training. Two different worlds."

But he didn't really feel in the mood to hold an intelligent conversation about music. He wanted to stand about, to go on feeling Charlotte's thigh against his as they stood together chatting to Maz's mum. He noticed that a little kid had fallen asleep curled up under the gram box; another lolled on a chair, legs hanging. Katie and Hiroshi were kissing by the stairs close to Maz who was fussing with his bass, tuning it and adjusting the amp. He glanced at his watch and saw with surprise that it was almost midnight. Aaron's mum was talking to Young Jasper's friend who looked a bit hippyish, Jasper thought, like her; Aaron stood behind her hoping for attention and not getting it. He caught Jasper looking at him and came over. Jasper would have liked not to bother but Charlotte made space for Aaron, putting her arm round his shoulder.

Some visitors were helping Muir towards the front while MBC members carried his chair over. Maz jogged Jasper's arm. "Come on." The bell clanged again briefly and everything quietened. Muir was settled in his chair. The band, hastily reassembled, led everyone in singing Happy Birthday.

Muir's present was brought in. It looked like a twentieth

201

century mummy, a large person-shaped package wrapped in layers of newspaper. It was stood on end next to Muir. The nearest kids helped to unwrap it while people craned their necks to see what it was. A full-sized head of Muir gradually emerged from the torn strips of newspaper, followed by his body, a rough-hewn and stylishly naturalistic wooden sculpture. Some little kids tugged off the final wrappings revealing the big square-toed shoes on which the statue stood, firm and solid.

Muir teetered onto his own shoes and stuck out a hand. "How do you do," he said to his present. "Have you seen Muir, by any chance?"

"He always makes silly jokes," Charlotte murmured to Jasper, "and tells the same stories. Love it."

"Speech, speech!" the kids called out.

Muir sank back into his chair and lit his pipe. "I've had a jolly good century," he said, "but as the kite said to the hot air balloon, we can't hang about up here for ever. Wish I could. I'd love to know what'll happen in the next century – and the one after that." He shifted in his chair and paused. Jasper fancied he could see a tear running behind the fold of Muir's cheek. You could hear a tiny break in his normally deadpan voice. "Aye, that's all very well but my body is getting fed up with carrying me around and –" he raised his head "– I'm awfully pleased you've manufactured this chap –" he gestured to his statue "– to stand in for me. A quiet fellow by the look of it, you'll not get a lot of bother from him." You could hear the thread of sadness under the dryness of his wit. "I shan't be with you much longer I suppose, but I don't think that really matters. I set the ball rolling, you might say, but all of you will keep it rolling." His eyes blinked closed and opened again. "Getting on for seventy years since I began this place. I think I can safely say we are no longer an experiment. We've demonstrated that freedom works. It may not work for adults, I'm a bit pessimistic about adults, but it works for children. Freedom is like playing the violin, the younger you start, the better you play."

Maz's father smiled and nodded. Jasper considered Muir, his shapeless corduroy jacket, his leathery old face, his relaxed personality. He wondered what image he could possibly develop which could match his gently tongue-in-cheek, slightly dour style. But of course he didn't have to match it, he thought. A quietness had fallen on the kids, on everybody, a stillness.

Muir sat on in his chair and nobody said anything. A perfect smoke ring drifted up from his pipe and lost itself against his image on the ceiling. "I really must be going soon," he said finally. Everyone cheered again.

MBC began cutting up cake over by the gram box, dishing it round.

Everyone cheering again, the clock in the lounge tinnily chiming midnight under the din and the kids, apparently spontaneously, circling round Muir's chair clapping and chanting, "Muir, Muir, Muir . . . more Muir . . . more Muir!" and other slogans which they seemed to make up as they went along. Muir took a large red handkerchief out of the pocket of his corduroy jacket and wiped his eyes. His chair was picked up with him in it, supported on all sides and a great procession began: kids, staff and a trail of visitors streaming behind, a colourful, ragged crocodile weaving and singing. Somebody had produced a tambourine which Katie was shaking as she danced. Leah shimmied next to her on her platform heels. Aaron and Tamara pranced along side by side. The crocodile danced out of the front door and began slowly making its way round the house and back to the front door again.

Aaron suddenly felt tetchy and bored. "Race you to the tree," he said to Tamara.

"Left my shoes in the lounge," Tamara shouted over the din. "Anyway I want to stay in the procession."

Aaron shrugged sulkily and Tamara lost sight of him in the crowd. Mumping again, she thought vaguely.

Maz had leapt onto his bike as outrider, Hiroshi danced ahead in his oriental robes shaking the tawse. Muir sat, impassive, silent, pipe unlit in his hand, held aloft in his wooden chair.

Which is why everybody was outside when it happened.

*　　　*　　　*

*Dark over here. Lights over there. Music. Hungry. My
bones aching with hunger. I put what I'm holding in the
first crook of the tree, grab the rope, put my foot in the loop.
I wish, I wish, but I can't go. No, I can't go, I can't leap into
space, feel the wind take me. Stay there! the bugger says,
stay where you are. Stay in your place. I close my eyes. The
roughness of the rope against my hand. Real? Is this real?
Real. Real. Everything's gone slow. I do not know my place.*

*I take my foot out of the loop. Climb. Climb. Take it with
me, up the tree, climb up the outside of the world. To the second crook. Crookedy-crook. Branches scratch at me, catch
my clothes, my jagged beard, come at my face. Shapes,
lights, music flicker up to me. It hurts my eyes. It hurts my
ears. Head pounding, bashing against the trunk. It's me
shouting out. The shout floats, drops, fades, drowns in this
fucking carnival of an island. I am nobody.*

*I spy the boy, that boy, riding on his bike up and down the
singing, dancing procession. A dervish at the front. An old
man in a chair. I'm the savage. Savage in my tree, my darkroom. Pictures, just pictures, floating up from the tank. The
carnival disappears, rises again. Girls. Girls in long dress-
es, bright-haired girls floating along in the tank, the big
tank down below – the island, the distant impossible island.*

*I'm frightened, very frightened. There is no way out of the
room. His voice speaks out of the darkness: "Evil little bastard! Devil's runt!" His fists knock me out of the world.
"Come over here, Devil's runt . . .come over . . ."*

*　　　*　　　*

Aaron was frightened of going over to the tree on his own
in the dark but he dared himself to do it. He'd climb up and
have a few swings and then he'd sit in the fork until people

204

started wondering where he was, came looking for him. He'd only just started being cool enough to go off the big beech swing; it had taken him a while and he'd never done it in the dark before. It wouldn't have felt scary at all with Tamara there and he wouldn't have mumped. "Jutht a bitch,' he said under his breath as he edged away from the procession into the darkness and skirted the back of it. As he expected, his mum was singing away, arm-in-arm with the ponytail guy. He took a quick sprint to the wall of the old theatre and put his back against it. He felt safer when nothing could spring him from behind. Now he had to get to the tree, which meant crossing the expanse of darkness beyond the front lawn. He'd heard that foxes came there at night. He kind of liked the prickling feeling he got when he was on his own in the dark and scared. A bit like on the swing but your stomach didn't feel so nice. He dashed through the long grass across to the big beech and spread his arms against its huge trunk. Maz said there was an owl in this tree sometimes. Aaron thought he could hear it flapping and rustling, though it didn't hoot. You couldn't climb up, not with the owl and he could hear it now, must be a huge owl, pecking and flapping about above his head. He even thought for a second he could see it, up through the leaves, a darker shadow in the dark tree. But how was he to go back when the space was full of foxes? He wished he'd brought Blanket but Blanket was in his room and that was a hundred miles away, on the other side of the procession. He could smell a sort of garagey smell and he thought he heard rain on the leaves. He flattened himself against the trunk, closed his eyes and felt in his pocket for the last of his gum. After a while things went quiet in the tree. He began to climb towards the fork.

*   *   *

I open the can; pour the stuff everywhere; the leaves, the branches. I pour it on my head, my parched, hungry body, rub it on my face, my beard. It takes years. Centuries. I feel

*the skin on my face go chill and slippery. It runs in my eyes
stinging and blinding, wets my fatigues. Fumes fold around
me, my head swims away, pounds and shatters against the
tree. "Come over to me," he says. I see his mouth fall open.
His dead eyes fix on me, waiting, impatient, angry. "Come
away from there," he says. "Not for the likes of you." And I
can hear them coming for me, I can see the first dark shape
climbing up for me, down there below the leaves. A terrible
grief envelops me, endless, black, wintery grief. I stare at the
beautiful carnival on the island, shimmering and melting
into the distance beyond this ferocious, final night. I am
unravelling into the tree. I am no one. My eyes bleed with
grief.*

I strike the match.

*　　　*　　　*

A noise like an enormous gas cooker lighting and the big
beech is a huge circle of fire streaming its yellow tongues into
the sky. The high point of the celebrations, a giant set-piece, a
flaring treeful of fireworks. "Oooh!" they gasp. Jasper knew
immediately, remembered what had been worrying him,
remembered Tamara's words in the meeting – "I saw a man in
the tree." Everyone stands looking at the burning tree, realising, transfixed by the scream wailing from its heart. A long
snake of fire swings out of the big beech, a blazing body in its
mouth. The mouth screams and screams. The snake parts
from the tree, the body falls to the ground, rolls over it strik-
ing fire to the grass. The snake arcs gracefully after the body,
laying a line of flame across the ground. People start forward
but the fierce heat of the fire holds them back. More run for
water. Ivy flames in a line along the wall towards the old theatre. People calling for blankets, extinguishers, sand. The two
bobbies on their walkie-talkies. The screaming stops. Only
the fierce crackle and suck of fire; a smouldering, still shape
on the grass.

At last a big red engine tears down the front drive and men

in yellow oilskin suits and hats take over, play hoses on the tree, tenderly cover the body and take it away, shepherd the onlookers to the back of the house, towards the pool.

The reporters snapping and snapping, gabbling into their mobiles.

Tamara, pulling at Jasper's sleeve, trembling and crying. "Where's Aaron?"

A few people saw the firemen, later, carrying a second blanket-covered stretcher, running with its light burden even though it was too late. Something they found at the foot of the big beech after they'd quenched the flames. A bundle readily identified by the rather unusual metal buckle on the belt Aaron's mother had bought him in Eliston only that day.

CHAPTER TWENTY

Muir floated in the pool, a tough, straight tree trunk with its folds of furrowed bark. He was trying to order the sequence of events. He felt miserable whilst being pleasantly aware of the pale September sun on his face and the soft lapping of the water, still carrying the summer's warmth, easing the loose skin of his body. He hadn't expected to be around to greet the autumn term, but here he was.

They were, the authorities, as he understood it, diverted towards another crusade – how to flush out solitary pae-dophiles with violent tendencies in advance of their violent tendencies coming to the boil. The call had gone out for greater security for schools, fingers had been pointed at various authorities for ignoring the warning fingers which had previously been pointed. The press had vilified other sections of itself for not checking the sources of its prurient picture-printing.

The heat was off Coralford for the time being.

The social services were pleased with the prompt, disciplined response to the recent conflagration. A team of Ofsted inspectors, headed by a friend of Jasper Bignold, had spent a week at the school and issued a balanced report.

Muir himself had written a number of letters to the press pointing out that the real culprit in the recent tragic events connected with the school, was the repressive education system itself – all the time you persist in coercing children, you produce warped, destructive personalities. Why didn't the authorities do something about that instead of wrapping barbed wire fences round children, which was bound to result in more of the same? A few of his letters were printed, but Muir didn't suppose it would make much difference. The fact was that when someone was brought up unfree, it was virtually impossible for them to understand what child freedom was . . .

He tried not to preoccupy himself with the fire itself, Aaron's death or the thought of young Maz in the darkroom. He tried to thank his lucky stars no one else was killed or injured. But inescapably his dreams were disturbed by the percussive clap of explosions or the charred remains of children's bodies or he was in a dark, windowless place, utter blackness pressing in upon him.

Jasper and Charlotte, he remembered, would be back tomorrow. They would finalise the arrangements for taking over in due course. Charlotte he felt sure, would keep Jasper along the right lines . . . and the kids themselves. He would talk to them about it all at next Saturday's meeting. He closed his eyes and floated.

Jasper and Charlotte had been in Greece for some weeks. Jasper had felt the absence of Aaron like a cold space clinging round him. Aaron's shade followed him round the school, he felt the clasp of his muddy legs round his waist as he embraced Charlotte, felt Aaron breathe against him in the night when she moved position, glimpsed his sad, grubby face as the light began to show through the curtains. He dreamed his fingers were parting Aaron's tangled hair looking for the transparent pinkish circle of his soul. Charlotte stroked and kissed the tears from his face each morning when they woke, her own eyes red from lack of sleep. "We must go away for a while," she said finally, and Jasper had nodded, saying nothing. Charlotte had written Muir and Helga to say they would be a little late getting back.

At the beginning of the new term there had been a meeting and it had been decided to plant a beech tree for Aaron near the old burned one. Someone had proposed they plant a tree for Robert Jarvis too – "After all he was a human being" – but the meeting had voted against the proposal. Instead they had decided to make a plaque to put on the wall near the remains of the big beech explaining what had happened for the benefit of future generations. They were making it in the workshop, but people kept bursting into tears, not being able to get on with it.

Tamara and Katie had planted Aaron's tree, carefully laying his blanket, space bandit and green computer game at the bottom of the hole before easing in the roots, tamping down the soil and watering it. Maz had made up a little tune and played it on his acoustic guitar. He tried to imagine the tune somehow winging up to Strumm or some sister planet where Aaron, clad in a silver spacesuit, smiled and sulked and chewed. But it didn't work. MvS was dead and so was Aaron. The rest of the school watched the ceremony holding hands in a big circle, silent and miserable.

Muir thought of these events as he did a careful breaststroke towards Helga who was just finishing her widths at the shallow end. He wished he could have died without having to suffer such images. He felt curdled, emptied of happiness.

The only other person at the pool was Maz. The early morning was still his special time. He stood on the small diving-board on the edge of the deep end. He didn't go over towards the big beech any more. Tried not to look at it. The blackened remains of its limbs reminded him of things he didn't want to think about again. He'd been a kid, then, and now, too suddenly, he was a grown-up. Nearly.

The sun slanted across his body, warm on his shoulders. The trees outside the pool fence were turning to rich reds and purples, and beyond he could see the evergreen of the school woods. A cooing sound, faint. Woodpigeons, he thought, over by the carriages. He stretched his arms above his head and dived into the pool.

THE END

Also published by Seven-Ply Yarns:-

A Really Good School

by David Gribble

A satirical whodunnit set in a boarding school where the complacent staff consider rules about uniform more important than murder.

Exciting fiction with something to say

from

SEVEN-PLY YARNS

PO Box 217, Ipswich IP2 2NZ